12/06

oc 7/12/07 **WITHDRAWN**

THE
SNOW
ANGEL
A NOVEL

schaffner
press

Tucson, Arizona

Cover Design: Kay Sather
Cover Photos: Darren Clark
Author Photo: Brian Pietro
Book Design: Darci Slaten

LIBRARY OF CONGRESS COPYRIGHT
REGISTRATION NUMBER: Txu1-282-354

FIRST EDITION
PRINTED IN THE UNITED STATES
2006
Schaffner Press, Inc.
Tucson, Arizona

Library of Congress Cataloging-in-Publication Data

Graham, Michael (Michael A.)
  The snow angel : a novel / by Michael Graham. -- 1st ed.
    p. cm.
  ISBN-13: 978-0-9710598-5-6 (alk. paper)
  ISBN-10: 0-9710598-5-3 (alk. paper)
  1. Racially mixed children—Fiction. 2. Kidnapping
victims—Fiction. I. Title.

PS3607.R345S66 2006
813'.6--dc22

                                            2006030309

FOR *GAIL, my wife and best friend,
who believed in me and made me believe.*

IN MEMORY OF...
MARY ALICE GRAHAM, *my mother;*
MRS. LUCILLE JONES, *who taught
a little white boy about the pain of bigotry;*
DAVID HAMMERLE, *a gentle policeman
who died much too young;*
and PATRICK J. HOWARD,
who carried the message that saved my life.

TABLE OF CONTENTS

PROLOGUE

It snowed hard that day, the Sunday before Christmas, the first serious snowfall we got that year. After a dry summer and autumn, we needed it for sure.

Still, no one was happy with the lousy weather, except maybe the city's children. This first snow was the kind kids pray for—heavy and crunchy, perfect for snowballs and snowmen. "Good-packing," that was the term for it. I'll never forget the creaking of all that good-packing snow under our boots that raw December day.

Nor will I forget the snow angel, not as long as I live. None of us will.

Before his abduction, Darryl Childress had been playing alone in his family's expansive yard, which covered a full acre. He was dressed in blue cold-weather gear and red gloves. The snow was already knee-deep on his seven-year-old legs.

The brick ranch-style family house was in a remote section of the Seventeenth Precinct, an upper-middle-class racially integrated neighborhood out near the city limits. The residence stood by itself in a cul-de-sac adjoining a stand of woods – maple and pine, mostly. It was only partially visible from the street. There was a large wreath on the door and the house was decorated with Christmas lights, Santas and oversized candy canes.

Darryl Childress was something of a local celebrity. He was a mixed-race kid well known to the city's children and their parents due to numerous local television commercials in which he had appeared. He was a born charmer. There never was a hint of danger in the boy's life. So that Sunday, believing he was safe, his parents had given him permission to play outside while they dressed for church.

First, Darryl went to the back yard. Then, at some point, he lay on his back, facing the sky. Maybe he stuck out his tongue to catch snowflakes, the way kids do. We do know that he moved his arms up and down at his sides, laterally, as if flying. In good-packing snow, this leaves the impression of a person with wings—an angel. Darryl did a good job of it.

Then, judging by his tracks, he walked around the north side of the house and out into the front yard. There he turned his attention to building a snowman, locating it on the median strip between the sidewalk and the street. Being a natural ham, he might have picked this spot so passersby would be sure to notice his handiwork.

Darryl had just begun rolling the first snowball to make the snowman's body when two male suspects, one white and one black, pulled up in a late-model sedan with tinted windows, later determined to be a gray Chevrolet Malibu. The men got out of the car and engaged the boy in conversation. How long they talked is anyone's guess.

Inside the house, Darryl's mother, Louise, happened to walk past the Christmas tree in the front window. She glanced outside just in time to see the two strangers pull her only child into the front seat of the car.

Shrieking, she ran outside in a desperate race to get to her son. Skidding across the snow-covered lawn, she slipped and fell twice, the second time landing on her face. She looked up to see the Chevrolet fishtailing on the ice as it sped away with her only child inside.

Responding to his wife's screams, Stephen Childress rushed out into the cold, still in his bathrobe. He ran to her as the car rounded a corner and disappeared. He knelt down next to her in the snow and held her tight. Louise screamed and screamed. Helpless, Stephen looked heavenward, unable to believe that something this bad was really happening.

By the time the first patrol car pulled up, five minutes after the 911 call, the snow had momentarily stopped. In fact, just for a little while, the sun broke through, causing the snow to glisten.

My partner and I arrived minutes later, young bluesuits whose only involvement was to help secure the scene. One of the first things we noticed was a child's red glove lying near the curb, next to some tire tracks where another officer was already posted. Our sergeant sent us around back to guard the snow angel until the crime lab and photographers showed up. I remember being struck by how small the angel looked.

Half an hour later, a north wind picked up again and brought more black clouds. Soon heavy snow was falling again, blowing in our faces. We got the pictures okay, but the forensics search was hurried in an attempt to beat the weather. Soon the snow angel was obliterated. That's the kind of day it was.

Like just about every other cop who was there that Sunday, I was haunted by memories of the red glove and the snow angel. So five years later, after I left police work to become a writer, I decided to look up the detectives who had handled this crime. Perhaps there was some kind of a follow-up story, something of human interest.

To my great surprise, I learned that in fact something *good* had come of it all, something very good indeed. One might even call it a miracle.

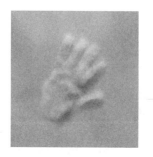

DAY ONE - SUNDAY

Ralph Kane sat on the edge of his bed in a ratty east-end rooming house, contemplating the Beretta in his hand. Kane—Detective III, badge number 2342, forty-seven years of age, sixteen years in Organized Crime Intelligence—was trying to settle on the best way to kill himself.

He was a short man with a graying military haircut, wiry, without a trace of fat. His right cheek bore the scar of an ancient knife wound. His constantly-moving eyes missed nothing.

Outside the window, heavy snow was falling. Across the street a Christmas tree in the upper window of a two-flat blinked on and off, mocking him. From a church down the street a ridiculous bell pealed out "Joy to the World."

Kane considered the options. Whenever a cop took himself out, he did it with a gun. That was the code, show the world you have balls.

But Kane had a problem with that. A nine-millimeter leaves a large exit wound, and someone would have to deal with the mess. Besides, being alone in a room like this, it was possible that no one would hear the shot. Days could go by before anyone discovered him. As much as he disliked his landlady, he couldn't do that to her.

Of course, if he capped himself somewhere else, a stranger might find him—maybe even some little kid. Kane recalled cases where a child was the first one to come across a gunshot death. That's a terrible thing to do to an innocent.

Systematically, he considered other methods. He rejected the spectacular ways—jumping from a high building, running in front of a train, driving into an expressway overpass. People who resorted to such methods, he believed, were selfish exhibitionists. An average citizen who witnesses something like that is troubled by the memory for life. Kane's fight was with himself, not strangers.

Poisoning was too complicated, requiring too much preparation and knowledge of chemistry. Kane never worked Homicide, so he wasn't up on such things. He might screw it up, end up a brain-damaged invalid.

Ditto a pill overdose or drowning. Besides, the river was too cold this time of the year. Carbon monoxide was a good way, but he had no access to a private garage. Hanging was too messy, and there was the same problem with finding the right location.

Kane lay the gun down.

He crossed the room to his portable refrigerator and opened another beer. Then, automatically, he turned on the radio. Hearing "The Little Drummer Boy," he snapped it back off. He took a pull off the beer, then started to pace about the small room.

He thought back to the times past when he had considered suicide, all the times he had held back. Cowardice, *that* was his secret shame. Never mind the medals, the bravery citations. He was yellow, just like his old man had always said.

He thought about his only child, Pete, dead from a drug overdose at seventeen, six years ago. And his ex-wife, Jennie, now drinking herself stupid in a little shack in northern Michigan. What could he have done to change things for them?

Not only was Kane a coward, he was a guilty coward. A fresh wave of self-loathing washed over him. He picked up the remote television control and snapped it on. A preacher, in love with his own voice, droned on about the "true meaning of Christmas," now just five days away.

He glared at the television in disgust. *What planet does this pious prick live on? How can a rational human being believe that loving-God shit? Assholes like him should spend a couple of years in some war zone. Pick one.*

Kane muted the television, walked to the window and

looked out at the street. Already his department car, a green Pontiac, was covered with snow. *There,* Kane decided. *That's where I'll do it, inside the car. Locked.*

The more he considered the matter, the more he realized that the unmarked police car was the perfect place to die. A forty-five-degree angle up into the mouth would drive the slug through the car roof, not out the back window where it could hurt someone down the street. Locking the doors would prevent some passing dirtbag from stealing the Beretta. He'd radio for assistance just before he capped off the round. That way, the person who found him would be a fellow cop.

Having made the decision, Kane suddenly felt almost giddy. This would be his final fuck-you to this city and this police department.

His mind started moving in other directions. Absurdly, he wondered if his low-life "customers" would miss him. He thought about the militia group he'd been working, and the latest LCN conspiracy. How about Vito Vitale, and Aldo Giacalone, and Carmine Lucci? What would the *goombahs* say when they found out old Ralph Kane ate his gun? It was creepy, now that he thought about it, but those shitheads were the closest thing he had to a family.

Kane let his mind linger there for a moment. No other cop could ever get close to those pricks, not the way he had. For sure, not the current batch in OCI. Like that college punk, Van Horn, who prided himself on being the youngest lieutenant in department history.

Kane took another swig of beer. He thought about last night, sitting in Harvey's Place, idly listening to a new blues group. Out of nowhere, Harvey had asked him if it was true he was planning to pull the plug.

The question startled Kane. How had Harvey guessed? Then he realized the old bar owner was talking about his *retirement.* The word was out, Harvey had informed him, that Kane was about to retire.

So Kane had set him straight. "Don't believe what you hear on the street," he told Harvey. The city's dirtbags couldn't wait for old Ralph Kane to retire. But he didn't have his twenty-five years in yet.

Kane let his mind wander back to the early years of his police life, to the incident with the Caldwell kid. He winced, then went back even further, to the Marine Corps—and that nightmarish day when Saigon fell. The memory of that horrible day had been coming back a lot lately, and not just in his sleep, the way it used to. Now the nightmare kept popping up when he was awake, with the clarity of a technicolor movie.

He forced Saigon from his thoughts and, instead thought about Angela, and what was probably his last chance ever for happiness. He remembered the early weeks with her, when he was on the wagon. Their lovemaking had been a ballet, the closest Kane would ever get to a spiritual experience. But then he had to screw it up by drinking **again**.

Kane was puzzled by the memory. It had been three years now, and he rarely thought about her any more. Maybe it's always this way with men who are about to kill themselves, he thought. Maybe they always review the regrets.

Then, at last, he thought about his brother Billy, also dead. His only sibling had been murdered two years earlier inside Statesville Prison. Kane tried to imagine Billy's last thoughts as a fellow convict shanked him...

Fuck this sentimental bullshit, he told himself finally. He set the beer on the counter, put on his mackinaw and picked up the Beretta. He studied it for another long moment. *How will it feel? You see hundreds of these things. But you never <u>know</u>, do you?*

He shoved the pistol in his belt and unsnapped the deadbolt on the door. The wall phone rang. Reflexively he grabbed it. "Kane."

"Ralph, this is Roberta Easterly."

Kane was startled. He took a deep breath before

answering. "What can I do for you, Inspector?"

"We've got a caper going down," she said. "A bad one."

Of all the fucked-up timing. "I'm off today. I have plans."

"It's a kidnap, Detective. A child."

"Why are you calling *me*? I don't work that detail."

"Because it looks professional, and no one in this city has better informants."

Kane pondered that. "It's a little boy," Easterly added quietly. "He's seven years old. We need you."

Kane shut his eyes. Then he shook his head. "I'll be there in a few minutes."

1029 hours

When he received the same summons Isaiah Bell was in church– a white man's church, no less. Wearing a trench coat over a dark blue suit and red tie, Bell stood with his family in a middle pew of St. Aidan's, watching the congregation sing. The floor was wet in several places where worshippers had tracked in snow. Everyone, including the Bell family, wore galoshes.

Bell covertly inspected the Christmas-decorated church, and the congregation. The Bells were the only African Americans here. His wife Vera, twenty years his junior, sang with feeling: "I once was lost, but now I'm found…"

The kids, Cassie, ten, and Ikey, eight, dressed in warm clothing, were less than enthusiastic about the hymn. But they were well-behaved children, and quietly endured the Sunday ritual with these strange white people. They knew how important good behavior was to their parents, especially here in the new neighborhood. If they missed the old church, with the raucous gospel songs and *amen!* shouts, they did not show it. Bell burned with love for them.

Ike Bell was nearly fifty-four years old. But, except for the graying hair atop his coal-black face, you would never know it. He was a huge man, maybe six-five, built like a linebacker —which, indeed, he once had been, before leaving school for the Special Forces and Vietnam. Now, still rock hard, he had the arms and hands of a man who could break a person in half.

Bell's cell phone went off. As the Gang Intelligence Unit's weekend duty officer, he had to keep it on at all times, but had it set to the vibrate mode, so no one else would hear it during the service. He checked the number. It was a headquarters extension. Vera looked at him quizzically. He shrugged. His wife just shook her head, knowing what to expect.

Bell waited for the hymn to end, then discreetly slipped out of the pew. The other parishioners sat down for the sermon and glanced at him politely as he quietly walked toward the back door. He heard the pastor begin the homily, a pleasant man who, just two weeks ago, had welcomed Bell's family to the neighborhood:

"Our lesson this morning concerns the promise of Christmas, the promise that culminates in the miracle of the Resurrection—the promise of human redemption…"

Bell feared the minister would think him rude. But the man knew what he did for a living. When welcoming the family to the congregation, he had made it clear that he appreciated the police and "all the heroic things you people do to keep our community safe." His brother Mike was a cop in Detroit, he revealed, adding something about the Archangel Michael being the first policeman.

The speech was a little too self-conscious, Bell thought at the time. He decided, for Vera's sake, to give the guy the benefit of the doubt. Still, he fought the old cynicism: how warm would these people be if he were some African American janitor? He knew that from now on the Bells would be the parish's "black family," even though no one would ever say it that way. How many of the people in *this* community had ever suffered? He thought about mothers in gang-infested neighborhoods whose children had to sleep on the floor to avoid bullets flying through the windows. What did these people know about that world?

But, still, Vera liked St. Aidan's better than any other church she had investigated in the three months since they'd moved into their "new" thirty-year-old house. She was nondenominational and ecumenical. She didn't care about the messenger. All she wanted from a church was to hear the *real* message of Christ. So far these people were doing a pretty good job.

Bell opened the church door. Wind-driven snow blasted his face. The stuff was coming down even harder, a thoroughly rotten morning. He paused to light a furtive cigarette. Vera would raise hell if she saw him. He hadn't been able to quit, which he had promised when the department doctor first got on his case. *Here I am, sneaking my drug like a common hype.*

Bell hated this time of the year. The winters were endless, and this one was just beginning. Someone in olden times must have put Christmas in late December for just that reason, to bring a little joy to an utterly depressing season.

He crossed the parking lot to the family station wagon, in case this was going to turn into a long conversation. The snow was already halfway up to his knees. For the thousandth time, he wished he had joined the Los Angeles PD back when he was discharged from the Army out in California twenty-eight years ago.

Instead he had come here, to an entirely strange city. At that time, even before affirmative action, the department was actively seeking African American recruits. The city fathers foresaw an explosive race problem. They needed black faces on the job. So they authorized bonuses to black military veterans, and young Ike Bell had responded to their ad in *Army Times.*

Now, three years past retirement age, Bell still clung to the job because his wife and kids needed the money. That's what happens when a confirmed bachelor finally marries late in life. He reined in his regret. Not only was it futile, if he had stayed in California he wouldn't even *have* this family.

Bell wished he could be more like Vera, a trauma nurse at Central Receiving. He admired his wife's faith, and the love she had for her fellow man. He would give anything to be like her. But he had too many old resentments.

They were very different people, he and Vera. He had seen far too much of life's ugly side. And, despite her entreaties, he supposed he'd never get over this race thing.

He knew his anger was justified. But he also remembered how his father had driven himself crazy with resentment, until it finally killed him. And he remembered what that did to his mother. Vera was right; such rage was toxic. And Bell always feared that his father's madness might be genetic.

So now here he was, all these years later, in this dismal northern city, having just moved his family into a lily-white suburb to get away from the gangbangers who were destroying their old community. At times, Bell was not overly fond of the black race, either.

He got in the station wagon, turned on the motor for heat, and dialed the headquarters number. "Major Crimes, Officer Williams," a black voice answered.

"This is Detective Bell, from GIU. Someone paged me."

"Stand by."

Bell was puzzled by the source of the call. What could Major Crimes want from him?

Then, realizing that he was still smoking, he rolled down the windows and turned on the fan. He knew he might already be in trouble: Vera had a sensitive nose. He flicked the cigarette out into the snow, just as a female voice came on the line: "Detective, this is Inspector Roberta Easterly, commanding Major Crimes."

"I know who you are, Inspector."

"I'm sorry to interrupt your weekend, but we need you. We have a very nasty kidnapping going down."

"Kidnapping? I work gangs. Kidnapping belongs to Criminal Conspiracy."

"You also have the best network of black informants in the city." She paused. "It's a child, Detective. A black child, seven years old. It looks professional. We're bringing in specialists from all over the department."

Bell looked at the clean lines of the modern suburban church, at the spire reaching up through the snow. He sighed, remembering what he always told young cops when they complained about the job: *no one drafted you.*

"I'm at church with my family. With this weather…I have to go home for the department car."

"Get down here as soon as you can. And don't tell anyone. We're trying to minimize media exposure."

"Yes, ma'm." He turned off the cell phone, wondering who the hell he would tell. But Roberta Easterly was one of the most respected command officers in the department. So he did not question the legitimacy of the call. *This will get my family some attention,* he thought, *pulling them out in the middle of the service.*

Bell rolled up the windows and climbed out of the station wagon. He stopped and picked up the soggy cigarette butt, dropped it in a trashcan, then walked back to the church. He stomped the snow off his feet before entering.

1110 hours

The snow again had stopped falling by the time Kane pulled the green Pontiac into the side street adjacent to the ancient headquarters building. He wore jeans and an old mackinaw.

Platoon Two was into their midwatch shift change, so the street was jammed with blue-and-whites. There never was any place to park around here. Kane pulled alongside a fire hydrant and placed the blue Kojak light on the dashboard, a time-honored practice. Lately the squints in Admin had been issuing reprimands for such infractions, but today Kane didn't give a damn. *Let's see them summon a dead man to an ass-chewing.*

He reached into the glove box and pulled out a pint of cheap whiskey. He took a long pull off it, then popped a breath mint into his mouth.

He got out of the car and noted that the wind had shifted. Now it was blowing in from the south, so the air was warming up again—typical for this time of year. Next it would probably rain on top of the snow, then freeze again. He silently cursed the weather. He rubbed his chin and remembered that he hadn't shaved.

On the way up the front steps of headquarters, he passed a pair of detectives who worked Central Holdup. They pointedly looked away. Kane ignored them.

As an intelligence officer, he was as much a spy as a detective. His job was to collect information about crime syndicates, keep track of things—who was who, and what they were doing. That information provided deep background for other investigators and prosecutors. Kane himself never had to gather actual evidence, testify in court, or work with a partner. It was the perfect job for a loner.

Kane had long known that he was the most distrusted man in this police department. Internal Affairs regarded him as a borderline criminal. It all began with that ancient Caldwell case, even though he had been cleared of any wrongdoing, and had continued ever since.

The police brass and IA also knew Kane's brother Billy had been a burglar and extortionist. They assumed that was the reason Kane himself was so good at getting information about the city's hoodlums: He thought like them. And if he thought like them, how different could he be *from* them?

Kane was almost proud of this reputation. Billy once asked him why he stayed on the job. "It's a game," Kane had replied, "matching wits with these idiots." And occasionally his work actually helped nail some prick who was victimizing the truly innocent. Part of Ralph Kane was still an altar boy.

Plus, God knew, he didn't want a boring life—or one like Billy's. So what else could he do?

Kane passed through the revolving glass door into headquarters, then badged his way past the security checkpoint. In the lobby, on the way to the elevator, he passed a gaily decorated Christmas tree. *You can't escape the Christmas horseshit anywhere, not even here.*

* * *

Now dressed in jeans, sweatshirt and black leather jacket, Ike Bell pushed his white Ford down the expressway into the city, code three. Traffic was light because of the snow. Bell had not informed Dispatch about the light and siren. New directives required command authorization for plain-car code-three runs. The Third Floor had gotten the word from the City Attorney about liability. But Easterly had told him to get in as fast as possible, so he took that as command authorization.

Bell turned on the AM radio as he splashed along in the number one lane. Under the rise and fall of the siren, a black councilman debated with the white head of a homeowner's group about the city's endless racial tensions. After all these years, the police of this city still behaved like an occupying army, the councilman declared, harassing people of color at any opportunity.

"That's because 'people of color' are the ones committing

most of the crime!" the white man spat sarcastically.

"That's a racist comment!" the councilman said.

"Oh, yeah? Get a scanner and listen to police calls, any night of the week!" the white man shouted. "Listen to the descriptions of the criminals!"

"That's a very small percentage of black people!" the councilman shouted back. "Most of their victims are other black people!"

"Which is exactly why *you people* need to support the police…!"

Bell, sick of this endless debate, changed stations. He heard "Jingle Bells" and turned the radio back off. He exited the expressway and rolled through the deserted downtown streets.

1206 hours

By noon, a task force had been mobilized, two dozen of the city's savviest street cops, drawn from various precincts and detective squads. All but three were male. Now they were assembled for a briefing in the headquarters gymnasium, out of sight of the press.

This being a Sunday, the usual media people were not hovering around headquarters. A couple of television crews had shown up at the crime scene after hearing something on the police radio. But a quick-thinking precinct lieutenant told them it was a domestic quarrel over child custody, nothing more. The weather was so nasty that no one stayed. They didn't realize that this was the home of the local child celebrity, so the task force had a few hours head start on the story.

Here at headquarters, a rumor was circulating among the cops: an in-house beat reporter from the *Daily Times*, a guy widely regarded as an egotistical prick, had gotten wind that something big was brewing. But Chief of Detectives Byron Slaughter had pigeonholed him. A child's life was at stake, Slaughter warned, and if the reporter said a premature word to his editors or anyone else, his wife would learn about the police-officer girlfriend he had on the side. The reporter saw the wisdom in keeping his mouth shut. And the rumor only further enhanced the cops' considerable respect for Slaughter.

Now, awaiting the briefing, Kane stood alone against the back wall of the gym, arms folded. He wore the Beretta in a shoulder rig over a denim shirt.

Clear across the room, Isaiah Bell sat with his enormous body sprawled across a folding chair. Kane covertly studied him. He'd heard Bell had found religion. *The asshole probably prays to some Black Christ…*

Bell glanced around and spotted Kane staring at him. Their eyes locked momentarily before Kane looked away. *Mother-fuck,* Bell thought, *this just isn't my day.*

He knew exactly why Kane was here. From an operational point of view it made sense. But Bell had spent the last twenty-three years avoiding the little bastard. You can do that in a big police department. It had worked out fine, until today.

Inspector Roberta Easterly, still a looker at forty-five, walked in to conduct the briefing. In her business suit, she looked more corporate executive than cop. She was flanked by Slaughter and the city's new Chief of Police, Jefferson Mosely, also wearing suits.

Mosely, an African American, had been in town for only a month. He was still floundering around in this new department, here in one of the nation's most dangerous cities. The word on Mosely was that he still hadn't even learned the names of the major streets.

The city's police, already stung by the appointment of an outsider, were openly suspicious of the newcomer, freshly hired away from Dallas. Many a secretive phone call had been placed to contacts in the Dallas P.D., who universally described Mosely as politically crafty but a second-rate cop—and a backstabber. He knew how to play the racial angles, they said, so he had been popular with the so-called "black community" in Dallas. But the rank-and-file Texas officers, white and black, detested him.

Now, at the briefing, Mosely wisely deferred to Byron Slaughter and Bobbie Easterly. He was smart enough to appear in civvies. The old-line cops resented an outsider wearing their cherished uniform, regardless of title.

On the other hand, even the most reactionary males in the department respected Easterly. She pre-dated affirmative action, so had made rank the hard way. It helped that, as a rookie, she had won the Medal of Valor for rescuing a wounded policeman under fire.

So the working stiffs didn't think of Easterly as a woman. To them she was a *cop*. Behind her back they called her "Ballsy Bobbie." Her passion in life, which she had honed to an art form, was catching evil people who did terrible things to good people. Everyone in the room would go to the wall for a skipper like Easterly.

The rank-and-file held Byron Slaughter in similar esteem. At fifty-six, he was at the second level of department command, his pay grade equivalent to that of a Deputy Chief. There were two other Deputy Chiefs—both of them away for Christmas—plus a fourth Deputy slot, which was vacant.

"Okay, listen up," Easterly addressed the task force. "I'm sorry to screw up your weekend. But you people are the best of the best, and we really need you."

Easterly held up a blown-up photograph of a light-skinned black boy, his smile radiating innocence. He seemed familiar to many in the room.

"Here's our victim, age seven," Easterly said. "His name

is Darryl Childress. Darryl's a child actor who has appeared in several local fast-food commercials. Perhaps you or your kids have seen him on TV. I don't have any children and I don't watch much television, but I'm told he has a large following. Kids apparently love him."

Easterly checked her watch. "Darryl was grabbed by two male suspects a little less than four hours ago from the front yard of his family home in the Seventeenth Precinct, the 14000 block of Lawndale Avenue. He was in the yard building a snowman. His parents were inside dressing for church. They're professional people—he's a teacher, she's a nurse. It's a racially mixed marriage—he's white, she's black. This is their only child.

"Darryl's mother happened to look out the window and got a fleeting look at the suspects. She saw them pull the boy into a car. In the struggle, he lost one of his gloves, which we've recovered. The vehicle is a late-model gray sedan with tinted windows, make and plates unknown. She didn't get a look at their faces. But she's positive one is white and the other black. They took off eastbound.

"That's all we know. The forensics people are at the scene trying to reconstruct what's left of footprints and tire tracks. Unfortunately, the mother ran outside and trampled the snow. Then the first radio car pulled up in the same spot and the officers interviewed her curbside—right where the bad guys grabbed the kid. And it's been snowing off and on since. So I don't think we'll get anywhere with physical evidence."

She looked around the room at the cops taking notes. "We're expecting a ransom demand. So we have a second command post under the direction of Criminal Conspiracy set up at the house. We've taken all marked police vehicles out of the area to minimize unwanted attention. The parents' number is unlisted, but these guys obviously were well-prepared.

"You'll be assigned to four six-man squads, each with

a team leader from CCB. Our operating frequency is Tac Four. The assignment sheets are up here on the desk. The first order of business is to canvas the neighborhood, see if anyone remembers a white guy and a black guy hanging around together. Ask the neighbors to keep it quiet."

"What about the FBI?" asked a black cop. "We have to work with those fools?"

"We'll bring them in only if we have to," said Slaughter. He spoke with a soft Tennessee accent. "We'll have to if this looks interstate."

"I think we can pull our own weight," added Easterly. The assembled officers murmured appreciatively.

"What about rewards?" asked another cop.

"The new guidelines require authorization from the city council," Easterly said. "This is Sunday. We can't get that until tomorrow, at the earliest."

Slaughter shook his head. "With all the racial crap going on with this council, I wouldn't count on it. Those people can't agree on the time of day. Besides, once we go to the council with this, the cat's out of the bag."

"But a kid's life is at stake!" a cop protested.

"You know that and I know that," said Slaughter. "But we're dealing with egos here. Political egos." He looked pointedly over at the new chief, Mosely. "There's none worse."

Mosely glared powerlessly back at him. Slaughter had also been a candidate for this job, the candidate favored by the troops. Besides, he was long past retirement eligibility, so he could say whatever he thought.

Easterly pointed to a tall stack of photos. "Pass out copies to everyone you contact."

The briefing ended with that. Easterly's adjutant, a grizzled Detective Sergeant named Stanislaus Jablonski, handed out the team lists and pictures of the boy.

Kane and Bell were not on any list. The two men waited

until the others filed out. Then, without speaking to each other, they approached Easterly.

"Excuse me, Inspector," Bell said.

"Don't worry," she said. "You're not working together." She looked back and forth between them. "I've heard there's bad blood between you two. Put it aside, at least until we clean this up."

"If we're not working together, what *are* we doing?" Kane asked.

"You're both on your own. Whatever you do is off the books." She looked back and forth between them. "That's how you usually work anyway, isn't it? A couple of lone wolves?"

"It's how *I* work," Kane said.

"Okay, then. You get out among the white dirtbags. Bell, you work the blacks. I want you to cast very wide nets. Find out *anything* that's on the street telegraph. Make any deals you have to, short of a free ride on a murder. And you both report directly to me."

Bell and Kane each picked up a stack of photos of the missing boy. Then they left the gym by separate doors.

When they were gone, Jablonski turned to Easterly. "Ain't love grand?"

"What's that all about, Stan? I've never heard the details."

"It happened before you came on the department, when Kane was a rookie and Bell was three or four years on the job. They both worked Patrol in the Tenth Precinct. Kane was partnered with a redneck named Lucas, who was a known racist. Lucas blew away a black kid in an alley one night— his name was Colson or Caldwell, something like that. He was fourteen or fifteen years old. The kid supposedly pulled a gun, but word went around that Lucas planted it on the corpse."

"And that Kane covered for him. Yeah, I vaguely remembering hearing about it."

"It was a big deal for awhile. Lucas was cleared by a Board of Review, primarily thanks to Kane. So there was a lot of bitterness on the part of the black officers. Kane was a kid, but he took a lot of heat."

"Was Bell involved?"

"Not in the shooting. But he was heavily involved with the Afro-American Police Officers Association, as they called it back then. He was one of their organizers. He was pretty militant. That was the term they used in those days, *militant*. This AAPOA, they conducted their own investigation, came up with some stuff about Lucas' background that made him out to be a bigot, which of course he was. Bell and the other AAPOA officers tried to pressure the D.A. to take it to a grand jury, but he refused."

"I remember reading about that, too, all the tension on the street."

"Not just on the street, boss. A lot of the white coppers hated Bell, same as a lot of the black coppers hated Kane." Jablonski paused, remembering. "It was a different department back then, Inspector. Women in this building didn't have it easy, either."

"Oh, *how* I remember." Easterly smiled sadly. "You don't need to remind *me*."

"Everything's changed now. Bell saved a white copper's ass one night, and that gave the more reasonable white guys a more reasonable point of view. Most of the old-time rednecks are retired now, or dead, and Bell's got a great street rep. So that shit's all ancient history around here."

"Except for Ralph Kane."

Jablonski just shrugged. "Except for Ralph Kane."

1245 hours

Roberta Easterly washed her face in the women's room on the fifth floor of the ancient police station, examining her graying hair. She was pleased that she still had some of her good looks. But one thing was sure: her days posing as a call girl were long past.

She dried her hands, then walked down the corridor to her office, passing photographs of the city's police chiefs, portraits dating all the way back to the Civil War. All, of course, were men. She entered her office, closed the door, sat down at her desk and put her head in her hands. She needed to slow down and think.

Easterly began mentally cataloguing each of the righteous kidnapping cases during the seven years she had been in this job. She couldn't recall any with this M.O.

A memory like hers was a mixed blessing. It certainly made the job easier—at least it did back in the old days, before computers. But it didn't help her insomnia on those lonely nights when her husband slept peacefully next to her.

She thought about those female officers she knew who had married other cops. In some ways it would have been easier to have a police spouse, someone who had personally experienced the "Horror Show," her private name for the parade of atrocious memories.

On the other hand, marriage to a good-natured adoption lawyer like David Goldman helped in other ways. David provided a different perspective, reminding her regularly that life also included happy things.

She smiled as she thought of him. Nearly twenty years now, and she still loved the old bugger—more than ever, in fact. David had had it rough as a kid, to be sure, growing up with asthma and poverty. But somehow he had turned adversity to his advantage. There must be something genetic about an optimistic disposition; both of David's sisters were the same way.

She decided to call him. He'd still been asleep when the Control Center summoned her into work this morning. So he hadn't a clue about what she was going through today.

Now, as their home phone rang, she examined their framed wedding picture. He had put on a lot of weight since then, and his hair was thinner. He was just an average-looking guy, but he had a great heart. That was the most important organ in the human body, she had long ago decided, the heart. She had known lots of people with great minds and no heart, and she had no use for them.

She was still working Patrol when they married. David had just finished law school. Adoption law was still new to him, and he loved it. Helping discarded kids find happy homes became his life's passion. He had never regretted the choice.

On the other hand, she and David had never regretted the decision not to have children of their own. Easterly realized long ago that she did not have good "mother genes," as she put it. And David was so involved with his work that any paternal instincts were buried deep inside.

The answering machine kicked in, David's pleasant voice. She remembered that he was going into his office today, too, to prepare for a hearing tomorrow. "Hi, babe," Easterly told the machine. "I just wanted to tell you I love you. This is a nasty caper we're dealing with. I could be here all night. Page me if you need me."

She hung up and the intercom buzzed. "Inspector, the family's in the interview room," Jablonski reported.

Easterly was startled. "Here? Who's minding the phone at their house?"

"The boy's aunt, the mother's sister. I'm sorry, skipper. They both wanted to talk to the officer in charge."

"I'll be right down." Easterly took a deep breath, bracing

herself. Then she walked back out of the office.

1325 hours

Kane drove out to Vito Vitale's mansion on the West End. He muted the police radio. He didn't want to hear the endless reports of human depravity. Sunday afternoons in the winter were noted for domestic violence.

For the time being, he had decided to put suicide out of his head. That would come later, once this job was done. *If there is a God, he's a sadistic prick with a bizarre sense of timing.*

Now, as he drove through the sloppy snow, Kane reviewed Vitale's history. Vito was seventy-four now. He had moved here as an orphaned teenager from upstate New York, nearly sixty years ago. He had earned his La Cosa Nostra pedigree the hard way: petty theft, strong-arm enforcement and collection, a little arson, a lot of narcotics. Vito made his first bones at eighteen when he killed an eastside shylock for welshing on a debt to old Santo Angelini.

But that murder wasn't just a routine Mob clip. What had caught the attention of Angelini and his *consigliore*—and the police—was the method Vito employed: he had bound and gagged the little guy, so the legend went, then put a hole in his brain with an electric drill.

To do such a thing, you had to have balls of iron. You also had to be more than a little nuts. So that was Vito Vitale—brilliant, ruthless and very close to psychotic.

Kane considered the irony that there were those on both sides of the law who used identical adjectives about him. Maybe that was why he and old Vito got along with each other, in their way.

There's one big difference: the only killing I ever did was approved by my government.

Kane pulled up to Vitale's gate. The mansion, he noted with amusement, was decorated with Christmas lights. He took another swig from the bottle, then pushed the button on the intercom.

* * *

Bell thought about Jefferson Mosely as he drove slowly through the city's sprawling ghetto, checking Willis Henry's haunts. The Central Division frequency murmured in the background but Bell barely heard it.

So far, Bell was unimpressed with the new chief. He sized him up as one of those mediocrities who make careers out of being black. A friend in the Dallas gang squad, a black man, had put it bluntly: "Jeff Mosely wouldn't make a pimple on a policeman's ass. What he is, he's a professional spade."

That assessment soured Bell's stomach even more. There were plenty of qualified officers, of both races, at the command level of this department. Any of them might have made a decent chief. Bobbie Easterly, for one, would have been a brilliant appointment.

But the city council, wary about where the latest grand jury investigation might lead, and unnerved by endless racial tensions, had decided they had to "go outside." They also had to hire a black face. The Reverend Cecil Washington and the NAACP had all but threatened civil disobedience if they didn't get "one of our own."

So that was how Jefferson Mosely had come to town. The council had awarded him a five-year contract. No one, of course, even questioned the appointment; no one wanted to be accused of racism. And now, if Mosely fucked up in the job, it would reflect badly on all black cops. *Around and around it goes.*

Bell lit a cigarette. He caught sight of a black Salvation Army Santa ringing his bell outside a cut-rate store. He forced himself to concentrate on Christmas. He thought about the black dolls Vera had bought for Cassie, and about the bicycle he had picked out for Ikey. He wondered if his children still believed in Santa Claus.

What would it be like, Bell now wondered, to have your only child snatched off the street by a complete stranger? How could you not go mad behind such a thing? His fingers tightened on the steering wheel as he felt the pain of people he had never met. He remembered why he was a policeman.

Bell turned down Martin Luther King Drive. A dozen 79 Trey Bloods stood around the liquor store at the corner of Lincoln, dealing rock cocaine. Bell felt his anger rise. *These shitheads are the reason we're over our heads with a new mortgage, the reason my children lost their playmates. What would Doctor King think about punks like these?*

As he passed, one of the Treys glared at Bell. He jammed on the brakes. He climbed out of the Ford and stood behind the open door. "LeRoy, you and your homies get your black asses off this corner!" he commanded in a booming voice.

Half the Bloods turned to walk away. The rest stood their ground. If they were afraid of the giant policeman, they weren't about to show it. "Who be talkin', mothah-*fuckah?*" demanded one of them, knowing exactly who he was.

Bell jerked the Beretta from his shoulder holster and held it loosely at his side. "Jonas, you have five seconds before I blow your balls off!"

The Bloods sauntered off, glowering back at him over their shoulders. Bell spat. "Fucking pussies."

Then, with a grimace, he remembered his renewed spiritual commitment—and his badge. He holstered the gun and climbed back into the car, angry at himself for losing control. What if someone important had seen that, someone from the ACLU or NAACP?

Fuck it, he finally decided. *Someone has to stand up to the world's bullies.*

***

Roberta Easterly was also having a rough time keeping her emotions in check. Usually she was more in command of her feelings than this. But the parents of Darryl Childress were getting to her. Darryl's father could not stop talking about the little boy, as if recounting every detail of his son's life could somehow keep him from harm. He spoke about him in the present tense, and for the third time he mentioned the boy's love of that Christmas song "The Little Drummer Boy."

"Every time it comes on the radio, he stops everything and listens," the young redheaded man said. "He's such a sweet little boy, it's like he wishes he could play a drum for the Baby Jesus."

Easterly listened patiently. Normally her patience was calculated, waiting for some compulsive-talking suspect to slip up and incriminate himself. But now the patience came from an agonizing sense of powerlessness. She felt this man's pain to the depths of her soul, yet she had no answers to give him. All she could do was listen.

Darryl's mother, Louise, was a thin woman with a medium-brown complexion. She normally would be neatly groomed, Easterly calculated, but now she was a haggard mess. She sat next to her husband, staring into space like a zombie. These had been the worst five-and-a-half hours of her life.

"I feel so helpless," Stephen Childress implored. "What can we be doing?"

"Only what I said," Easterly replied. "Think. Think of everyone you know. Try to remember anyone who might have a motive, a grudge, anyone who might have asked for money, any of Darryl's fan mail that seemed strange. Think of any black and white males who hang out with each other, someone around the neighborhood, or at work…"

Childress looked over at his wife. "It's funny," he said. "We're the only white and black people we know who hang out together. It's a sad commentary on this city. I don't even see much of it in the schools any more…"

Childress shook his head, lost in a terrible dream. He was running out of things to say. Then an idea came to him. "I'd like to talk to your officers, let them know what kind of boy Darryl is."

"I don't think that's necessary, Mr. Childress."

"Just to motivate them."

"Sir, my officers don't need to be motivated. They're professionals. And most of them are parents themselves."

"Please, Inspector. I just want them to know how we feel."

Easterly softened. "I'll tell you what. We can videotape a message. I'll play it at the next briefing."

Childress considered that for a long minute. "All right," he said finally. "We'll tape it."

Louise began to cry softly. Utterly helpless, Easterly sat down and took her in her arms. As the woman sobbed, Easterly gently stroked her hair and fought to keep her own composure.

1415 hours

Kane waited in the high-ceilinged living room of the Victorian mansion, looking over at a life-sized statue of the Virgin Mary. Pallid and otherworldly, "Our Lady" stood open-armed over a gurgling marble fountain. Even after all these years, it still amused Kane the way these goombahs put on the pretense of religiosity.

Two of Vito Vitale's torpedoes stood silently across the room next to a Christmas tree, watching Kane. Unlike the old days, when aspiring mobsters dressed the part, these two looked more like punk rockers, with shaved heads, earrings and plenty of tattoos. *Fucking idiots. Don't they know what good descriptions those tats make?* Kane memorized their faces and tried to picture them in twenty years…

"Mr. Vitale will see you now," announced a servant girl.

Kane rose and followed her. She was vaguely pretty. He made a mental note to find out what he could about her, to see if there was some ugly secret in her life, something he could use to squeeze her. You couldn't ask for a better-placed snitch.

Then he remembered that soon he would be a dead man. *Stick to this caper. You're in the last act.*

They walked down a block-long marble corridor. "He's in the study," the girl said. *Study, my ass. The only thing this puke ever studied was the sports book.* But today, Kane told himself, he'd play the game with Vito. For a change, the police needed the Mafia.

"Officer Kane, a pleasure," Vitale said as the girl opened the door. He stood before a crackling fire, wearing a smoking jacket, of all things. Kane shook the old capo's hand, suppressing his cynical amusement. *This bastard's seen too many movies.*

Vitale gestured for the girl to close the door. He poured two brandies. "It must be something important for you to come to my home unannounced the Sunday before Christmas."

"It is." Kane accepted the brandy and filled the old mobster in on the kidnapping.

"What makes you think we had anything to do with this?" Vitale asked.

"I don't. But you might be able to find out who did."

The *capo* examined the picture of Darryl Childress for a long moment. "Sweet-looking child," he said finally. "For a nigger."

"A person can't help what he's born."

Vitale studied his old nemesis. He looked again at the child's photo. There actually seemed to be a spark of humanity in the old killer's eyes. "Any man does something bad to a kid, he should have his balls cut off and stuffed in his mouth."

"I figured you'd see it that way."

"How can I help you, Ralph?"

"You have people wired in everywhere, all over town," Kane said. "I know who they are, where they are and what they do."

Vitale smiled. "So you want us to report whatever we hear."

"I want more than that. Put the word on the wire that we want this kid back—alive."

"We?"

"You and us. The outfit and the cops." He took another sip of the brandy. "We'll consider it a marker. A big one."

Vitale thought about that, then smiled. "Fuck markers. It's Christmas. This one's on the house."

"You're getting generous in your old age."

"We all have kids, Ralph." He studied the tough little detective. "Hell, we all *were* kids." He pointed to Darryl's photo. "Give me a dozen of those pictures."

1502 hours

Ike Bell pulled up to the Red Bird Pool Hall, across the street from Amos Brown's Barbecue Shack and adjacent to a Main Line subway stop. He parked the Ford at a hydrant, then got out slowly, checking the street for hostiles. He noted the Christmas lights on the front window of the pool hall, and the wreath on the door. Then he trudged through the snow and into the place.

Rap music pounded from the jukebox. Bell stopped at

the door and searched in vain for Dizzy Dean Jackson, the proprietor.

Then, sure enough, he spotted Willis Henry, aka "Killer Willis," aka "Big Gun." Henry, the buffed-out shotcaller for the Eastside Rolling Crips, was orbiting a pool table, lining up an eight ball. Half a dozen Eastside homies stood around basking in reflected glory. Unseen, Bell stood there with his hands in his jacket pockets, watching.

Henry, now pushing thirty, was an "OG"—"Original Gangsta"—with the Rollers, the gang's leader by dint of muscle and longevity. A cigarette dangled from his lips, dropping ashes on his baggy pants. But Henry, oblivious to the ashes, was riveted on the shot. He rammed the ball home. Grinning, he slapped the hands of his followers.

"Yo, Willis," Bell finally called out in a booming voice.

Henry spun around. "Aw, man! What the fuck *you* doin' here?"

"Put that much attention into something righteous, you could be a millionaire."

"It's Sunday, Deacon. Why you hasslin' me?"

"My badge don't say nothin' about days of the week." He smiled. "Chill out, Willis. I just want to talk to you."

Two of the Crips moved closer to Henry, protectively. The OG waved them away. "I'll take care of this shit," he said.

"Let's go outside," Bell said.

"It's cold outside."

Bell shrugged. "Have it your way." He pointed to a booth. Henry grabbed his bottle and they sat down.

"You want a beer?" Henry asked. Bell shook his head. "Still on the wagon?"

"Almost two years," Bell replied.

"You go to those meetings?"

"Sometimes. Why you askin'?"

"My momma's back in the program. She strugglin'."

"I hope she makes it."

"Hear you had a little run-in with some Treys."

"News travels."

"Bell-man, I got people watchin' ever-*thang*. We better than the fuckin' CIA."

"That ain't saying much. I worked with those fools in Vietnam."

Henry thought about that. "My daddy was in Vietnam."

"Never knew you *had* a daddy, Willis."

"He got his black ass killed over there. 'Friendly fire,' they called it."

"Sorry, man," Bell said sincerely. "There was a lot of that shit."

"Don't make me no mind," Henry shrugged. "Didn't even know the nigger. Motherfucker knocked up my mama—she was just a *teenager*—then ran off to war to get away from what he did."

"People make mistakes."

"That's for goddamned sure." Henry fired up a joint and inhaled deeply, testing the limits. "You didn't come out in this weather to talk about fathers and sons."

"Yes, as a matter of fact, I did," Bell said, ignoring the dope. He pulled out the picture of Darryl Childress. "This child is someone's son."

Henry studied the picture. "I seen that kid on TV. Pizza King commercial, that's what it was."

"Someone kidnapped him this morning while he was building a snowman, snatched him right out of his front yard. Black dude, white dude, working together."

"What you leanin' on me for? I would *never* mess with no kid. Besides, my people don't hang with white motherfuckers. We sure as shit don't caper with them."

Bell lit a cigarette. "I wasn't accusing you. I just want your help. You and your homies."

Henry just stared at the old detective. "Help the *po-lice*?"

Then he laughed. "Man, that's the goddamnedest thing I ever heard! What you gon' do, man, give us honorary deputy badges?"

"Willis, you got a little brother around that age? A cousin, maybe?"

"Man, I got a *chile* that age."

"Well, how would the *chile's* mama feel if some strangers grabbed him?"

"I know how *I'd* feel about it."

Bell leaned forward and looked Henry deep in the eyes. "Then help us, for God's sake."

Henry pondered that. "You gon' ax the Bloods, too?"

"Maybe. We need all the help we can get." He pointed to Darryl's photo. "This baby's too young to know about all that red and blue bullshit."

Henry studied the picture. "Got some white blood in him, don't he?"

"Who doesn't?"

Henry thought about it. "I'll see what I can find out," he said finally.

"Thanks, Willis."

"You owe me one, Bell-man."

"Only if we find the boy."

Henry pointed to the picture. "Gimme ten copies. For the *honorary deputies.*"

Trudging back to his car, Bell thought about the anonymous, long-dead soldier who had fathered Willis Henry before being killed by his own comrades. He tried to picture what the man might look like now had he survived the war, but all he could see was the face of an old African American master sergeant named Mathers.

Then it suddenly occurred to Bell : *Willis Henry looks just like a younger version of Mathers. In fact, the fucker could be his son.*

Bell stopped to take a breath, blindsided by this sudden connection. Mathers had been a lifer, the grizzled NCO who first explained to young Bell the realities of military life for a black man.

On Bell's first classified mission in 'Nam after special weapons training, he had found himself ferried out to the boonies in an unmarked chopper, a Huey assigned to the First Air Cav but loaned to the CIA. He found himself sitting across from a very young and very small Viet Cong prisoner, who was bound and blindfolded.

An ARVN intelligence officer, a major, started interrogating the VC as the chopper lifted off the ground. He was backed by a pair of South Vietnamese thugs in civilian clothes. They left the door open on the starboard side.

Young Bell and old Mathers were sitting next to each other, watching, trying to comprehend the questioning. Mathers was returning to the field after being treated for minor wounds. They were the only Americans aboard, other than the pilot. They watched the Vietnamese major grow more and more animated as the helicopter ascended, but the VC said nothing whatsoever. He couldn't have been more than seventeen, Bell reckoned.

Suddenly, with no warning whatever, the two thugs grabbed the kid, ripped off the blindfold and casually shoved him out the door. Bell caught a glimpse of his eyes as he dropped to his death. It sickened him like nothing ever had before.

After they had safely landed, Bell approached the old sergeant and told him he was disturbed by what they had witnessed.

"Kid, keep your fucking mouth shut," Mathers commanded. "That's just the way these people do things. You'll get your black ass in deep shit if you say anything."

"In training, they told us to report shit like that," young Bell insisted.

"Are you that naïve? The Pentagon puts that bullshit out so the press will think we're policing ourselves. So the average white American in the suburbs can keep believing we're the noble saviors of mankind." The old master sergeant leaned close to Bell and spoke urgently. "Listen, slick, you know how easy it is for a black man to disappear over here? Keep your yap shut about this or you're just another dead nigger."

Two weeks later, Mathers himself was killed in an ambush. So Bell put the incident out of his mind, for the most part. He heeded Mathers' counsel and said nothing. But now, all these years later, it still bothered him.

Bell reached the Ford. Fuck it, he told himself as he opened the door. That was then, this is now. Mathers was right. Quit thinking about that shit.

1627 hours

The makeshift command post had been expanded. The gymnasium now was filled with card tables, folding chairs, telephones and computers.

Roberta Easterly sat in a corner with two detectives from the Criminal Conspiracy Bureau, Forrest and McEwan. Forrest was white, McEwan black. "What do you think the odds are?" she asked somberly.

"There shoulda been a ransom demand by now," said McEwan.

"Could be these punks aren't as smart as we think they are," Forrest said. "The phone's unlisted."

"Maybe we should break silence, publicize our hot line," Easterly said. "They have to know the Childress home is full of cops, that we have a bug on the phone."

"Also could be they're just fucking with us," said McEwan. "You know, for sport."

Then a phone did ring, a few feet from Easterly. Jablonski grabbed it and turned to her. "Ralph Kane checking in."

Easterly shook her head. "Nothing new at this end," Jablonski told Kane. "We're combing the neighborhood, coming up with zilch."

Kane sat talking on his cell phone in his idling Pontiac on a block splotched with graffiti. He watched the snow start to fall again. Dusk was approaching. "The media blackout still on?"

"For the time being," replied Jablonski. "But the citizens we've talked to—those people watch the news. When they don't see a story at six, someone's sure to tip off the vultures."

"That's the way it goes in a democracy," Kane said sarcastically. He signed off and pulled away from the curb. He continued slowly down the slippery street to a closed auto repair garage under an El overpass. The presence of a dozen old cars at the curb told him the West End Outlaws were holding their usual Sunday gathering. In dry weather, the vehicles would be Harleys.

Kane considered the firepower that was likely cached inside. The Anti-Terrorism Squad had been leaning heavily on these scrotes lately, ever since the firebombing of the Spanish Pagans' clubhouse two months ago. Right at the moment, police-Outlaw relations were at an all time low.

Fuck it. These guys have no beef with me. I've always been square business. And even these assholes were kids once.

Kane was grateful that Vito Vitale had reminded him of that elementary fact. He tried to picture Tiny Lawless, the Outlaws' leader, as a baby. The thought amused him.

Kane took another belt from the flask, then drove around to the slushy alley. Burglar bars covered both rear windows.

Kane got out of the car, dodging puddles. It was turning cold again. In a couple of hours, this alley would be solid ice. *Fuck this weather!* He pulled up the collar on his mackinaw and felt the reassuring weight of the Beretta in the shoulder rig. He banged on the steel door.

"Who the fuck's there?" boomed Lawless' surly voice.

"Your friendly neighborhood po-lice," Kane called back. "Open up, Tiny."

It took a full minute for Lawless to comply. The Outlaws, Kane suspected, were hurriedly stashing whatever dope they'd been consuming. Meantime, an El train clattered overhead.

Sure enough, when the door creaked open, Kane could smell marijuana. Tiny Lawless' immense, tattooed body blocked the doorway. "Since when you working Sundays?" he demanded.

"Leonard, does your mama know you use drugs?"

"You got a warrant? Because if you don't have a warrant..."

"Lighten up, little man. I need some help." Kane handed the giant biker a photo of Darryl Childress. "This boy's been kidnapped."

"What the fuck's that got to do with us?"

"We're trying to save his life."

"My people don't fuck with kids."

"I know. That's why I'm asking for help."

"*Help?* What kind of help?"

"Information—you know, from your 'associates.' Nose around, ask a few questions, turn over a few rocks..."

Lawless stared at him. "Son of a bitch, you have balls. Your gestapo's been leaning on us for months, calling us terrorists, and now you want *help.*"

"That's them, this is me. Have I ever screwed you over?"

"You all work for the same company."

"Is that a no?"

Lawless examined the picture for a long moment. "I've seen this kid somewhere."

"TV. He's been on TV. Pizza commercials. Cute little guy, ain't he?"

Lawless studied the detective, then looked back at the

picture. Finally, he shrugged. "Come on in. It's cold out here."

Kane followed the pot-bellied Outlaw through the dank garage. Four huge motorcycles covered with tarps stood to one side. Absurdly, a scrawny little Christmas tree stood near them, lights flashing.

In Lawless' office sat six leathered-up bikers, holding beer cans and glaring at him in an attempt to look menacing. Kane knew them all; he had memorized their rap sheets. Mostly they were petty thieves or weed dealers, although some may have been dealing crank. All wore identical black leather Outlaw jackets. Other than their various sizes and differing tattoos, they were virtual clones.

These assholes think they're bad-asses and rebels, but they're all in uniform, just like corporate ladder-climbers. Everybody has a costume. With them were four young girls, heavy on makeup and mascara, also dressed in leather. *Underage, no doubt—someone's children, runaways.*

Statutory rape was a common offense on Outlaw rap sheets. Kane made a mental note to tip off Vice if these fuckers declined to cooperate.

The room remained dead silent. Kane sniffed the air. "Who's holding the weed?" he asked. "You, Mumps?"

The wiry Mumps Rafferty glared at Kane. "You jamming us for smoking a little gage?"

"No, I'm asking for some. That bud smells good. Marin County, that's my guess. I haven't tasted any good cannabis in a long time. Fire up some of that shit."

Weasel Warren, with a bad complexion and covered with tats, looked over at Lawless in astonishment. "Is this fucker for real?"

"Go ahead, *give* me a joint," Kane insisted. "You can take a picture of me smoking it if you want. That way you'll know I'm not gonna burn you."

Lawless shrugged in amazement as he handed Kane a

joint. The detective lit it, inhaled deeply, held the smoke, then exhaled. He repeated the ritual, then smiled and handed the reefer back to Tiny. "Nice stuff," he said to one of the girls, who was staring in disbelief. "Bet you never saw a cop do *that*."

"Man, you are something else," said Lawless.

Kane, lightheaded, just laughed. "I came to enlist you citizens in my own private army." He held up the photo of Darryl Childress. "This boy here is our mission."

1812 hours

Night had fallen. Christmas lights twinkled even here, in the bleakest of slums.

Ike Bell checked in with the command post, then called Vera to tell her he'd be working late. "So what else is new?" she asked. But she said it lovingly. It was just the way things were, being married to a detective. She didn't even ask what kind of a case it was.

Vera reminded Bell that she herself was working tomorrow. Now that they had moved, her commute was much longer. That meant the children had to spend more time in day care. And this week and next they were on Christmas vacation. So the babysitting costs would be substantial.

"I'll take some comp time next week," Bell promised. "I can watch them myself."

"Sure thing," said Vera, not believing it.

Bell said goodbye and hung up, once again angry about their forced relocation. He examined the graffiti on the nearby walls. This particular desecration was the handiwork of an offshoot Crip set, the One-Twelve Killahs. *Who needs the KKK when black terrorists control our streets?*

He tried to check his rage. Hate the sin, love the sinner; that's what Vera would say. *Sure thing.*

He pulled up his jacket collar, crossed the street, and walked slowly into The Lucky Deuce, a strip bar. He paused just inside the door and surveyed the room.

A buxom chocolate-colored woman with dyed blonde hair gyrated her naked pelvis before a group of noisy lowlifes to the tune of "Jingle Bell Rock." Half her admirers wore sunglasses, one an absurd peaked red Santa Claus hat with a white pom-pom. Four or five drunks were scattered about in the otherwise empty dive.

Garland McQueen sat in his usual place in a rear corner, next to an exit sign. He was smoking a Cuban cigar while playing cards with three of his cronies. Bell flashed on their rap sheets. All were small-time, low-profile wannabes.

But there was nothing low-profile about McQueen. Today he wore a purple suit which made him look like a singer from a sixties Motown group, topping off the ensemble with a wide-brimmed purple hat. *No wonder white people have stereotypes about us.*

The Lucky Deuce was the legit front for McQueen's gambling operation. Vice Ops had tagged him for bookmaking several times over the years, but each time he had skated, aided by expensive lawyers and—more than once, it was rumored —an expensive judge.

Bell walked toward McQueen, exaggerating his gunfighter stride for the benefit of his audience. With his peripheral vision, he watched the room. How many of these dirtbags had outstanding warrants?

McQueen looked up, the cigar clenched in his teeth. He forced a smile and, without rising, slapped Bell's hand. "The Deacon! My *man!*"

"A minute of your time," Bell said quietly, nodding toward McQueen's rear office.

"You back workin' Vice?"

"No. It's something else."

"Whatever you say, brother," said the old racketeer. He

lay his cards face-down on the table, stood up and led Bell back to his office. The walls were covered with nude shots of former McQueen employees.

"How's business, Queenie?" Bell asked, casually inspecting the pictures.

"If that's an official question, let me call my lawyer."

Bell held up a photo of Darryl Childress. "Someone kidnapped this kid this morning, out front of his house. The media doesn't know about it yet. We think it's professional, a ransom caper."

"My people are into *adult* entertainment. We don't fuck with kids."

"You hear me accuse you of anything? I'm asking for help."

The old hustler considered that, then broke into a gold-toothed grin. "Help. The man's askin' for help. How about that shit? My oldest main ad-versary comes askin' for *help*."

"This ain't about you, Queenie. Or me, either."

McQueen took a fifth of bourbon from a drawer. "Little taste, Deacon? Some Christmas cheer?"

"I'm off the sauce."

"Oh, yeah? How long?"

"Coupla years."

"Good for you. Some of us were worried."

"Don't give me that jive, *Garland*. You and your boys would be just as happy if I turned tits up."

McQueen grinned again, pouring a shot for himself. "Ike, you and me, we gettin' too old to be enemies. What can I do for you?"

Bell laid a dozen glossies of Darryl Childress on the cluttered table, next to a porno magazine called "Black, Beautiful and Barely Legal."

"Put the word on the wire," Bell said. "We'll be kindly disposed toward anyone who helps us find this child."

"Is there a reward?"

Bell picked up the porno magazine and idly thumbed through it. "This your publication?"

"One of my an-cillary businesses."

"You sure these girls are all eighteen?" Bell asked. "Maybe I'm getting old. But some of them look pretty young to me."

"What are you driving at?"

"I didn't think we had to *reward* people for helping to save an innocent kid."

McQueen thought about that and nodded. "Christmas *is* a shitty time to kidnap someone's baby."

"Yeah. A real shitty time. You gonna help us or not?"

McQueen belted down the whiskey. "I *love* children, Ike, you hear what I'm sayin'? How can I help?"

2003 hours

Once again, Kane and Bell stood on opposite sides of the police gymnasium, avoiding each other. Each had privately briefed Easterly, without revealing names or giving much detail. Between them, they had mobilized an army of the city's criminals in the search for Darryl Childress and his captors.

Now the room was filling up with plainclothes officers, many of them new faces. Since noon, the task force had almost doubled. A nerve center was manned by six uniformed cops working computers and communication equipment.

On the way in, Kane had stopped for a chat with another biker gang, the Brightmoor Satans. He also looked up a recent parolee who had been hanging around with a new militia group. Everyone had pledged cooperation.

Kane had long since ceased being impressed by the human race. Once in a great while someone rose to something better than himself, something close to heroism. But most people behaved badly most of the time; that was Kane's world view. Today, however, Kane was surprised how easy it had been to recruit these scrotes into the cause.

It must be the season, he finally decided. Even criminals were bombarded by Christmas hype, coming from everywhere. *Goodwill toward men, all that shit.*

Plus, the Childress kid was cute and semi-famous. The city's dirtbags, having a lot of time on their hands, watched a lot of television. So they all sort of knew the kid. That's another reason they were helping.

Across the room, Isaiah Bell was having similar thoughts. After leaving McQueen, he had cruised the ghetto for a while, pondering the situation. Sometimes, when working a case, a detective needs to slow down and let his mind wander. That's how hunches arrive.

While thus reflecting, Bell had spotted the city's main dope dealer, Cleveland Talmadge, in his chauffeured Town Car. Bell had put the blue light on the roof and pulled Talmadge over. The drug dealer went into his usual indignation routine, accusing Bell of harassing him because he was with a white woman. Bell let him run his mouth, then pulled out the picture of the missing child.

Talmadge shut up. He, too, recognized the boy from television. By the time the conversation was over, Talmadge had vowed to take out a contract on the life of anyone who harmed little Darryl.

"No," Bell had cautioned. "We want the kid back safe. Ask your people to help with that."

Now, leaning against the rear wall of the gym, watching Kane across the room, Bell wondered what the reaction would have been had the boy not been a celebrity.

Bobbie Easterly walked to a microphone at the front of the gym and waited for the room to fill up. Next to her was a huge television set. Absent was the boisterous laughter which usually attends a gathering of cops.

"All right, listen up!" Easterly commanded. "Here's what we know: a vehicle—we now believe it was a late-model Chevrolet with tinted windows—was seen circling the block just before Darryl was grabbed. We're putting a neighbor under hypnosis, to see if she can remember any more details.

"Other than that, no one saw anything except Darryl's mother. You already know what she gave us. The lab didn't find much. As we feared, all footprints and tire tracks were trampled or covered over. We did find some fibers from Darryl's coat. We think they were pulled loose when he struggled. Other than that and the glove, there's no physical evidence."

She paused and shut her eyes for a brief moment. "We're hoping, of course, that matching fibers will be found on the suspects—when we arrest them. Maybe we'll get lucky and find the other glove. There still has been no ransom demand. We're worried about the silence." She looked around the room. "That's all we have. Any questions?"

A detective raised his hand. "Inspector, when are we going public with this? We've already told the entire neighborhood about it."

"But the bad guys don't necessarily know that," Easterly responded. "We'll keep a lid on it as long as we can."

"Publicity might help the cause," argued another cop.

"Maybe, maybe not. We don't know what kind of people we're dealing with here. It's a calculated risk either way." She thought for a moment. "Believe me, Jim, the Chief of Detectives and I are anguishing over every facet of this thing. We may change our minds, depending on developments. We know we can't keep it quiet for long. Any further questions?"

No one raised a hand. "Okay, then," she said. "Everyone who's worked eight hours or more, go home for some rest. I want you fresh in the morning."

The troops started to rise. Then Easterly remembered: "But before you go, at their request, we have a message from the boy's parents."

She nodded at Stan Jablonski. He killed the lights and activated the television. The Childress couple filled the screen, Louise sitting silently beside her husband.

"I—we are the parents of Darryl Childress," Stephen said. "We want to thank all of you from the bottom of our hearts for what you are doing for us, and for our son. We just wanted you to know a little about the kind of boy Darryl is, and why we miss him so much.

"You see, he loves Christmas. His favorite Christmas song is 'The Little Drummer Boy...'"

His voice trailed off. Then he composed himself.

"Many of you have seen Darryl in his TV commercials. So you know what a charming boy he is. But there are other things about him which are truly extraordinary."

Childress held up a photo of Darryl seated on the lap of a black Santa Claus. He spoke faster, hurrying through his thoughts. "This picture was taken just last week. When Santa asked him what he wanted for Christmas, you know what he said?

"He said he wanted an end to war. He'd seen war news from the Middle East and Africa. He said he didn't want any more children to suffer because of grown-ups.

"You see, Darryl is a precocious child. Somehow he has this talent—this gift—for getting inside the shoes of other people, for feeling their pain.

"Darryl always shares his toys with other children. And when he outgrows his clothes, he always..." Louise began to sob. Stephen put his arm around her. "He always insists that we take his old clothes to the Goodwill, so some less fortunate boy can have nice things, too.

"That's the gentle soul you're looking for, officers." He

put his face in his hands and sobbed. "Please find my son!"

With that, the screen went dark. The room was dead silent. Jablonski left the lights off for a second. When he turned them back on, everyone in the room sat grim-faced.

"Okay, gentlemen and ladies," Easterly said softly. "You new people hit the streets. The others report back at 0700."

The cops solemnly filed out of the gym. Easterly looked over at Jablonski, hope fading from her eyes.

2135 hours

Vera Bell fixed her husband a late dinner of soul food—chitlins, ham and collard greens. She had been raised here in the north and didn't care much for such cuisine, but sometimes indulged him when he ate alone. Bell had come from Deep South poverty, where such dishes were dietary staples.

Cassie and Ikey were in the den, watching a Charlie Brown Christmas special. While his wife cooked, Bell finally described the crime he was working.

The disclosure hit Vera hard. Her years in Central Receiving had toughened her to many things. But the violation of children still got to her. "Don't tell the kids," she said quietly.

"They'll find out soon enough."

"Well, don't let it be tonight."

"The mother's a nurse. Her name is Louise Childress. I don't suppose you know her."

"Black?"

"Yes."

Vera searched her memory. "No, I don't think so." She bit her knuckle. "My God, what a horrible thing for a mother."

Bell wanted a drink. He remembered that he hadn't been

to a meeting in several days, and he silently vowed to get to one as soon as he could. *Maybe a meeting where there are other cops.* "Ralph Kane is in on this one," he said quietly, almost as an afterthought.

His wife stopped her work and looked at him. "Ralph *Kane?*"

"Just my luck."

Vera studied her husband. "Ike, that old resentment will eat you alive."

"It's okay as long as I don't see the—as long as I don't see him."

Vera saw the pain in her husband's eyes. She put down the knife and went to him. She put her arms around his huge body and clung to him. "You're still my hero, you know."

Bell rocked her gently. "And you're mine."

They held each other tight for a long moment. Then Cassie and Ikey walked in on them. Cassie tittered. Bell scooped up both of them in his arms. He went into his tough-guy imitation. "Okay, punks, it's time for bed."

They laughed hilariously as he carried them past the Christmas tree and upstairs to their rooms. They did not notice the pain deep in his eyes.

* * *

Easterly stretched out on her office couch, hoping for some rest. Jablonski had gone home. She had told the cadet who replaced him to summon her with the slightest fragment of news.

Now she stared at the ceiling, going over and over the kidnapping, trying to put herself in the minds of the thugs. Without any hints, she was drawing a blank.

The biracial nature of the crime puzzled her. You just didn't see many salt-and-pepper crimes any more, not with the racial friction in this part of the country. In a perverse sort of way, this was diversity at work.

Then she reflected on the biracial marriage of the Childress couple, how difficult such a thing must be. Her own marriage to David Goldman crossed cultural lines. She was a WASP, he a Jew. But neither of them was religious and both were white. They weren't stared at everywhere they went.

Then a horrifying thought hit her. What if this caper wasn't professional at all, but a kinky thrill crime? Suppose the kidnappers had a thing for little boys? She didn't want to think like that. She and David had gay friends, none of whom would think of harming a child. But a good detective has to consider every possibility. In the absence of a ransom demand...

She sat back up, unable to rest. The thoughts of her husband comforted her. *Dear David.*

She went to her desk and called home. David answered on the second ring. "Hey, tough guy," he said lovingly.

"I just wanted to hear your voice," she said.

"A rough one?" He knew better than to pry for details.

"It's a little kid, David. A kidnapping."

"Oh, God!"

"Say a prayer, if you remember any. This one doesn't look good."

There was a long silence while he absorbed that. Finally he said, "Bobbie, do you have any idea how much I love you?"

She smiled. "I was hoping you'd say something like that."

* * *

Kane sat in Harvey's Place, sipping a scotch and listening to the blues singer: *"...We're having a party, for the sad and the lonely, and it's Members Only tonight..."*

He idly watched a young couple fondling each other in a nearby booth. It annoyed him. *Why don't you just take her somewhere and fuck her?* He gestured at Harvey for another shot.

"You need a woman, Ralph," said the old barkeep, eying the couple.

"I've had plenty of women."

"I see you're even more cheerful than usual."

"Can you just serve my booze without the commentary?" Kane descended deeper into his thoughts.

He wondered what Angela was doing these days, if she was still with that stockbroker or banker, whatever he was. Stability, that's what she said she wanted.

What she really meant was that she had grown tired of his drinking and his anger. She implored him to stop drinking, to seek help for whatever it was that bothered him. *How could I expect a woman like that to understand a man like me?*

Kane winced at the thought. He couldn't blame her. Hell, he didn't even understand himself.

He belted down the next shot and closed his eyes, trying to visualize the kidnapping. Instead, his mind once again conjured up the girl in Saigon. He tossed a ten on the bar. "See you around," he muttered to Harvey.

"Careful driving," Harvey said. "It's snowing again."

Kane got up and walked out into the night.

2340 hours

A full moon streamed into the bedroom through a break in the fast-moving clouds. Bell, unable to sleep, and still unaccustomed to the new house, watched the show. The barren tree swayed in the wind. The temperature must really be dropping, he thought.

Bell looked over at Vera, sound asleep. Her body was still in great shape. The nature of her job kept it that way. Vera

Lincoln Bell was one wonderful woman, he thought, far too good for him.

Before getting in bed, Vera had knelt down and said a prayer for little Darryl Childress. She had invited her husband to join her, but he had been too embarrassed to do such a thing. So he had merely watched her.

Now he thought about Cassie and Ikey, who was only a year older than the kidnap victim. Their usual Christmas excitement was subdued this year. Last week they had attended the Christmas play at their new school, the only black children there. Bell could feel their pain.

Then he remembered that his mother would be arriving Christmas Day from the family farm near Mobile. He hoped this crime would be resolved by then. He was supposed to pick her up at the airport.

Bell reflected on his mother, fighting senility, and of his surviving family in Alabama. He fretted that Eddie, his oldest brother, was still drinking. More than once since Bell had sobered up, he had been tempted to go south and try to rescue Eddie from himself. But it wouldn't have done any good. Even God couldn't have stopped Bell's own drinking, not until he was ready.

Then Bell tried to picture his father, known as Big Ed, who had been murdered by a self-inflicted gunshot wound at the age of thirty.

That's how Ike had come to regard his father's death—not a suicide but a murder. Big Ed was a gentle soul, tormented to the end by the memory of having witnessed the lynching of *his* father by the Ku Klux Klan. So his suicide made the crime a double murder, by Bell's reckoning, a double murder that took twenty-three years.

Horace Bell, a sharecropper, had gone to town to drink one night and—so the story went—insulted a white woman. Forty-eight hours later, night riders dragged him from his bed and hanged him from an elm, right in front of his family.

Bell's father was seven years old at the time. He'd never gotten over it.

Seven. The same age Darryl Childress is now. The same age I was when Big Ed shot himself.

Bell didn't want to be thinking about his father. It was one of those intrusive thoughts which came to him from time to time, unbidden, a ghost. He had very mixed feelings about the man.

Edwin James Bell had never been the same after Horace Bell was lynched, or so went the family lore. Bell never knew him to be anything but slightly peculiar. He was a good person, never abused the children or anything like that. But he was withdrawn and dreamy, rarely laughed, and often displayed sudden emotional reactions. Sometimes that frightened little Isaiah. It always confused him.

Ike Bell's only pleasant memories of Big Ed were of their occasional bass fishing expeditions in the flat-bottom boat they kept behind the barn. But that was so long ago, and Bell had been so young, that the memories were vague. Someone —Bell never knew who it was—had taken a black-and-white photo of the father and son on the river. As far as Bell knew, it was the only picture ever taken of him with his father. But it was a bad picture, and Bell could barely recognize his own face, let alone his father's.

Big Ed had ruined even that good memory by his choice of suicide locations. He had stood next to that same boat behind the barn when he shot himself, so he fell forward into it. His big brother Eddie heard the shot and was the one to find the body.

The preacher at the funeral had called the suicide "senseless." But for Bell, it always had made perfect sense. The Jim Crow South was a society almost calculated to drive a black man insane. Now Bell reminded himself for the thousandth time that the man knew not what he was doing. It was almost a mantra he recited to himself when he felt himself getting angry at Big Ed for depriving him of a father. Sometimes it worked, sometimes it didn't.

Then he remembered how his own drinking had very nearly deprived Cassie and Ikey of a father. Thank God a counselor at the Vet Center had confronted Bell about it, and that he had gone for help. *Maybe the cycle is broken.*

The thoughts of his own children caused Bell once more to think of Darryl Childress. He wondered how Darryl would be affected by whatever these animals were doing with him at this very moment.

Bell couldn't bear to dwell on that. He slipped out of bed, went into the kitchen and poured himself a glass of milk. Then he donned boots and a parka and went out into the frigid back yard. There he lit a cigarette and watched the moon disappear behind a cloud.

He said his own silent prayer for Darryl Childress.

* * *

Kane sat alone in the dark, watching the flashing Christmas tree in the two-flat across the street. The Beretta lay on his lap. He took the last deep drag on a joint, then crushed the roach in an ash tray.

Kane lifted the gun, hefting its weight, inspecting it. Then he tossed it on the bed. He hoped he'd still have the courage to pull the trigger once this job was done.

He sat there feeling the dope work its magic, and took another belt from a pint of whiskey. He tried to visualize a long-ago Christmas Day, back when he and Billy were little.

It was futile. All detail was lost. All he could conjure up were fragments.

Kane pulled back the hair on his wrist and examined the ancient scar. He did remember the old man flinging the butcher knife at his mother. But his drunken aim was way off. Full-force, the knife hit little Ralph, who fortunately had covered his face with his hands.

When had that happened? Kane couldn't remember for sure, but it seemed it happened around then—he did remember a Christmas tree. Christmas always brought out the savage in his father.

He realized with a start that he didn't even have a picture of Billy—or anyone else in his family, for that matter. Including Pete. *What kind of an asshole doesn't even have a picture of his own son?*

Kane staggered to the window and stared at the tree in the apartment across the street. He wondered what kind of people lived there, whether or not there was love in that home.

He pulled down the blind so he wouldn't have to look at the goddamned tree any more. In the distance, he heard fire sirens. He lurched back to the bed and lay down, fully clothed.

As soon as he closed his eyes, the little girl in Saigon came to visit him again—just as he knew she would.

It was April 30, 1975. Although not yet twenty-two, Kane was a Sergeant, an E-5. Like most fighters in that war, he had aged long before his time. After his first bloody battle experience in '72, then months of training in an Okinawan jungle, he figured embassy duty would be cushy, almost a vacation. Instead, it had turned into a surreal nightmare.

Kane could picture the hordes of terrified Vietnamese civilians trying to enter the embassy vehicle gate that last day, or attempting to scale the concrete wall protecting the compound. The wall, between twelve and eighteen feet high, was itself protected by concertina wire and topped with broken glass. Outside, thousands of panic-stricken Vietnamese were crying for help, desperate to escape the approaching Communist forces closing in on the city.

Kane was among four dozen Marines under orders to hold back the throng. Some were on the rooftop, others were at the gate. Several Vietnamese women lifted up their children and held them out to the Marines, begging the Americans to take the kids to safety.

The Marines, of course, were powerless to help, and could only hold the people back. Behind them, one packed helicopter after the next left the embassy for a flotilla of U.S. Navy ships waiting a few miles offshore.

On the ground, Kane and the others carried M-16s at port arms as the swarm of begging people pressed against the fence. The rifles were locked and loaded, but they had orders not to shoot.

CIA officers inside the compound pointed out faces they knew in the crowd, civilians who had helped them, and who were terrified of reprisals from the NVA forces. Marines were sent outside the gate to escort those "sensitive people" inside, to be led to the waiting helos. The rest were refused entrance.

At one point, it was Kane's turn to leave the compound to fetch two of the lucky ones. In the crowd on the other side of the wall was a young mother dressed in blue, barely out of her teens, holding her three-year-old daughter. When she spotted Kane, she held out her child to him. Even with the language barrier, it was clear that she was begging him to take the terrified little girl to safety. "She can't come!" he shouted over the din of the panicky crowd, knowing the mother did not speak English. "She can't come!"

As Kane reached his designated evacuees, he heard the young mother wailing in anguish. For all these years, he had been haunted by that sound, and by the face of her crying daughter. He did not know why it was that particular mother and that particular child; there were dozens of them. But ever since, with great regularity, these two would visit Kane in the night. In that sense, the little girl *had* come to America.

What had become of them? Why wouldn't they leave him alone so late at night? *Maybe they were the reason the phone rang this morning…*

Kane instantly scoffed at that notion. *Things don't work like that in this life. The only reasonable thing to believe in was the random cruelty of the universe…*

But still another thought kept nagging at him: *Maybe, maybe just maybe, this job can somehow even the score.*

DAY TWO - MONDAY

0506 hours

It was the solstice, the first official day of winter. Isaiah Bell drove the unmarked Ford through the pre-dawn darkness downtown to police headquarters. He had slept only fitfully, and decided to get in early. He kept trying to change the pictures in his head, but the face of Darryl Childress wouldn't leave.

At this hour, the expressway was nearly deserted. No new snow had fallen, so the going was smooth. Bell reached for a cigarette, then remembered his pledge to Vera. He'd try to tough it out this time.

When he'd left, Vera and the kids were still sleeping. Bell had checked the muted television for any news of the kidnapping, but had found none. Now he searched the car's A.M. dial, and still there was no mention of it. He hoped that was a good sign.

He stopped on an all-news station. "The Butler Commission, investigating allegations of police brutality in the raid of a suspected drug house last month, has subpoenaed seven officers to testify," the announcer said. "The officers, all white, have been accused by community activists of beating four African American prisoners..."

Bell pushed another button: "...Mayor Webster said the charges against him are racially motivated." The mayor's voice came on the air: "I say to you, none of these complaints is worth the paper it's printed on. I'm being singled out for attack by the U.S. Attorney and the white-run media. As for the patronage issue, I have done nothing more than carry on the tradition of my white predecessors..."

Bell pushed another button and found rap music. *At five in the morning, for God's sake!* He turned the radio off.

Now he was in a really foul mood. He visualized that white motherfucker, Kane. He reached in his pocket and took out a pack of cigarettes. He studied the pack for a long moment, then took one out and lit it.

What was it about this American culture that bred so much hatred on both sides? Were whites and blacks so different in their perceptions that they *never* would see things the same way?

He recalled the way his mother had reacted to Big Ed's death, nearly going mad herself. Without the kindness of her church friends she might have. She had never been the same since.

The old bitterness welled up again. *Those are the genes I have in me, the hand I was dealt.* Vera always counseled forgiveness. She was convinced Bell could never be spiritually free until he forgave—*really* forgave—Big Ed for sending that round through the roof of his mouth.

Bell knew she was right. After he had sobered up and faced his past, he had come to understand that it wasn't Big Ed he really resented. It was those white terrorists who had destroyed the Bell family.

But then that left Bell with a spiritual dilemma—how to forgive the murderers? So far, he had found that impossible.

* * *

Ralph Kane awoke to a headache and thoughts of Darryl Childress. He forced his feet to the floor, leaned forward and cupped his head in his hands. He hoped to God that the kid was still alive. To his own astonishment, he realized that the thought was almost a prayer. He instantly dismissed that notion. *That's just crap from childhood.*

But then he sat for several more minutes, trying to make sense of a surreal dream he'd had about Billy. His brother, in a prison cell, kept beckoning to him, waving to him to come closer. But every time Ralph approached, Billy disappeared into thin air. It happened over and over, seemingly all night.

It was the first time in his life that Ralph had ever dreamed about his brother, at least that he remembered. *That was very strange. Why now?* Finally he shrugged it off. *Shit happens.*

He crossed the room and turned on the stove to make instant coffee. He reached up on the shelf and found a pint of whiskey, unscrewed the cap and belted down two quick blasts. Then he found his bag of weed and rolled up two more joints. He lit one and took two slow hits.

Kane turned on another burner for breakfast. Then, as the dope hit him, he decided against it. What the hell, he'd buy himself a meal. He was going to be a dead man soon. Why not spend a little money?

Kane turned on the television for any news of the kidnapping. Instead he found a stock market analyst in love with his own voice, babbling about the latest corporate merger and personnel "downsizing." *This asshole makes it sound like eliminating jobs is a good thing.*

Disgusted by his own species, Kane turned off the television and went in to take a shower. He decided not to shave again today.

* * *

Easterly was deep in some nightmare of her own when Stan Jablonski awakened her. The nightmare instantly vanished. Within five seconds, she could not even remember which one it had been.

She sat up on her office couch and focused her eyes. "God, Stan, what time is it?"

"Five," said the old detective. "Our esteemed Chief of Police wants to see you in half an hour."

"What's he doing in this early?"

"Getting ready to brief the FBI."

"FBI? Did something happen I don't know about?"

"Inspector, you're going to love this one. The kid's

parents went to the Bureau on their own. The father decided we needed their quote, 'expertise'."

Easterly slumped back on the couch. "Oh, Christ!"

"The boy being a cute TV star and all, I'm sure the Feebees just couldn't turn it down."

"Jesus!"

"Watch what happens now. We get the kid back safe, they grab the credit. If it goes bad, then it's our fault. The usual FBI trick."

Easterly shut her eyes, forcing herself to think. "We can't blame the parents. They're desperate."

"Well, I don't like the feel of it," Jablonski said. "This could screw up everything." He shook his head. "It amazes me how civilians buy all that Bureau PR."

Easterly looked down at her rumpled clothing. "If the Chief calls again, I'm taking a shower."

Sickened, she got up and headed for the women's locker room.

0530 hours

W alking in the pre-dawn cold to the neighborhood diner, Kane started to feel better, thanks to the booze and the weed. He passed a line of homeless people shivering outside the Catholic soup kitchen. They were of all races; despair might be the most democratic force of all. Kane wished the smarmy television market analyst and his downsizing friends could be forced to stand out here in the cold a few mornings.

Then Kane laughed at himself for thinking this way. It was like he was turning into a fucking *liberal*, or something. He had no illusions about these pukes, either. Most of them were there of their own doing, that was his view.

But then he passed an elderly woman, standing by herself, face bruised and eyes blank. Her inner lights were off—a living dead woman.

She bore a strange resemblance to his own mother—or what he imagined Blanche might have looked like had she survived long enough to wind up on the streets. Kane turned his head. He couldn't bear to look any longer.

Then, half a block down, he passed a much younger woman, barely out of her teens. She held the hands of two mixed-race children. The kids looked up at Kane with curious, bewildered eyes. "Excuse me, sir, can you please help us out?" the young mother asked. Feeling guilty about the old lady, Kane pulled a ten from his pocket and handed it to her. "God bless you," she said.

Then he put a quarter in a *Daily Times* honesty box, reached in and grabbed a paper. He walked into the diner, shaking off the cold. "Adeste Fideles" was playing on the jukebox. Kane paused at the door for a moment, his policeman's eyes scanning the clientele. Only a dozen customers were there, along with a fat waitress and a surly cook.

Six of the customers—construction workers—shared one booth. Three were black, one was Hispanic and two were white. He vaguely recognized one of the blacks from somewhere, probably an old misdemeanor lockup, or maybe a witness to something. If it were something serious and current, he would remember.

Kane made a point of memorizing BOLO mug shots. An aggressive detective had better "be on the lookout," always. His very survival might depend on it. Out on the street, you might encounter one of those pricks by mere chance, just by being in a felonious neighborhood. A wanted man was dangerous to any policeman.

Kane finally decided that this particular guy had done lightweight time somewhere but was not currently wanted. So he relaxed. He sat down at the counter, ordered coffee and opened the newspaper.

There was nothing about the kidnapping. But the page one lead was about a federal grand jury investigation into alleged corruption in Mayor Webster's office. *Good. It's about time someone told the truth about this crooked prick.*

The great thing about being a black politician was the immunity it gave you. If anyone even questioned your honesty, you could scream racism. The liberal press could be counted on to go along with it. And, by merely reporting it, they gave it the stamp of legitimacy. *What a country!*

Kane ordered eggs, bacon and hash browns. He was leveling off from the morning ration of booze. That was a good thing. He needed his wits about him today. He sipped his coffee and focused on Darryl Childress: *Where are you?*
The jukebox, as if on cue, switched to "The Little Drummer Boy," the Harry Simeone version. *What the hell gives with that?* Nothing, he finally decided; it's just a popular Christmas song.

The construction workers cracked up at some bawdy joke. Kane was still amazed that some men still found things to laugh about.

Outside the window, the old lady who looked like Blanche passed by slowly, pushing a shopping cart. Now, from inside the window, Kane did look at her, noting the details of her facial injuries. She probably couldn't even remember when and where it had happened.

Blanche's face had frequently borne bruises like that. Kane couldn't count the number of beatings she'd suffered at his father's hand. The fucker used to brag about the damage he'd inflicted. "The mark of Kane," he called it, and then he would laugh drunkenly.

I swear to God, if that asshole were still alive I'd take him out in the woods and shoot him. I wouldn't even think about ending my own life until I accomplished that.

His head started to hurt again.

0550 hours

Jefferson Mosely was in his political element. He was doing everything but kissing the ring of the FBI's Special Agent in Charge, a generic bureaucrat named Francis Demarest. Easterly and Byron Slaughter stood by, silently fuming.

Easterly wondered if she looked as haggard as she felt. She vowed never again to sleep on that couch.

"We certainly welcome the opportunity to work with the Bureau," Mosely said. "I've always had great admiration for your expertise."

"I only wish your people had notified us directly," Demarest scolded. "Why did we have to hear about it from the family?"

Mosely smiled like a whore on a street corner. "I'm trying to get some clarification about that myself."

"If we'd been told at the outset, we could have gotten our Evidence Response Team to the scene," Demarest said. "They might have found something your people missed."

Slaughter finally snapped. "You weren't notified because this is *our* case! There *wasn't* any evidence, and we don't need federal help!"

Good, Easterly thought, there's a *cop* in the room. She watched Slaughter and Demarest. For years, there had been a rumor that they hated each other. This exchange confirmed it.

Demarest persisted icily: "Chief Mosely, this is not only within our jurisdictional mandate, we're the ones with the experience and resources. You said so yourself."

Mosely looked pointedly at Slaughter. "Gentlemen, there's no point in animosity," he said.

"Yeah, it's a moot point now," Easterly said wearily. "We're in this together, like it or not."

"And we're primary," Demarest said smugly. "We take the lead."

Now it was Easterly's turn to snap. "That's not what I said! We work together, *as equals!* My Criminal Conspiracy people have a little expertise of their own."

Demarest looked over at Mosely, who again smiled. He turned to his two executives. "The FBI is primary," he said. "In cases of joint jurisdiction, federal supercedes local."

Slaughter flushed. "Where'd you find that in the law books?"

Mosely's smile vanished. "Chief Slaughter, do I need to remind you that I am the Chief of Police? Now you may not like the fact that your superior officer is a black man..."

"This doesn't have a goddamned thing to do with race!" Slaughter exploded. "Why would you make a comment like that, right out of left field?"

Mosely glared at him, then he checked his watch in a show of nonchalance. "We'll deal with this later," he said calmly. "In one hour, we're going into that gymnasium for the briefing. We're going to present a united front for the troops for the sake of that missing boy! Now check with your key personnel and find out what it is we have to tell them."

Easterly looked down at her shoes, fighting her own rage. *Of all the lousy times for male egos.*

Then she remembered that Jefferson Mosely had a five-year contract. *God help this city.*

0700 hours

Once again the gymnasium was filling with detectives and plainclothes officers. The cops milled around discussing the case as they waited for the brass to arrive. Without exception, their faces were drawn. Darryl Childress had troubled each of them all night.

Rumors were circulating. Already the cops had heard

about the FBI entering the case, and this news did not make them happy.

Furthermore, the assembled officers had learned the news media were now onto the story. They were less upset about that. It was inevitable that word would get out. Too many people had been questioned, and last night Patrol had pulled over numerous cars containing black children.

Bell sipped coffee from a paper cup, listening to a pair of hotheaded young black plainclothesmen bitch about "this latest harassment of innocent black citizens."

"Bullshit," Bell finally interjected. "What do you expect the patrol guys to do? Ignore some kid who might be Darryl?"

"They're only pulling over black people," one hothead said.

"The *victim* is black," Bell said.

"A light-skinned black," said the other. "And the suspects are biracial."

"Like the parents," the first added contemptuously.

"If the adults they're stopping are mixed-race, I can see it," insisted the second cop. "But they're pulling over every black family in town—even the ones with dark-skinned kids. And they're using phony excuses, not explaining the real reason."

"How's a patrol officer supposed to make those distinctions at night?" Bell demanded. "And what's thirty seconds to these people? A child's life is at stake."

He shook his head and crossed the room to the huge coffee urn, just to get away from the rhetoric. *What kind of morons is the Academy turning out these days?*

Then he spotted Kane across the room, watching him. What was that peckerwood looking at? Bell glared back, filled his cup, walked to a corner and leaned against the wall.

Kane noticed Bell's stare. He hadn't even been thinking about Bell as he stood idly gazing into space, letting the booze wash over him. Out in the parking lot, he had taken a couple more belts from his flask, just to shake off the cold, and to help clear his thoughts. But now Bell was standing there staring hatefully at him, for no reason. Kane popped a breath mint into his mouth

Someone called the room to attention. The cops rose listlessly to their feet as Mosely and the FBI agent appeared, followed by Slaughter and Easterly.

Easterly was trying to conceal her own foul mood. She and Slaughter were now having to take a back seat to Mosely and Demarest. It was, she knew, a dress rehearsal for the press briefings to come.

Mosely made a few perfunctory remarks. Then he introduced Demarest and promised him "the full cooperation of everyone in this room."

Easterly observed the silent, collective reaction. The old-timers had been through many changes of regime, so they knew how to read the political winds. Now the presence of Demarest confirmed what they'd already been warned about Mosely.

But even though the veterans were disdainful, they were pros, committed to saving the life of Darryl Childress. And in fairness, Easterly reminded herself, the city also was blessed with many dedicated FBI street agents, most of whom privately shared the locals' contempt for Bureau leadership.

Easterly was not concerned about problems at the street level. Instead, she worried that wrangling at the top might somehow get the little boy killed. She prayed she was wrong. Then she started wondering *why* Mosely was sucking up to the FBI. It had nothing to do with the welfare of the child. Even Mosely had to know the limitations of the feds.

No, she guessed, the new chief was simply covering his ass in advance. Mosely knew the press would crucify him if things went bad and the FBI leaked a complaint about inadequate local cooperation. With their tabloid mentalities, too many of the reporters covering the city these days were eager to find controversy in anything. Thoroughly dispirited, Easterly turned her attention back to the briefing.

"As you all know by now, there is still no word on the whereabouts or the safety of our victim," Mosely said. "There's been no ransom demand yet—or any other communication from the suspects. As most of you also know, the press is now aware of the case. But my Public Information Office has contacted all editors and news directors, and we've asked them to keep a lid on it for a few hours."

"Why?" challenged a cop sitting in the rear.

Mosely gestured for Demarest to answer. "People like these thrive on publicity," said Demarest. "We don't want to play into their hands."

"People like who?" demanded another cop.

The FBI man was taken aback by the hostile tone. His reply was defensive: "Like the ones who grabbed the boy."

"That sounds like you know who they are," challenged a third detective. "Would you mind *sharing* it with us?"

Demarest flushed with anger. "We don't have any idea who they are. It's just Bureau policy to keep a low profile..."

"If we go public someone might lead us to the kid," interrupted another detective. "Nothing else is working."

Yet another detective chimed in sarcastically: "If we go public we'll get a thousand phone calls. That'll require manpower. Maybe the city doesn't want to approve any more overtime."

Easterly could see the direction this was going. She needed to head it off. She took the microphone from Demarest. "Carl, I agree with the decision, but only for a few more hours."

That momentarily calmed the troops. Mosely nodded gratefully. *The bastard owes me one,* Easterly thought. *But now I'm playing politics.*

"So what's your best theory?" yet another cop asked. Demarest started to answer, but the cop interrupted: "I'd like to hear it from Chief Slaughter."

Slaughter took the mike, ignoring Mosely and Demarest, both angry. "We still believe it's a ransom job," he said. "We're guessing the kidnappers think the family's rich, because the kid was a TV star." He caught himself: "*Is* a TV star."

"A local actor doesn't make as much as you might think," Easterly added. "This isn't Hollywood."

"Our guess is they're delaying to build up pressure," Slaughter said, "so they'll get everything they're after." He looked at Demarest pointedly. "Of course it's all speculation. No one in this room has a crystal ball." The tension between them was apparent to everyone in the room.

Easterly took the mike again: "Our M.O. analysts have been working all night, running computer checks on everyone in the tri-state area who ever was even suspected of kidnapping. And we have the boy's picture in every radio car in the county."

"So what do we do?" asked one exasperated Homicide cop.

"The same thing you've been doing." On impulse, she picked up a blown-up crime-scene photograph of Darryl's snow angel. She held it high, so every cop in the room could see it. "Hit the streets and turn over every rock you find."

0815 hours

Kane drove out the Interstate to the headquarters of the White Brotherhood. It was a farm in the north end of the county, far from the city limits and out of radio range. Once more, as he preferred it, Kane was completely on his own. If he got in a jam, he'd have to rely on his cell phone.

Technically the Anti-Terrorism Squad—and the FBI —had jurisdiction over political extremists. But the White

Brotherhood overlapped politics and organized crime. As a gang dedicated to eradicating the black race, the Whites qualified as "political." But everyone in law enforcement knew they financed their operations with gun and methamphetamine trafficking. Thus they also qualified as a major organized crime ring.

The Brotherhood was born as a prison gang, a self-defense group for white convicts locked behind the walls with hate-filled blacks. The penal system was their only recruiting turf. The Whites wouldn't admit anyone who hadn't been in prison.

As a result, this tribe was far more dangerous even than the right-wing militia groups springing up all over the nation. Most of those people were pussies, in the view of the White Brothers, emotional weaklings who needed assault rifles to prove their manhood and anti-government ideology to justify their own failures in life.

The Whites, on the other hand, didn't need to prove a thing. All they needed was an outlet for their racial hatred. A widely-publicized study recently claimed that most White Brothers had been abused children, needing a scapegoat, someone to justify their rage.

What crap, Kane mused as he left the city behind. *Lots of people are abused as children and don't become thugs.*

As he drove, Kane reflected on an animated argument he once had with Billy about that very subject, during one of his brother's paroles. Inside Statesville Prison, Billy had gotten chummy with the White Brotherhood's founder, a psychopath named Eric Klemmer. *Charismatic,* that had been Billy's description of Klemmer.

After his release, Billy had told Ralph that he himself was flirting with the idea of becoming a White Brother. Ralph had told him he was crazy. The Whites were neo-Nazi bullies. He and Billy had fought about it. A short time later, Billy violated his parole, and not long after that he was dead.

Kane again wondered about his dream last night. Except for the girl in Saigon, he rarely remembered details of his dreams. But now his brother seemed to be reaching out to him. *That's weird, fucking weird.* And Kane couldn't stop thinking about Eric Klemmer.

So, after this morning's briefing, he approached Roberta Easterly to tell her about a hunch he had. He did not disclose that it had come to him as the result of a dream.

"I'm thinking it's possible the kidnappers are prison pals," he said. "A white guy and a black guy normally don't caper together, unless they have history with each other. Prison is a logical place for criminals to get that kind of history."

Easterly considered that for a long moment. "Could be," she said finally.

Then he told her about Klemmer. "This guy's wired into the entire penal system," Kane said. "His people are so racist they just might keep track of convicts who cross color lines. And he *was* a friend of my brother's."

"It's worth a shot," she shrugged. "Nothing else is turning up. Play on his bigotry."

Now, twenty miles out of the city, Kane started second-guessing himself. This felt like a huge waste of time, chasing a lead that had come to him in his sleep. But he couldn't think of anything else to do in the cause of saving Darryl Childress.

He reached in the glove box and took out his flask. He belted down two huge gulps, finishing the bottle. Then he got off the freeway at the next exit, in search of a liquor store.

* * *

Kane's prison theory had triggered a new line of thinking for Easterly. The more she thought about it, the more sense it made. She asked Jablonski to locate Ike Bell.

In the meantime, she was summoned to yet another

high-level meeting. This time it was in the Press Relations Office. The meeting was a background session for the city's "media," preparing them for the end of the news embargo. Byron Slaughter was conspicuously absent.

As the news crews were assembling, Easterly stood watching the self-involved reporters smiling their phony smiles at each other. They all had been given photographs of Darryl. But, she suspected, there wasn't a "journalist" in the room who genuinely gave a damn about the kid.

Easterly despised these people. She remembered when the city was blessed with some really good police reporters, all of whom worked for newspapers, not television. When she was a brand-new detective, the city supported not one but three daily papers. In those days, there was arm's-length respect between the professionals of both trades. The cops even tolerated reporters digging into police wrongdoing, as long as they got their facts right.

But that was twenty years ago, before the word "media" had been invented, before real-life violence had become entertainment. It was before the sound-bite mentality of the illiterates who ran television news, whose credo was "if it bleeds it leads." It was a time when a beat reporter actually knew the locations of the precinct stations, before hacks like these took to calling themselves "journalists."

Christ, I'm getting old. Remember what David says: "bend with the times, girl, or get left behind."

One of the reporters spotted Easterly. She was a young white female named Nanci York, the newest pretty face at Channel 3, just arrived from a station in Cincinnati. York approached Easterly privately. "Inspector, my sources tell me a lot of civil rights are being violated in this search for the boy."

Easterly was taken aback by the question. She was in no mood for this, not now. She answered curtly, through clenched teeth: "That *boy's* civil rights were violated by being kidnapped."

York started to write that down. Easterly held up her hand: "If you quote me I'm going to take that notebook and shove it up your ass, one page at a time." While York stared in disbelief, Easterly walked away, afraid of her own further reactions.

She crossed the room and stood near Jefferson Mosely who was deep in conversation with a sycophantic young lieutenant named Dunsmore. Easterly knew Dunsmore's type well. He was a squint.

"Squint" was a derisive term for a career police bureaucrat, an "inside" officer who spends as little time as possible out on the dangerous streets. Squints work their way into administrative jobs, where they can make rank fast because they are in a position to play the right political cards. Real cops are thus disadvantaged in promotional competition. As a result, squints often wind up running police departments— Mosely himself being a prime example.

Easterly was close enough to hear Dunsmore inform the chief that last night's felony numbers were the lowest in years. "It must be the weather," Dunsmore was saying.

"Don't say that to the press," Mosely replied. "Find a way to get some mileage out of it."

"Yes, sir."

"Link it to our increased Christmas patrols at the shopping malls."

"Sir, last night the malls closed at six."

"Well, figure out something, Lieutenant," Mosely said. "That's what we're paying you for."

"Yes, sir," said the squint.

Then Mosely noticed Easterly listening. He smiled self-consciously. "Crime seems to be going down, Inspector. That's good news, isn't it?"

"Yes, sir," she said cynically, "that's good news."

This asshole's an even bigger whore than I thought.

0845 hours

Bell stood in front of Easterly's desk, awaiting her return. He idly scanned the pictures and awards on her wall. There were no staged, happy-faced photos with dignitaries or politicians. This woman was for real.

After several minutes, Easterly walked in hurriedly, her face furrowed. "Sorry to keep you waiting," she told Bell.

"Yes, ma'm."

"Detective, do you have any informants inside the Black Liberation Family?"

"They're political," Bell said. "That's outside my turf."

"That's not what I asked you."

Bell thought for a moment. "There's a couple of gangbangers who joined the BLF in prison. But they're not exactly friendlies. I'm the one who put them there."

"Someone has a theory that our salt-and-pepper team might have hooked up with each other in prison. Do you think your customers could find out something about that?"

Bell rubbed the back of his neck. "One of them does owe me a favor."

"Offer money if you need to, up to a thousand bucks from the confidential fund—if the information pans out."

"I'll try, Inspector. But I wouldn't hold my breath. These people don't like us."

"Do what you can," she said.

"Yes, ma'm." Bell saluted and walked out.

0930 hours

Kane knew he was being photographed the moment he pulled up to the concertina-wire fence surrounding the sprawling White Brotherhood compound. The surveillance vehicle was a telephone company van, parked a hundred yards down the unpaved road. He assumed the watchers were feds—FBI, most likely, or maybe ATF or DEA. Or maybe a joint task force. Their van sat right out in the open, where they could take clear pictures of anyone visiting the Whites. It also exposed them to any sunlight that might randomly pop through the clouds.

But there would be no sunshine this day. Huge black clouds were again gathering in the north. More heavy snow was on the way, of that there was no doubt. Kane knew well the discomfort of the agents inside that van. In the early days, before he had been made a pariah, Kane himself had sat on countless such "plants," and been paired with innumerable partners from his own department as well as other agencies.

Kane regarded intelligence stakeouts as the most boring work in all of law enforcement, except for maybe paper-shuffling admin jobs. You freeze your ass off, improvise how to relieve yourself, and sometimes spend hours cooped up with insufferable pricks eating smelly sandwiches. If you're lucky enough to be teamed with righteous guys who won't rat you off, maybe you can drink a little beer. That helps with the cold and boredom.

And sometimes, like these guys, you do nothing to hide your presence. You make sure the dirtbags know they're being watched. Inducing paranoia—one of the few remaining joys of police work.

However, this poses an obvious problem. No one will caper if they know you're watching. To make a case, you need an undercover operative, or a snitch, or a flipped witness, or a wiretap. With an open surveillance, you'll never catch anyone committing a crime. *It's all just a big game, around and around, endlessly.*

Kane was certain these particular watchers knew who he was. Cloak-and-dagger operations are a small, arcane sub-specialty within the police world. Everyone in it knows everyone else, at least by reputation.

Perversely, Kane enjoyed fucking with other cops. As he got out of the Pontiac, he waved to the faceless agents. They would go nuts speculating why Detective III Ralph Kane had shown up here. Who knows, they might even open a corruption case. By then, of course, he would be dead and buried.

Amused by that scenario, Kane lifted the telephone at the gate. He had called ahead, so Eric Klemmer knew he was coming. At first Klemmer had been hesitant about seeing him. But he couldn't overcome his curiosity about Billy Kane's big brother. Now one of Klemmer's disciples buzzed him in, instructing him to follow the left fork up the hill to the farmhouse.

The private road was so slushy and muddy that Kane wondered if the Pontiac would make it. The department was too cheap to buy snow tires, even for vehicles like this, which might have to go anywhere. Most of the White Brothers, Kane knew, drove four-wheel-drive trucks.

While picking his way along the uphill road, Kane reviewed what he knew about Klemmer. The man was brilliant, no doubt about it. He had earned three university degrees while in prison. He also was a first-class sociopath.

Now pushing sixty, Klemmer had spent most of his life behind bars. As a kid, he had been a car thief. Then he'd graduated to stickups, specializing in armored car takedowns. He was suspected of several murders, but no one had ever tagged him with one.

Rumor had it that Klemmer's racist attitudes stemmed from a gang-rape he suffered as a youngster in a reformatory. But, of course, he had never admitted to that.

Klemmer "got political" only in recent years, when he began studying the speeches of Hitler. He then went on to form the White Brotherhood as an offshoot of the old

Aryan Nation. Billy had admired Klemmer for his brilliance and ruthlessness. He once described Klemmer to Ralph as "Satanic."

Finally Kane arrived at the farm, half a mile off the main road. Klemmer stood on the porch in camouflage fatigues, cradling an ugly assault rifle. Kane vaguely recognized the weapon as Israeli. *Satanic, my ass. This guy's just another aging shithead.*

Flanking Klemmer were two heavily-tattooed, muscular thugs, each with a prison pallor. Kane surmised that they had recently done stretches in maximum security. Even in this shitty climate, the average person picks up a little color just by being outdoors. Kane parked the police car and approached the porch. "So you're William Kane's big brother," Klemmer greeted him.

"Yeah. You can ditch the tommy gun."

"I just wanted to make sure you were alone." He handed his weapon to the torpedo on his right. "You want to talk in private, take a little walk?"

"It's too cold to walk," Kane said.

"Then we'll go down to the basement." Klemmer motioned him inside. As he entered, Kane looked around behind himself, to see who else might be watching.

1015 hours

Ike Bell stood at the entrance of a mosque-like fortress, smoking and rehearsing his approach. Gangbangers were one thing. Most of them were idiots. Who but a moron would get into a firefight over the color of someone's jacket, spraying bullets all over a neighborhood filled with women and children?

But the BLF—these people were something else

altogether. They made the old Panthers seem tame by comparison. Their sworn enemy was the white-run corporate oligarchy, exemplified by banks.

Bell was not sure he disagreed with the political sentiment. But he failed to see how bank robbery, armored car stickups, kidnapping and murder were political acts. Furthermore, the badge in his pocket made *him* the enemy. *Be careful here. Be real careful.*

Bell looked up at the overhead security camera. He crushed the cigarette underfoot, then banged on the heavy door-knocker. "Who's there?" a surly voice demanded over the intercom.

"My name's Isaiah Bell," he called back. "I'd like a word with Malik Karanga. He knows me."

"You look like a cop."

"I am a cop."

"You got a warrant?"

"Just get Malik."

Bell waited, knowing he was being videotaped over the closed-circuit television. He also was convinced that the postal truck down the street was filled with federal agents. He now lived in a world where everyone taped everyone else.

Bell knew that, despite their criminal activities, the Black Liberation Family had little to fear from law enforcement. Because the BLF admitted only ex-convicts who had been in prison with them, the feds couldn't run an undercover agent into the group. Besides, any penetration attempt would be regarded as racist harassment. So no law enforcement administrator in the country had the guts to take on the BLF. The politically-correct, safe people to go after were all on the radical right. White guys.

After three minutes, Karanga appeared at the door in a black jump suit. He also wore two automatic pistols and an ammunition bandolier. A smirk crept across his face when he recognized Bell. Then he smiled widely, displaying two gold teeth.

The smile exuded arrogance. Beneath the graying goatee, this was still the same Tyrone Jones whom Bell had arrested for drug dealing two decades before. He had abandoned his given name in prison, denouncing it as a "slave name."

"Long time, Brother Bell," said Karanga. He did not extend his hand.

"You've come up in the world, Tyrone."

"Malik. It's Malik."

"Malik. Like I said, you've come up in the world."

"Hey, I was a chump in my youth." Karanga's smile faded. "What are you doing here?"

Bell pulled out a picture of Darryl Childress. "This little boy got kidnapped about twenty-four hours ago. Salt-and-pepper team, a white dude and a black dude. We think they might have been friends in the joint—maybe even married."

"We heard about it."

"You did?"

"The Eastside Crips been showing the little motherfucker's picture all over town. Can you dig that? They even stopped doing business." He laughed. "That means the crime rate oughta be going down."

That news startled Bell. Karanga studied his reaction, then laughed again. "Don't you think that's funny, Crips working with the po-lice? It would make a great sitcom."

"So what do *you* hear?" Bell asked. "*Your* people ever heard about such a team?"

"We don't pay attention to that shit."

"Well, then, can you reach into the prisons for us, shake loose some information?" He gestured imploringly at his old adversary. "Malik, we really need to know."

"If it was biracial, you can bet the white guy was running things."

"Does that mean you *have* heard something?"

"Don't go putting words in my mouth. I don't *know* shit. I was just – *speculating.*"

Bell stared at the aging thug. *Fuck this shit.* "Malik, I saved your life one time. You remember that?"

"No. That was Tyrone Jones you saved."

"If I hadn't tipped off Tyrone Jones, there wouldn't be a Malik Karanga."

Karanga looked up at the security camera. "I wondered how long it would take, you calling in that particular marker."

"If I hadn't warned you about that hit, you'da been in the ground fifteen years now."

"So I owe you, is that it?"

"Don't fuck with me, *Malik!* The street rules haven't changed, just because you've seen the light." Bell felt his gut churning. He fought to control himself. "For Christ's sake, this is an innocent little child! A *black* child!"

"Bell, you got a lot of balls coming here. That saving-my-life shit is old business. You're the motherfucker who *cost* me eight years of my life."

"You did that to yourself. Nobody forced you to take down that liquor store."

Karanga considered that. "Let me see the picture," he said.

Bell handed over the photograph. Karanga examined it. "Interracial family, from what I hear."

"What difference does it make?" Bell asked.

"Rich kid, right? Which parent is black?"

"The mother."

"The mother. Usually it's the other way around." Karanga sneered. "You know something, Dee-tective Bell, it wouldn't bother me a bit if they blew the little half-breed away." With that, he ripped the photograph in half.

Bell lost control. With his huge left hand, he seized Karanga's throat and started squeezing. With his right, he jammed the muzzle of his Beretta against Karanga's temple. "You motherfucking piece of shit!"

The security door flew open and three BLF toughs appeared, leveling assault rifles. Karanga thrashed around in the detective's grip, choking. Bell spun him around to use him as a shield. Then, squeezing Karanga's windpipe in the crook of his elbow, he leveled his own gun at the trio.

"Go ahead, shoot!" Bell yelled. "Let's see how many homies gonna die—right here, right now!"

The thugs froze in place. Slowly Bell backed down the stairs to the street, dragging Karanga with him. Karanga thrashed about in the chokehold, fighting to breathe. With his peripheral vision, Bell saw three federal agents leap from the surveillance van and crouch low, brandishing automatic weapons of their own.

For a very long moment, there was a standoff. The BLF men remained frozen. Moving backward, Bell eased down the slippery sidewalk toward the agents, dragging the gasping Karanga along with him. He hissed in the revolutionary's ear.

"You *are* a piece of shit, you know that, Tyrone? I'm sorry I saved your black ass. If those feds weren't behind me, I'd blow your fucking brains out right now."

When he reached the crouching agents, Bell wrestled Karanga down to the snow. The agents quickly disarmed and handcuffed him. "So what do we do with this guy?" one asked.

Bell didn't answer. Out of nowhere, a crowd was gathering, all black. Bell looked at them, then holstered his weapon. In disgust, he started to walk away. One of the feds shouted after him: "Hey, man, you gave us a prisoner! What the hell do we do with him?"

"As far as I'm concerned, you can dump the motherfucker in the river!" Bell answered, loud enough for the onlookers to hear. He just kept walking, not looking back, shaking with rage. He didn't even notice that heavy snow was falling again.

Kane sat on a wooden chair in the dank farmhouse basement, trying to place the familiar smell. Eric Klemmer leaned against a huge, cluttered workbench, staring at Kane's face.

"Something bothering you?" Kane demanded.

Klemmer smiled. "You bear an uncanny resemblance to Billy."

"Why does that surprise you? I was his brother."

"You still *are* his brother." He shook his head. "It's like looking at a ghost."

Kane fought a smile as he considered the irony of that statement. His own imminent death had become a private joke.

"I was fond of Billy," Klemmer continued. "Most men I've encountered in various prisons have been Neanderthals— even the Caucasians. But Billy—Billy was always reading, improving his mind. I wanted him to be my Minister of Information."

Kane held his tongue. He looked away from Klemmer to examine the room. Across from the furnace, Nazi and neo-Nazi paraphernalia covered an entire wall. The intersecting wall was covered with exotic firearms, notably assault weapons.

"I assure you that everything you see there is perfectly legal," Klemmer laughed. "If it weren't, would I let a cop in here?"

"I'm not your typical cop," Kane said.

"I know. Billy told me about you." He got up and began pacing about. "You know, sometimes it's just luck of the draw, the way we turn out. Billy said more than once that he always expected that *you* would wind up in prison." He smiled again. "Did you know your brother said things like that about you?"

Kane shrugged. "Billy was always running his mouth off. That's why he kept getting caught."

"You can learn a lot about a man in a prison, if you pay attention. You also can learn a lot about his family."

"What are you driving at, Klemmer?"

"We'll get to that after you tell me why you're here."

Kane pulled out the picture of Darryl Childress and told the story. As he talked, Klemmer's eyes were riveted on the photo.

"Tell me something, Ralph. What on earth makes you think an organization like mine would help you find a little mongrel African?"

"Maybe a favor? Like a memorial. A favor to me, in memory of Billy."

"Why would you think that? We're the *White* Brotherhood."

Kane nodded. "I know. But I figured maybe you'd want to discourage white inmates from partnerships with niggers."

"Niggers?"

"Yeah. These assholes are salt-and-pepper, a white guy capering with a nigger."

Klemmer laughed. "I hope your Internal Affairs people never learn that you used that word. You do remember that unfortunate detective in Los Angeles, the guy in the Simpson case."

"Well," said Kane, "there's no one here but us kids. Not unless the feds have a bug in the furnace."

Klemmer shook his head. "So how do you know it was a white guy and a nigger? The kid must have had a lot of insurance, and the mother's the only witness. How do you know the *family* didn't arrange it? The kid's a jungle bunny. You know the value those people put on human life."

What a sick fuck! "No, this was a righteous kidnapping," Kane said. "Darryl was worth a lot more to them alive than dead."

Klemmer sat down and again examined the photo. "This boy represents race pollution at its worst. On TV, no less! I wonder what the Fuhrer would have done with the parents of such a child."

"Forget the parents," Kane said. "Think about the *kidnappers*. These guys get away with it, this'll just encourage more white-black partnerships."

"What are you talking about?"

"Klemmer, you know how tight crime partners are with each other—it's like a marriage. I don't have to tell *you* that. So a mixed-race team is sort of like—what's that old word? —miscegenation. And if they're fucking each other, then it's *homosexual* miscegenation." Kane shook his head in disgust. "I hear that kinda shit's going on all over in prisons these days."

Kane studied Klemmer's face in the dim light. *This psycho's actually buying this bullshit!*

Klemmer took a Galil machine gun down from the wall and fondled it. "I'll tell you what, Ralph," he said finally. "I'll see what I can find out. But there *is* a price tag."

"We've been authorized a thousand bucks. It's chump change, I know, but it's all they'll authorize."

"I'm not talking money."

"Then what *are* you talking about?"

Klemmer grinned, savoring this. "See, from time to time we could use some help from someone inside the police. Nothing heavy, just a little information."

"Raid plans. Undercovers. That sort of thing."

"Yes. And it also would be quite helpful to learn if any of our own members ever supply information to the authorities." He smiled murderously. "You see, we have a very active *counter*-intelligence operation. For our own protection."

So that's the deal. Billy's asshole pal wants me for a spy. He wants me to endanger other cops.

Kane almost laughed aloud. Klemmer hadn't a clue that

Kane was going to be a dead man as soon as this job was over.

"It's a deal," Kane said. "You get me something on these two scrotes, then you've got yourself a righteous snitch."

1112 hours

Easterly leaned against the wall of an interrogation room, frustrated. Her CCB captain, Nick Georgiades, and two of his female detectives, Alberts and Gregorio, were trying to coax information from a frightened Chinese woman whose command of English was limited. Next to the woman sat an interpreter, a young man with a worried frown.

The woman, Lin Loh, was the middle-aged housekeeper for one of the prosperous black families on Lawndale Avenue. Earlier that morning, before leaving her house, she had told her daughter about something she had noticed while driving to work the day before—a young black boy standing with two men outside an idling car, talking. Lin Loh, of course, had no idea what they were saying, and besides, she was concentrating on her driving because of the heavy snow. She had put the incident out of her mind, thinking it some sort of disciplinary matter. But it struck her as peculiar that one man was white and the other black.

Then, later that afternoon, plainclothes police had come to her employers' house, showing pictures of the boy. But no one had interviewed her. Out of fear, Lin Loh had kept quiet. Back in China, when the police came to visit, it could only mean trouble. And now, here in the new country, she lived in a neighborhood controlled by street gangs. She had decided to tell no one what she had seen.

The matter had troubled her all night. Because of the media blackout, she knew none of the details, although the little boy's face in the picture had haunted her dreams. And it had to be serious if so many police were involved. So she told her daughter about it in the morning before again leaving for work.

After four hours of anguished soul-searching, the daughter, who had a seven-year-old girl of her own, decided to call the police.

Gregorio and Alberts had been hurriedly dispatched to pick up Lin Loh. But now, here in the station, she was refusing to cooperate. Not only was she terrified, she was enraged at her daughter's betrayal.

The assembled detectives were almost shaking in frustration. They were desperate for an artist's sketch of the suspects, or for a hypnosis-recalled license plate number, anything. "Please, Mrs. Loh," Alberts pleaded. "We can't tell you how important this is."

The interpreter repeated the plea. The woman sobbed and shook her head, mumbling. "She repeats that she never saw anything," the interpreter said softly.

Detective Gregorio, herself the mother of three, was growing visibly angry. "Then why in the name of God did she tell her daughter...?"

Easterly held up her hand to calm Gregorio, who took a deep breath, shaking her head. "I'm going out for a cigarette," she said.

Easterly stepped outside with her. "Sorry, boss," Gregorio said. "I just don't have any sympathy." She examined her watch. "Every minute that goes by..."

"Liz, you're preaching to the choir." Easterly looked back through the one-way window at the trembling woman. "You know Faye Yang, works Central Holdup?"

"Yes."

"I think she speaks Cantonese. See if you can get her in here, code three."

Gregorio nodded and rushed off to Communications.

Easterly looked back through the fake mirror. *Damn this country. Why is everyone so frightened? What the hell went wrong here?* She decided to phone David for a dose of sanity.

1130 hours

Kane drove through another snowfall back into the city, straining to see through the windshield wipers. He wondered what his next move should be. Adding together the Whites, the Outlaws and the Mob, he had enlisted into the cause every major white dirtbag in the city. Then he found himself wondering how Isaiah Bell was making out on the black side of town.

Kane reached in the glove compartment for a joint. He stopped for a red light and fired it up. Any onlooker would just see a middle-aged guy smoking a cigarette. He took three strong hits, then stubbed it out.

The light turned green. The tires spun in the wet snow before gaining a purchase. Driving with one hand, Kane took his flask out of the glove box. He took two more belts, not even trying to conceal it. *Let the assholes burn me. I'm a walking dead man.*

Soon he felt the desired buzz. He replaced the bottle in the glove box, and glanced down at the photos of Darryl that were on the car seat. He turned them over so he wouldn't have to look at the boy's face. Then he rolled down the windows and turned on the fan to ventilate the Pontiac.

The citywide frequency cut in with an urgent message. Dispatch was trying to locate unit 4120, a Central Holdup detective car. Kane idly wondered why.

At the next red light, he glanced over at the sidewalk. A young mother was struggling in the snow with a baby carriage. She also clutched the hand of a little boy, who looked to be about five or six, muffled against the cold.

That had been about the age difference between him and Billy, Kane realized. He tried to picture Blanche as a young mother, but the chemicals in his bloodstream were making it difficult for him to think clearly, and try as he might, he could not bring her image into focus. Once again he found himself thinking of the girl in Saigon. He forced her out of his head and instead tried to remember Billy as a little boy.

The light turned green but Kane didn't notice. The driver behind him leaned on his horn. Kane felt the old murderous rage. He rolled down the window. "Fuck you, asshole!" he yelled back.

He realized that he had gone over the line. He was on duty and he was drunk. *Watch it, Ralphie. You don't want to show any weakness, not now. When the time comes to end it, you don't want to give the dickheads any easy explanations.*

He crept along the curb lane, studying the people on the sidewalk. He felt like a patrolman again, forcing himself to notice everything in the vague hope of spotting Darryl Childress. *Where are you, goddamn it?*

Instead he noticed another little boy, a white kid. He was hatless, and his wet hair was the color of Billy's. Kane flashed on the beatings in the basement, when Howard would take one or both of the boys to the coal bin and whip their bare backs with a leather belt.

That's what Klemmer's basement smelled like—home.

He could feel the sting of his father's belt even now. But he also felt something far worse—the wrenching powerlessness to protect his little brother. The memory of that helplessness made Kane feel sick to his stomach.

He inched along, his policeman's eyes still scanning the sidewalk. He just let himself run with the memories. His mind went back to the last time he saw Billy, on a Christmas visit to Statesville. It was the only time Kane ever visited his brother in prison. It was to be Billy's last Christmas.

The two of them hit some mutually raw nerves that day. Billy brought up something they had never discussed—the incident in which Howard crushed Billy's spirit for once and for all.

About half a mile from the neighborhood where the Kanes then lived was a sprawling parcel of undeveloped land, still covered with woods. In the middle of the woods was an open field known as "Skunk Hollow," and in the middle of the field was a large pond. The hollow was populated with all manner of wildlife, from mallard ducks and catfish to turtles and rabbits.

Ralph, about ten at the time, loved that hollow from the moment they moved into the neighborhood. It was a place of safety and peace. Sometimes he would go there alone after school and hide out, an hour or two at a time, taking a story book and sometimes his crayons.

One spring afternoon, Ralph was assigned to babysit little Billy. On an impulse, he decided to take his brother with him to the Hollow, introduce him to his sanctuary. It was a childish act of generosity; he wanted Billy to have a place to hide, too, once he was old enough to come and go by himself. The two boys took along a mason jar with holes punched in the cap, in the hope of catching a butterfly.

And, in fact, they did capture one, a big monarch, as it lit atop a flowering bush. For half an hour, the boys sat in the sun studying the confused butterfly, fascinated. Ralph thought they should release it, but Billy wanted to take it home to their bedroom. In the morning they would let it go. They slipped a few blades of grass into the jar so the butterfly would have something to eat.

On the way home, Ralph carried the jar, periodically checking on the butterfly. Billy spotted a small dog and went running after it, but in the pursuit, he fell and skinned his knee, tearing his trousers.

Both boys were terrified as they headed home. They knew

the wrath of Howard Kane awaited them. Billy started to cry. Ralph put his arm around him, protectively. "Come on, I'll say it was my fault."Without even realizing it, he hung onto the butterfly jar, when he just as easily could have released the poor creature right there.

Howard was in the kitchen when they got home. He reeked of cheap booze. Sure enough, when he saw the torn trousers and the butterfly, he flew into one of the worst rages the Kane boys ever suffered. He would not listen to Ralph's entreaties on behalf of his brother. The butterfly jar was on the kitchen table, near the edge.

"Kill it!" Howard screamed at Billy. "Kill that fucking butterfly!"

Billy just stared in panicky disbelief. His eyes went back and forth, from Howard to Ralph, pleading.

"I said kill that fucking *bug!* You bring *bugs* into my house, you kill them."

"No!" Ralph pleaded. "Please don't make him do that!"

"He tears his clothes, paid for with *my* hard-earned money, chasing *bugs!* I want you to tear the wings off that thing, make him die slowly!"

"Dad, no!" Ralph said, choking back tears. "It was my fault!"

With that, Howard backhanded Ralph hard across the face. Ralph went sprawling across the room, his nose bleeding and one of his front teeth loosened. He lay in the corner weeping helplessly.

"Faggot!" Howard sneered at Ralph. Then he turned back to the cowering Billy. "Another butterfly-collecting faggot! Both my sons, queers!" He started after Billy but staggered, bouncing against the dinner table. The mason jar fell and shattered. The butterfly was thrown loose onto the linoleum floor and tried to find its wings.

Howard looked down at the struggling insect. Then, staring straight into Billy's eyes, he crushed it underfoot, grinding it into the linoleum. "You fucking pansies," he grunted. Then he staggered into the living room, lay down on the couch and passed out.

Ralph Kane had just witnessed his first murder, the murder of his brother's spirit. Right then, an unfeeling hardness descended on his little brother, and Ralph watched it happen. He was never again the same, sweet kid.

And, from that day on, Ralph Kane never wept again either, not even in Vietnam.

The incident went unmentioned all those years, until the day of his last Christmas visit with his brother at Statesville three years ago. "Why did he do it?" Billy asked Ralph over the intercom, studying him through the plate-glass barrier. "Why would that fucker do a thing like that to an innocent kid?"

"I don't know," Ralph said. "I stopped asking questions like that a long time ago. He was an evil prick, end of story. Why are you bringing it up now?"

"I don't know, big brother. I guess I'm just trying to understand myself."

"Understand yourself?"

"Yeah. How did I get so fucked up?"

Ralph noticed that Billy's eyes were shiny; obviously he was fighting tears. For some reason, seeing his brother this way frightened him. So he said a hasty goodbye. Billy didn't try to stop him, just thanked him for coming. And in a few months Billy was dead.

Kane snapped back to the present. *Quit this sentimental horseshit. The world is full of Howard Kanes. You've got a job to do.*

But first he needed to go somewhere and sober up, just a little. Up ahead, he spotted a landmark from his boyhood, the spire of St. Michael's Catholic Church.

Old St. Mike's. Perfect!

Ralph and Billy had attended St. Mike's for a couple of years, between two of their many moves around the city. He remembered a kindly nun who once asked him about the bruises. Kane hadn't thought of that nun in years, and he could not recall her name. He wondered what had become of her, and of St. Michael's itself. The church was old and run-down even then.

Kane pulled into the church parking lot. He put the blue Kojak light on the dashboard, even though he was legally parked and didn't need it. He scanned the parking lot and his eyes stopped at the life-sized statue of St. Michael the Archangel.

Funny, he'd forgotten that stupid statue. All these years later, the celestial warrior was still standing atop his pedestal, keeping watch over the church, the picture of military bearing—ramrod straight, wings spread, right hand clutching his sword, sheathed in the cross-draw position. Michael, the first policeman—the patron saint of policemen. Kane remembered a priest once describing Michael as "God's personal guardian angel."

Or some bullshit like that. That's what those old Irish priests used to say. Half of them had fathers, brothers or uncles who were cops. Cops and priests, that's what Irish homes used to turn out. *So they made up this crap about what a holy and noble profession it was. All based on bullshit. Why would God need a guardian angel?* Kane laughed at the absurdity of it all. He stepped out of the car onto the ice, tested his footing, and walked into St. Michael's Church.

1140 hours

Bell drove through the ghetto, peering through the windshield wipers, silently cursing the weather. Clusters of poor people huddled in storefronts, waiting for buses. He thought about the whites in his new neighborhood. They all had fancy cars and never had to suffer like this.

Bell passed the family's old house of worship, The First Church of God's Messenger, and felt his anger rise again. He thought of his children. Vera's sister had agreed to watch the kids during the daytime for the rest of the week, thank God. Bell hoped all this time in day care wouldn't damage them. During his career, he had seen hundreds of kids damaged by the lack of loving supervision.

For the fourth time, the citywide frequency cut in with an urgent request for a specific Central Holdup unit. Bell surmised that a stickup somewhere must have resulted in a shooting. *That'll sure mess up someone's Christmas.*

Once again, reflecting on the confrontation with Malik Karanga, Bell turned his anger on himself. A suspension was the last thing he needed, money as tight as it was. He prayed the federal agents would be stand-up if Internal Affairs got involved. But that one fed sounded as if he could be a prick.

On the other hand, no one in law enforcement was in love with the BLF, that was for sure. And the Malik Karangas of this world don't go complaining to the NAACP or the ACLU, much less the white media.

So, if the feds did ignore the incident, the only people Bell needed to worry about were those civilian onlookers. They certainly would have no problem identifying him.

Worry about it later. That's all you can do.

Bell realized he had a far bigger problem. Anger was consuming him. He felt himself in spiritual danger. He also felt an urge for a drink. He needed to do something about that.

He found a coffee shop, parked the Ford and went inside, bringing along his briefcase. He stomped the snow off his boots, sat down in a booth and ordered coffee.

When the waitress was gone, Bell opened the briefcase and took out a leather-bound Bible. He lay it on the seat next to him, so no one could see what he was doing. He put on his reading glasses and scanned the book of his namesake, Isaiah. His eyes stopped at the passage he was seeking:

"The wolf shall dwell with the lamb, and the leopard shall lie down with the kid, and the calf and the young lion and the fatling together, and a little child shall lead them…"

Suddenly, Bell felt his eyes fill with tears. He could not even see the text. The big policeman removed his glasses and closed the book, hoping no one could see him. He brushed away the tears and asked God to remove the hatred from his heart.

* * *

Kane sat in the last pew of St. Michael's, trying to will himself sober. The place smelled exactly as he remembered, a musty mix of incense and candles. And, along with the aromas, the old church feelings washed over him, feelings long since forgotten.

Was it here or at St. Mary's where he had been an altar boy? Kane couldn't remember now, the family had moved around so much. And his religious phase hadn't lasted long, that was for sure. His father had ridiculed him for that, too. The only reason the old man sent him and Billy to parochial school was to teach them obedience. That, and their mother's insistence. Blanche didn't ask for very much, but she did get her way on that issue. Catholic schools were required for the salvation of the souls of her two boys.

Now, drunkenly, Kane tried to calculate how long it had been since he had last sat in this building. Thirty-five, forty years? And what was that nun's name? She had hugged him once, told him that whatever was bothering him, the baby Jesus understood. That had embarrassed him, and he'd pulled away from her. *She knew. She knew what I felt. She must have gone through it herself.*

Then his mind jumped to that last conversation with Angela, the night they had said goodbye. She said she would pray for him. The comment had filled him with contempt. How could a reasonable adult think like that? But now, suddenly, he longed to see her again.

He got up and began walking slowly around the drafty old church. It wasn't as big as he remembered. There were water stains in the plaster around the brightly-colored windows. His eyes followed the Stations of the Cross around the walls, depicting the gruesome execution of Christ, graphically portrayed, every step of the way.

What morbid shit. No wonder Catholics are fucked up.

Still, there was something comforting about being here. He remembered coming here as a child, all alone, when the church was empty. He would just sit in the back by himself, right there in the last pew, talking to the baby Jesus, seeking His friendship.

Fat lot of good that did. What a weird-assed kid I was.

But now he found himself kneeling before the altar, gazing up at the cross. "If You exist," he challenged under his breath, "help us find that little boy."

This was not what he had come here for. Kane stood up, holding the communion rail for support. As he turned he was startled by an aged priest walking toward him. "May I help you?" the priest asked.

"I'm a policeman," Kane said.

The priest waited. "Yes?" he finally asked. Kane knew the priest could smell the liquor on his breath.

He reached into his coat and took out a folded picture of Darryl Childress. "This little boy's been kidnapped. We're looking for him. His name is Darryl."

"How dreadful!" The priest examined the photograph. "I'm afraid I haven't seen him. Why would you think he's around here?"

"No reason," Kane said. "Just doing everything we can."

"Of course." The priest smiled gently. "My brother's a policeman. In Wisconsin. Officer, would you like a cup of coffee?"

"Thank you. I have to get back to work."

"Well, good luck."

Kane gave the priest a little salute and walked down the aisle, hoping he wouldn't stagger. Then he stopped and turned around. "Do me a favor, Father."

"What sort of a favor?"

"Pray for this kid, this Darryl."

"I had planned to do just that."

"Good. Pray he doesn't suffer." Kane turned and walked back out into the snow.

1312 hours

The ransom demand finally came just as Easterly was in her office finishing what passed for lunch.

Faye Yang had been located interviewing witnesses to a filling station heist. Now she was down the hall working gently on Mrs. Loh. Easterly decided to leave them alone. The fewer non-Asian faces around the better.

So, while she waited, Easterly had Jablonski bring in a pizza, and they split it. Then she noticed that the lunch was from a Pizza King, little Darryl's television employer, and her stomach suddenly turned sour. She ate one piece, then put her half of the pizza in the little refrigerator.

Despite the investigative saturation, and despite the citywide Patrol alert, nothing had turned up. Ralph Kane had phoned in the results of his meeting with Eric Klemmer. It was hopeful. But she knew better than to expect anything from the White Brotherhood. And Isaiah Bell had informed her that his BLF contact had flatly refused to help.

So Easterly was fighting despair. She also was feeling her age. She reminded herself that the human body can produce only so much adrenaline before it takes a toll. Her body had pumped enough for two lifetimes.

She was just closing the refrigerator when the hotshot line rang. Jablonski grabbed it. He beckoned to Easterly. "Saul Epstein," he said. She picked up the extension.

Saul Epstein was one of Easterly's CCB investigators; they didn't come any better. He was whispering into his cell phone. "Boss, I'm at the Childress house."

"Let me have it, Saul."

"The bad guys called. The kid's alive."

Easterly closed her eyes. "Thank God!"

"They put the boy on the phone to his mother. The Feebees taped it. They want a hundred thousand bucks. The feds are dummying up a package. The drop's set for fifteen hundred."

"Where?"

"They won't tell us."

"*What?*"

"The feds won't tell us. Operational security, they're calling it."

"Good God! Let me talk to their ranking agent!"

"Skipper, it won't do any good. Their SAC is here personally. He's been talking to Mosely. Mosely agrees with him. He's turned the entire operation over to the FBI."

"Oh, for Christ's sake!" Easterly felt her knees weaken. She sat down. This stupidity was beyond comprehension.

1345 hours

Ike Bell stopped at the eighth-floor Gang Intelligence Unit to pick up his paycheck. Payday was last Friday, but Bell had been out in the field. An hour ago Vera called his cell phone to remind him that they needed the money in the checking account.

The bullpen was vacant. The GIU lieutenant, Sammy Grimes, was alone in the office, sitting in his glass cubicle that had been decorated with a fake Christmas wreath. Lieutenant Grimes, a wiry African American, seemed like an old man to Bell. Bell was always startled to remember that he actually was older than Grimes. He wondered how he himself appeared to the younger cops, and winced.

Bell thought back to the old days, when he and Sammy were young patrolmen in what was then one of the most racist police departments in the nation. There was nothing good about the good old days, at least for black cops. *What do these kids just coming on the job know about what we went through?*

Bell opened the pay envelope and shook his head at the meager net. This was the pay period when union dues and the pension came out.

Grimes spotted him and came out of his cubicle. "You hear the news?" he asked.

"What news?"

"There's been a ransom demand."

"God!" Bell exclaimed. "The kid?"

"Still alive. Talked to his mama, in fact. You'd better get downstairs."

Bell shoved the paycheck in his coat and hurried to the elevator. He waited a few seconds, then raced for the stairwell. He ran down two stairs at a time, then hurried into the gym. Several officers were standing around a coffee urn. "What's going on?" Bell asked.

McEwan from the CCB looked up. "The FBI's setting up a ransom drop. They won't tell us where."

Bell was stunned. "What the fuck are you talking about?"

Forrest, McEwan's partner, just shook his head. "They're

afraid of us screwing things up. Can you believe that shit?"

Bell stared in horror. "And we're sitting still for that?"

"What choice do we have?" Forrest said.

"Jesus! What else do we know?"

"Nothing," McEwan said. "The federal radio frequency is encrypted."

"A Bureau friendly told Saul Epstein the kid was pleading with his mother to help him," Forrest said. "They haven't hurt him yet. But the poor little bugger is scared shitless."

Bell shut his eyes tight, not wanting to visualize that, or the anguish of the parents.

"They want a hundred grand," Forrest continued. "They'll make another call to a specific phone booth with further instructions. The feds are putting together a package. They'll try to grab the fuckers at the drop."

"But there are two of these guys—at *least!*"

McEwan nodded cynically. "The federal geniuses think one will act as a scout while the other makes the pickup."

"Leaving the kid where?"

"Who knows? Tied up somewhere, that's their guess."

"How did they come up with that information?"

"From their crystal ball," said McEwan. "They issue them to all FBI supervisors."

Bell felt nauseous. "So all we can do is sit here and wait?"

"Wait and pray," McEwan said.

* * *

A mile away, in the disguised storefront where the Organized Crime Intelligence Bureau was housed, a half-sober Kane sat with his feet on his desk, seething about these latest developments. Three other OCI officers were typing reports into their computers and ignoring him.

The college-boy lieutenant, Van Horn, stood next to a

Christmas tree across the room, watching him. Kane knew Van Horn would love nothing better than to get him fired. And, at this precise moment, he didn't give a flying fuck.

Van Horn had volunteered for OCI just to get his career ticket punched; Organized Crime looks good in an ambitious policeman's personnel file. It had nothing to do with the job. It had been the same way with half the officers running the war in Vietnam. Like them, this slick little asshole was beneath contempt.

Now, sure enough, Van Horn beckoned to him. *Here we go, the big reprimand.* He swung his feet off the desk and sauntered over to Van Horn. "You rang?"

"Your breath stinks," the kid said. "You'd think someone as close as you are to a pension would be more concerned."

"Lieutenant, if they shitcanned every detective who drank on the job, they wouldn't have anyone left." He smiled disdainfully. "Any *real* detectives, that is."

"Does the captain know you drink on duty?"

"Kid, what the hell do you think an OCI cop does? The people I deal with don't hang out in the Mormon Tabernacle."

"Don't call me 'kid'!"

"You are a kid. I was doing this work when you were in elementary school."

"I want to see your activity log. I'm sure you entered all these, quote, 'people you deal with.'"

"Go fuck yourself." Kane realized his voice had carried. The other guys in the unit were looking.

"What did you say, Detective?"

"I'm on detached duty, answering directly to Inspector Roberta Easterly of the Major Crimes Division."

"I know that."

"Then you also know I don't need an activity log, and I don't need to account to you."

He walked back to his desk and grabbed his overcoat.

Van Horn stared at him murderously as he headed out of the office. "You've just killed your career!" Van Horn shouted.

Kane laughed out loud as he opened the door. If the little prick only knew what he was planning.

Then another thought hit him: *When I shoot myself, they'll blame it on the booze. 'Just another alcoholic cop,' that's what they'll say. 'The dumb bastard wasn't in his right mind.'*

The idea sickened him.

1432 hours

Easterly leaned against a wall in Mosely's plush office, clenching her jaw, trying not to explode. Demarest, the FBI chief, was justifying his hijacking of the Childress case: "We've had far more experience in these matters than any local police department. And we operate on a need-to-know basis. The more people involved in an urgent operation the greater the chance of a security breach…"

"Security breach!" shouted Byron Slaughter, his face red. "We're not talking about some goddamned espionage case!"

"That's enough!" snapped Mosely.

Demarest was growing increasingly defensive. "Human life is at stake here!"

"You're telling us something we don't know?" Slaughter countered. "How many kidnappings have you personally worked? I've worked at least a dozen."

"Then you know that involving too many people increases the chance of something going wrong!"

"Let's hope to God you people don't get that boy killed!" Slaughter shot back, clenching his fist.

"Chief, I said that's enough!" Mosely shouted.

Easterly was proud of Slaughter. She wished she could do something to hurt Demarest, badly, right then. She forced herself to remember that this was not about her, or about this police department, but a terrified little boy, alone and desperate for their help.

Easterly checked her watch and tried to speak calmly. "The drop's in half an hour," she said. "What do you want us to do?"

"Nothing," Demarest said. "Having all those officers out there can only screw things up. Your Captain Georgiades is over at our shop. We'll keep him briefed. He can report to you as soon as something happens."

"What do we know about the suspects?" Easterly asked.

"The voice on the phone had a southern accent. There's disagreement among our agents whether it's the white guy or the black guy talking. Our tech people are doing voiceprints."

"What *difference* does it make which one it is? " Slaughter persisted. "They're in it together!"

"Just to get everything straight, for when we go to court," said Demarest. He sounded downright smug.

"Let's hope we *get* someone in court," Easterly said bitterly to Mosely. "*Federal* court. Because that'll mean the kid's been recovered safely."

Then she turned to Demarest, no longer caring what Mosely thought. "Let me tell you something, Mr. Demarest: If this thing goes bad, I'm taking this entire investigation back. And I won't care a bit if the press finds out how you commandeered it."

She turned and walked out of the chief's office, leaving the three men standing in silence. She walked back to her own office, fast, fearing that she had just cut her own throat.

* * *

For the next hour, police headquarters nearly shut down as every detective in the building awaited the outcome of the ransom drop. The collective frustration was palpable. These people were not accustomed to inaction. But the federal radio encryption prevented them from even monitoring unfolding events.

By agreement with Mosely, the news embargo would end the moment the FBI reported back—whichever way things went. So the media now were assembled in the Public Information Office.

Easterly waited with Jablonski in her office. She called David twice, just needing a measure of comfort. As always, he gave it to her.

Bell waited in the gym with clusters of detectives detailed to the task force. Some of the cops played cards, others read. Most just sat there, talking quietly. A few violated the city-mandated no-smoking rule. Bell soon was among them. He found himself chain-smoking, and cursed himself for doing so.

Kane had nowhere to go. He didn't feel like being with cops. And he didn't feel like driving in the snow any more.

So he went out to the illegally parked Pontiac, furtively fired up another joint and let himself get stoned again. Then he boarded a downtown shuttle bus and rode it to the retail business district, ten blocks away.

Kane got off the shuttle and walked slowly through the snow. The air had grown bitterly cold but he found it sensuous, somehow cleansing. Must be the weed, he figured.

He found himself walking through Silverton's, the huge downtown department store. He felt as if he were in a dream. He stopped before a group of children waiting to talk to Santa Claus and stood there watching them, as if expecting to find Darryl Childress in line with them. A little Asian girl looked over at him, and for a moment she looked exactly like that girl in Saigon. *I'm going mad. I'm going batshit crazy.*

Kane walked back out of the store. Out on the sidewalk, he stood in the bracing air, silently commanding himself to get his act together. Then he got back on the shuttle and returned to headquarters. As he walked back into the warm building, he checked his watch. An hour had passed. He needed to relieve himself. He entered the men's room adjacent to the gym.

There at the washbasin stood Isaiah Bell, his face grim. The old enemies caught sight of each other in the mirror. They stood there for a long moment, sizing each other up. Finally Bell spoke: "The FBI screwed up the drop. The bad guys escaped."

That news slugged Kane in the gut. "No shit!"

"No shit."

"Then the kid's fucked."

"Yeah. The kid's fucked." The huge policeman flung a paper towel into the waste container and walked out. Kane once again felt rage overwhelm him.

1630 hours

Mosely and Demarest held a joint press conference, just in time for the city's six channels to go "live at five." The assembled news vultures were in a predictable frenzy.

Both men looked appropriately somber. They displayed a blown-up photograph of Darryl Childress and appealed to the public for help.

Easterly stood in the back of the Public Information conference room, arms folded, barely able to watch. Byron Slaughter was nowhere to be seen. Neither of them had been invited to join the two executives at the podium.

Mosely displayed large sketches of both suspects. Faye Yang had come through. Speaking gently in Mrs. Loh's native tongue, Faye had finally persuaded the frightened housekeeper to cooperate.

But the drawings were nondescript. To Mrs. Loh's recollection, neither man had anything distinctive about him—except the black thug had very dark skin and the white had very light skin. Otherwise, there was nothing you would notice if you passed them on the street. They were what old Stan Jablonski called "generics."

Mosely, at least, did not identify Mrs. Loh. He alluded instead to a "secret witness." Easterly prayed the poor woman would not go mad with fear.

Nor did either executive say anything about the ransom drop and subsequent screw-up. Demarest deftly turned away questions about both. A number of things could not be disclosed, he claimed, because to do so "would compromise our investigation and jeopardize the life of little Darryl."

This dog-and-pony show was more than Easterly could bear. She left the room unnoticed, before any of the press people thought to ask her something.

Out in the hallway, she encountered an agitated Ralph Kane. The detective clearly had been drinking. "Inspector, what the hell happened here?"

"All I know is what Saul Epstein told me," Easterly said. "And all Saul knows is what the FBI told him."

"Which is…?"

"The bad guys changed the location three times. The final drop was set for the North End Mall, a trash can near the big Christmas tree. They promised they'd release the kid somewhere safe as soon as they got the money."

"And?"

"The agents set up surveillance a few yards away. They planned to move in when they saw someone reach into the trash. But the crowd was heavy, this being Christmas. A lone black male blended in, moved up fast and grabbed the entire trash can."

"Jesus fucking Christ!"

"There was a foot pursuit. The agents had to elbow through a swarm of people. The guy was able to fish out the package and disappear." She shook her head. "They didn't even get a look at his face."

"What a clusterfuck!" Kane said.

"We're just lucky he didn't open fire. We could have lost more children."

Kane shut his eyes, angrily envisioning the incident. "It couldn't be any worse for *this* kid."

"No, Ralph, as a matter of fact it is worse. The ransom package was fake, just a bunch of newspapers. They didn't use any real cash at all."

"Not even as a wrap-around?"

"No. Just newspapers."

"Shit!"

"Precisely," she said. Easterly stared at the tough detective. She was astonished at the depth of the pain she saw on his face.

Kane turned and walked slowly away. "Thanks," he said, over his shoulder.

Now Easterly wanted a drink herself.

1710 hours

Vera Bell called Ike's cell phone as soon as the sensational story appeared on the five o'clock news. She watched it on the television monitor in Central Receiving's emergency waiting room. Night had fallen on the city.

Bell answered the phone in the gym. Across the room, a score of angry cops was gathered around three television sets, channel-flipping. "Are they going to find this baby?" Vera asked.

"I don't know," Bell said.

"Are you all right?"

"I'm not going to drink, if that's what you mean."

"I'm sorry. It's just that I worry about you."

Bell sighed. "I need to retire, I swear to God."

"Yes. Maybe we need to start thinking about that. A second career, maybe real estate..."

"The TV even ran one of the kid's Pizza King commercials. Can you believe that?"

"Ike, everyone in the city knows who that boy is. Publicity might help find him."

"Sensationalism, that's all they care about. Anything for ratings."

"I love you, Isaiah," Vera said. "I'll see you at home."

"I don't know what time that will be."

"Just take care of yourself. The child is in God's hands."

"Sure thing," Bell said. As he signed off, he hoped desperately that she was right.

Across the way, phones were ringing on the cardboard tables. Tips were already coming in, but everyone knew that most of them would amount to nothing.

Inspector Easterly reappeared and took the microphone. She called for the troops to re-assemble. Bell walked back to join the others. He noted that Ralph Kane was not among them.

"Okay," Easterly said. "I know you're all upset. No one is more upset than me. But the question is: what now? The media had enough sense to put our phone number on the air, not the FBI's. We're bringing in several night watch precinct people to handle the calls. The rest of you get back out on the street."

A young detective raised his hand. "Inspector, we have a logistical problem. We don't have enough cars."

Easterly was exhausted. She hoped it didn't show in her voice. "If you don't have a take-home car, use your private vehicle. The city will reimburse you later. Use hand-held radios. We're still operating on Tac Four."

As the others pulled on their heavy coats, Bell approached Easterly. "Inspector, what do you want me to do?"

Easterly looked up at him as if not comprehending the question. Finally she nodded. "I hear you've been on the wagon a couple of years."

"We don't use that term, 'on the wagon.'"

"What term *do* you use?"

"*Sober*. We say we're *sober*."

"Well, see what you can do to help Ralph Kane."

"*Ralph Kane?*"

"Yeah, Ralph Kane. I think he's in trouble." She saw the revulsion on Bell's face. "I thought that's what you *sober* people do, help other *non-sober* people. Was I wrong?"

Without waiting for a reply, she turned and walked away, leaving Bell to stare after her, dumbstruck.

1802 hours

In the Acropolis Lounge, Kane sat alone at the far end of the bar. When drinking in public, he always sat where he could see all the doors, but as far as possible from them.

The Acropolis was a blue-collar gin mill in the Greekville section on the fringe of downtown. The joint was filled with the usual after-work crowd, but now they were uncommonly quiet. All eyes were on the overhead television monitors.

Kane was pacing his drinking, trying to maintain just the right buzz without overdoing it. He knew he might have to return to work.

He tried not to pay attention to the six p.m. news update. The smarmy chief of police, Mosely, and the crooked mayor, Webster, were appealing to the kidnappers to release little Darryl unharmed.

In Kane's estimation, both men were human maggots. Mosely was trying to cover his ass after the FBI fuck-up, and Webster was grabbing the chance to deflect attention from the grand jury investigation. *Give me an honest Mob guy any time.*

Kane picked up his beer and moved to the bar's back room, where he could pretend to watch a pool game. Right now, he would give anything to shut off his brain. But he had no such luck. The pool shooters stood around yet another television. On the screen, the anguished Stephen and Louise Childress were submitting to an "exclusive" interview by a breathless, concern-faking bimbo.

The Childress couple were people in hell, of that there was no doubt. Both wept as they talked about what a wonderful boy Darryl was. They begged the public for help.

So what do you think, Billy? What would it have been like to have parents who loved us that much?

Then the television again played an outtake from one of the boy's pizza commercials, with accompanying music – his favorite Christmas carol, "The Little Drummer Boy." There wasn't a word about the FBI blowing the ransom drop.

"Cocksuckers oughta be dead," commented one pool player.

"Torture them first," said a second.

"Let *me* have the motherfuckers, just for ten minutes," said the third, a weightlifter.

Kane went into the men's room to escape the television. He just wanted to get Darryl Childress out of his mind. Again he found himself before a mirror, staring at his image. He was beginning to look like an old man. He was never much to look at in the first place, but now he looked like shit. There were bags under his eyes and his hair was turning a yellow-gray.

You look like shit because you are shit.

Then a hideous realization hit him. He was not starting to

look like an old man. He was starting to look like a corpse.

Kane shut his eyes tightly, trying to blot out the pain. In machine-gun succession, a rush of pictures came at him. He saw the long-ago incident in the alley, the Caldwell shooting. He saw the swarm of desperate Vietnamese at the American Embassy. He saw Howard Kane towering over him, screaming at him for being yellow, because he hadn't stood up to the bully next door.

You are a piece of shit because you are a coward.

Kane once again feared he was going mad. He looked at the wall, where some moron had inscribed: "God is Dog spelled backwards."

You have that right. God is a son of a bitch.

That view was confirmed the instant he came back out of the men's room. The news anchor was breathlessly announcing more breaking news:

A child's body had just been found in a downtown alley.

1823 hours

Kane arrived at the crime scene, blue light flashing. The alley was on the seedy side of downtown, in a marginal slum. The snow had stopped and the sky had cleared, leaving stars vaguely visible through all the city lights.

The corpse lay half-hidden behind a dumpster. A radio car team, a Zebra unit, had been flagged down by a homeless man. The bluesuits both were youngsters and hadn't yet seen much death, and this one was horrifying beyond comprehension. One of the young cops hastily covered the dead child with a blanket while his partner called frantically for assistance.

The urgent call, of course, had been monitored by the news media. Homicide detectives had not yet arrived, but already three news helicopters were hovering nearby. A police aero unit kept them at bay while lighting up the alley.

Roberta Easterly, Isaiah Bell and other task force officers were also on the scene, awaiting Homicide and Forensics. Easterly stood with her hands deep in her overcoat pockets, shifting from one foot to the other, unwilling to accept this turn of events.

On her orders, everyone stayed outside the yellow tape. The snow had already been hopelessly trampled by a small army of winos summoned by the transient. Easterly didn't want any more interference with possible evidence.

Crunching through the snow, carrying a four-cell flashlight, Kane hurried up to her. His face was ashen. "Is it him?"

"Yes," she said softly. "It's him."

Kane ducked under the tape. Easterly grabbed his arm. "You don't need to see it, Ralph."

He pulled away. "Yes, I do." Despite herself, Easterly let him go.

Kane walked gingerly toward the dumpster. He went around behind it, turned on his flashlight, crouched down and gently lifted the blanket from the face of Darryl Childress.

The body was frozen. The boy's bloody right hand covered his face. The bullet had gone through his hand and into his head.

He knew it was coming! He knew it was coming, and he put his hand over his face to stop it!

The strength of his own revulsion stunned Kane. He had seen a lot of corpses in his lifetime. But he had never seen anything like this, not even in Vietnam.

He pulled the blanket back over Darryl's face. He stood up and looked over at the brightly-lit crowd watching him, barely able to see them. Dimly he made out the first arriving Homicide team walking toward him. "Officer, get the hell out of there!" a Homicide guy commanded.

He dream-walked back toward the tape and ducked under it. He was vaguely aware of Bell watching him, along with the others. So he kept walking down the alley until he was out of their sight. He stopped and pulled a flask out of his overcoat, uncapped it and took four long swallows. Then he leaned his back against the wall of a tenement and stood there, numb.

After a few moments, Kane began to weep, softly at first. Then he thought of Billy and Pete. The tears burst forth, uncontrolled. He turned around, propped his forearm against the wall and pressed his face into it, and sobbed from the depths of his soul.

Kane did not notice Ike Bell standing in the shadows, watching him.

1915 hours

Easterly sat in her unmarked car a block from the crime scene, talking to David on her cell phone. She watched the arriving television crews and the crime-scene detectives lit up by the circling aero unit. "I have to give a statement to the press," she told her husband. "Mosely dumped the whole thing in my lap, the gutless bastard."

"Listen, kid, I know you're upset. So be careful what you say."

Easterly smiled bitterly. David knew her all too well. "Everything inside of me is screaming," she said. "I want to tell the world what I think of Mosely and that FBI toad."

"And nobody could argue with you. But the timing is wrong. What this city needs from you now is for you to catch the killers."

"You're right," she said softly. "As usual."

David softened his voice. "How are you? Really?"

Easterly felt the fatigue course through her. "I have a

new picture for the Horror Show. The worst one yet." She inhaled and held her breath. "The little boy had his hand over his face. The bullet went through his hand into his head."

"My God!"

"The corpse is frozen…" She fought nausea. "David, what kind of a *hero* can execute a seven-year-old child?"

"I trust that's a rhetorical question."

"You still opposed to the death penalty?"

David ignored the question. "Any physical evidence?"

"We're excavating the scene, looking for slugs," she said. "But we don't expect to find anything. We're pretty sure he was killed elsewhere and dumped here."

"It's a good thing you have that witness."

"Witness?"

"The sketches. I saw them on TV."

Easterly sighed. "Yeah. The witness."

There was a long silence as David let her feel her pain. Finally he asked, "Have I told you lately how much I admire you?"

Easterly smiled. "David, when this is over, I want to spend an entire night with you just holding me."

"That can be arranged."

"I'll see you at home. I'll be damned if I'm going to spend another night in the office."

"Good."

"But first I have to go deal with the vultures."

"Remember to save the criticism until it will do some good."

As she hung up, Easterly felt overwhelming gratitude for the goodness in her life. Then, walking back to the crime scene, she noticed Kane leaning against his car, alone. He was just standing there, staring off into space.

Where does a man like that find love?

B ell stood in his son's bedroom, silently watching the boy sleep. Ikey had wanted to wait up for his daddy, Vera said, but he was just too tired. He and Cassie had been playing all day with Shawn and LaDonna, their cousins.

Bell said he hoped they weren't playing violent video games again. He also hoped he and Cassie hadn't seen the news tonight. No on both counts, Vera reported.

Now, looking down at his sleeping son, Bell said a silent prayer of thanks that his own children were safe. Instead of complaining about the expense of moving, instead of focusing on the privileges of white people, he should be grateful that they could afford to live here at all.

But Darryl Childress had lived in a safe neighborhood, too.

Bell reflected bitterly on the plight of black children in America. Especially male black children. At this time in history, right here in the land of the free, it was so dangerous to be a black boy-child.

He quietly shut the bedroom door and went downstairs. Vera was waiting in the kitchen. Wordlessly, she handed him some hot chocolate.

"Thank you," he said. He sipped the chocolate and looked out the window at the snow-covered back yard. "I saw something strange tonight. At the crime scene."

"What was that?"

"Kane was hiding in the alley. He was crying."

"*Ralph* Kane?"

"He was drinking from a flask, and he was crying. He didn't know I saw him."

"From what you've told me, I didn't think he was human."

"He's a racist son of a —." He caught himself.

Vera stroked his arm. "You never know about people, Ike."

"He coulda been one of those Klansmen who lynched my granddaddy."

"Maybe he changed."

"Sure," Bell said.

He walked to the back door, pulled down an old parka from a hook and put on some rubber boots. He grabbed an axe leaning next to the door and turned on the backyard light. Then he went outside, to a pile of logs left by the previous owners.

Bell began to chop the wood, slowly at first, then faster and faster, venting his fury. He remembered the police aero unit lighting up the sky earlier, and then saw the young Viet Cong being thrown from the Huey. Past and present began to merge in his fevered brain as he chopped faster and faster, causing splinters to fly like shrapnel.

Vera watched from the window as her husband took his rage out on the wood. She closed her eyes and prayed for him.

She also prayed for the souls of Darryl Childress and Ralph Kane.

* * *

Kane drove aimlessly through the Christmas-lit city, paying scant attention to where he was, or even which precinct. Now the city's snow was lit by a full moon. The main streets were plowed and salted. Kane drove slowly, as if on patrol, sobering again, trying to pull himself together.

He realized he was in the wealthiest part of town, the Sixteenth Precinct. His anger came up again. All these over-privileged pricks in their luxury cars...Kane never could shake his deeply ingrained resentment of the rich.

Get over it. There are more important things to think about tonight.

His breakdown in the alley had frightened him. Nothing

like it had ever happened to him before. He needed to suck in his gut and regain control. Losing control is dangerous for a policeman.

He tried to keep his mind off the face of Darryl Childress. But he had inadvertently memorized the boy's features, having become so intimate with the photograph. Thus, in a bizarre way, the child had become a part of him. Then, to see him dead behind that dumpster…Kane shuddered violently.

Now, to distract himself from Darryl, he started paying attention to the police radio. Except for three or four holdups and the usual rash of car clouts, the air was quiet tonight. For some reason, in fact, the radio traffic was far lighter than normal at Christmas time. *Probably the weather.*

He tried to picture what the uniformed officers were encountering on each call, how they were reacting, what they felt. A lot of the voices rogering the radio sounded young, and several were female. *Babies. They're nothing but babies. Was I ever that young?*

He considered the toll this job took. Police work had never been a joyous profession. But, for the kids just coming on these days, it was even worse. This generation had never known America as a safe place. During Kane's lifetime, police work had mutated from law enforcement into a form of hit-and-run warfare. Sometimes he felt as if Vietnam had followed him home.

Now Kane drove past a strip mall standing where Skunk Hollow had once been. A child-abuse-in-progress call went out over the citywide hotshot channel, a code-three run clear across town in the Twenty-seventh Precinct, some fresh atrocity. A Lincoln unit answered up, some bluesuit working alone.

Don't go in there without backup. A man beating a child is capable of anything.

This was one of the worst times of the year for child battering. Old Howard Kane wasn't the only daddy who turned into an asshole at Yuletide.

Kane called to mind the day long ago when, at seventeen, he had dropped out of school and left home for good. Howard had been even drunker than usual and had mocked Ralph savagely, insisting that he would be back within two days. But Kane had fooled the bastard. He'd used fake documents to get into the Marine Corps, and never saw his father again.

He and Billy had talked about this that day in Statesville, a few minutes before Billy brought up the butterfly story. Billy revealed what had happened after Kane left to serve his country. Until then, Howard had two sons to brutalize. But Ralph's departure left Billy the sole target.

I never should have left him there like that. Running off to war was just another form of cowardice.

Again Kane snapped himself back to the present. He looked out the window at the night streets, observing the people he passed. There were a surprising number of them, despite the snow. Last-minute shoppers, he guessed. He studied them, like an anthropologist. He didn't feel like a member of the same species. He never had.

He passed into a seedier part of town. The crack dealers were out, of course, and the hookers. People of the night needed to work, regardless of the season or the weather.

Then he passed a homeless encampment, and was struck by the number of men he saw wearing military jackets. Was this still the country they had fought for? Was this still the country *he* had fought for? They were white and black and brown; war may be the most democratizing force of all.

Stop this, goddamn it. You're getting emotional again.

But then he passed a storefront church, decorated for Christmas. "Jesus Saves," said the sign. With that, the impact of Darryl Childress' murder hit Kane all over again, hard. He was seized with rage. Christ himself would not be able to forgive such an act of savage cruelty.

Then Kane thought again of Pete, whom he never really

knew. Kane and Jennie had split up shortly after Pete was born. Kane had faithfully kept up the support payments, and he sent gifts at Christmas and the boy's birthday. But, he had always told himself, it was Pete's good luck that he was gone: he carried Howard's genes.

In fact, after Pete's birth, it had terrified Kane to see how much like his own father he had become. Leaving them was one of the few decent things he had ever done. He always hoped Pete had been able to see it that way.

Jennie, of course, knew about the curse of Howard Kane, and probably had explained it to the boy. But she had her own problems, so Kane never knew for sure what she had told him.

And now he never *would* know. A bad batch of heroin had seen to that.

A hideous feeling of loneliness overwhelmed Kane. He was accustomed to unpleasant feelings, but loneliness was rarely one of them. Now, for some reason, he felt an overpowering need to be with someone. He pulled over to the curb and found an old number in his wallet. Silently cursing himself for his weakness, he punched out the number on his cell phone.

Angela answered on the second ring. When she heard his voice, her tone went flat. She had been expecting someone else.

"How have you been, Ralph?" she asked.

"Fine," he lied. "You?"

"I'm fine. Why are you calling me?"

"I don't know. It's Christmas. I was—I was just thinking of you."

"I'm married now. We're expecting a baby in February."

This was the last thing Kane expected to hear. Somehow he had figured that Angela would always be there if he needed her. "Congratulations," he said weakly.

"At my age, can you believe it?"

"I'm glad you're happy."

"My husband's name is Larry. He's a city fireman. He's on duty tonight. I thought this was him calling."

"I'm sorry it's not." He paused, trying to picture her pregnant. "Listen, I apologize for bothering you. I was just feeling kind of lonesome. We've got this big kidnapping and murder case, maybe you saw it on TV…"

"I don't watch the news. I don't want to get upset while I'm pregnant."

"Right."

"Have you been drinking?"

Kane shut his eyes tight against the pain. There it was again, that tone of voice. He fought the impulse to lie. "Yeah, a little bit."

"Ralph, get some help. While you still can." There was a long pause. "Listen, I *do* want to wish you a Merry Christmas. But I don't think you should call here again."

With that, she hung up. Kane stared at the dead receiver.

Tonight. I'll do it tonight. I couldn't save Darryl Childress. He was my last chance, and I failed again.

2301 hours

Bell sat in his television room, channel-flipping to the various accounts of the ghastly crime. The ghouls had spared nothing in their scramble for ratings.

Channel 2 ran a garish logo, "A City Weeps." It referred to Darryl as a "local celebrity."

Channel 4 played "The Little Drummer Boy" over a slow-motion shot of grim-faced morgue attendants wheeling the gurney from the dumpster to their black van.

Channel 7 ran a black border around the screen, over

a year-old Pizza King commercial featuring Darryl laughing and sharing a pizza with Santa Claus.

Channel 11 re-ran the emotional appeal of Darryl's parents for the release of their son—even though by now the entire city knew the child was dead.

Channel 13 ran a man-on-the-street story, filmed in a department-store appliance section. Interviewees were crowded around scores of television sets—all, of course, tuned to Channel 13. The reporters cut back and forth between white and black citizens, all commenting about how horrifying the crime was.

Bell turned off the television and reflected on the irony. *Is this what it takes to bring the races together, the murder of a child celebrity?*

But none of this, of course, was Darryl's fault. Bell thought about the boy's parents. He tried to imagine what they must be going through right now, and hoped they hadn't seen the sleazy television coverage.

Bell's guts screamed for a drink. He needed to get to a meeting soon, or do something else to ensure his sobriety.

But that would have to wait. The important thing now was to catch the motherfuckers who had done this to Darryl.

2332 hours

Kane again sat on his bed with the Beretta in his hand. He couldn't get Darryl out of his mind. He took another hit from a joint. He set the pistol down and crossed the room to his little television set, turned it back on and rewound the VCR tape. *Why in the name of God did I tape the news tonight?* He hadn't the faintest idea. All he knew was that he couldn't let go of the boy.

Or maybe it's the other way around. He won't let go of _me_. Like that girl in Vietnam.

Kane sat down and watched the entire story again, all the way through. Then he rewound to Darryl's Santa Claus commercial, which he watched one more time. With the remote control, he froze the tape on the little boy laughing in sheer delight.

What was it like for you? What was it like to <u>know</u> they were going to put a bullet in your head?

He crossed to the refrigerator for a beer, oblivious to the newscaster's addendum to the tale of horror: "In more positive news, police announced that street crime was reduced dramatically today, for the second day in a row. All categories of offenses were down—a whopping thirty-two percent compared with last year's Christmas season.

"A spokesman for police chief Jefferson Mosely attributed the drop to the massive police presence out on the streets in response to the Childress kidnapping.

"'This proves our theory that more officers on the street will prevent crime,' the spokesman said."

Kane returned with the beer and shut down the VCR. He thought for a long moment, then went to his closet. He fished around on a shelf and pulled down another videotape. He wiped thick dust from it and returned to the television.

The video was an old documentary about Vietnam. Kane sat down with the remote control. He fired up the joint, then drank down half the beer. Then he fast-forwarded the tape to the most significant event of his own life.

There, in fuzzy but living color, was the evacuation of the American Embassy in Saigon. And there *he* was, Sergeant Ralph Kane, USMC, wielding his M-16, holding off the terrified Vietnamese civilians from the embassy gates.

The little girl and her young mother were not in this film. They had not yet arrived when this footage was taken. But there were scores of people just like them.

Now, alone and drunk in his seedy room, Kane wished

that they *would* magically appear in the video tape, that little girl and her mother—if only for a split second. That way the child would be alive. She would be alive forever.

But it was not to be. Kane felt certain she was dead. Just like Darryl Childress. *This country betrayed us by sending us there, then it betrayed these people by pulling us out. That's been my life, just a long series of betrayals.*

Kane froze the picture again and looked closely at himself as a young Marine. He sat there with the beer in his hand, staring at the screen.

A boy. That's all I was, just a scared boy trying to be a man.

2342 hours

Bell stood quietly in his back yard, looking up at the full moon through the naked branches of an old maple tree. The snow glistened around him.

Then he heard crunching footsteps. He turned to face Vera. She wore a heavy coat over her nightclothes. "Are you coming to bed?" she asked gently.

"In a few minutes."

She smiled at the moon. "You see something that beautiful, you could almost forget all the bad that exists in the world."

Bell said nothing. Vera put her arm around his massive waist. "Were you thinking about the little boy?" she asked.

"Yes. And about Ralph Kane."

Vera held him tighter. "You're going to hate what I'm about to say."

She hesitated. Bell looked down at her. "Well?"

"Why don't you try loving him?"

"*Loving* him?"

"Loving him. It's what Christ taught. Love your enemies."

She squeezed him. "Ike, you know that."

"I also know what the motherfucker did."

"I know, too. I've heard it a hundred times." But she knew better than to argue with him. "Have it your way. It's cold out here. I'm going back to bed."

As she walked back to the house, Bell closed his eyes tight. *"Loving* him," he echoed bitterly.

But then he turned and followed her inside.

* * *

Shitfaced now, stripped to his shorts, Kane rummaged through his chest of drawers. Finally he found the old shoe box he was looking for. He returned to the bed and spilled out the contents. Everything dated to a time when he still felt it was important to save things, a time long since passed.

There were a few pictures from Vietnam, a much-younger Kane with the kids in his first combat platoon. He knew for sure that at least three of them were dead, because he had been with them when they died.

God only knew where the rest of them were now. Unlike most Marines, he had made a point of forgetting his comrades as soon as the war was over. And now he couldn't even remember their names.

He came across a dozen old mug shots of major scumbags he had locked up early in his police career. That was back when he still believed he could make a difference. *How many of these pricks had had fathers like Howard Kane?*

Then he found his police academy class picture. All thirty rookies were spit-shined and eager, hat brass polished and Sam Brownes gleaming across their shoulders. *How many of these pricks had had fathers like Howard Kane?*

Finally he found what he was looking for. There was his Silver Star, and his police Medal of Valor.

He held the tarnished medals loosely in his hand. It had

been years since he had even looked at them. The actions in which he had earned them were only vague, receding memories now.

Kane unfolded the crinkled citations and scanned them: "…rescued two fellow Marines, wounded and pinned down by enemy fire…," "…disregarding his personal safety, he shielded an injured citizen while exchanging gunfire with the bandits…"

Kane laughed aloud. Earning these medals had been the greatest con job of all.

He picked up the Beretta and examined it again. Then he put it back down.

No. Not tonight, not yet. You have one last job to do.

DAY THREE - TUESDAY

0600 hours

The clock radio on Roberta Easterly's side of the bed came to life with an insufferably cheerful announcer babbling about the weather: "Old Mother Nature continues her crazy ways. It'll be bright, sunny and warmer today. But another bitter cold spell, a real 'Arctic Express,' is scheduled to arrive by the day after tomorrow—which, as we all know, is Christmas."

"Scheduled"? Where do they find these morons? Easterly reached over and silenced the fool, annoyed that these were her first thoughts of the day. She realized she was drenched with perspiration, and wondered if it was early menopause. No, she finally concluded, her genetic coding was kinder than that. Her mother hadn't reached the change until fifty. Maybe she was getting the flu.

She looked over at David, who was snoring. He wasn't due in his office until 9:00, and it was only a mile away. So he always got an extra hour of sleep, which normally Easterly did not mind. But this morning she resented it.

She reset the alarm for 7:00, the time *he* had to get up. Then, just as the digital clock hit 6:02, she remembered Darryl Childress. She was stunned to realize that for two full minutes she had blocked the murder from her consciousness. Just about the most hideous thing she had seen in a lifetime of hideous things, and for a few moments she had *forgotten* about it!

It must be some kind of defense mechanism, she finally told herself. *What an amazing thing the human mind is, no matter how rational and analytical. Even mine.*

She shuddered at the memory of Darryl's corpse behind that dumpster, thrown away like an old rag. No wonder she'd been sweating. How often in a lifetime does a human being encounter something that evil? Even a veteran cop in a violent city?

Easterly went in the bathroom to towel herself off. She put on her robe and went downstairs. She turned on the coffee and went outside for the newspaper, and was greeted with the caress of warmer air. Stars were shining. The dawn would bring some sunshine.

She lingered outside for a moment, studying the placid suburban street. The huge moon was down low, nearing the horizon, barely visible between the barren trees. At this hour, in a place like this, such horror seemed incomprehensible.

But, back in the kitchen, there it was. The *Daily Times* headline screamed at her: "CHILD ACTOR FOUND SLAIN; Kidnapped Boy Shot, Dumped in Alley." An accompanying photograph showed evidence technicians at work, crouched down on their haunches next to the dumpster. Easterly herself appeared in the photo, watching in the background, with her hands deep in her overcoat pockets. The cutline called her "an unidentified police detective."

Alongside the photo were the sketches of the two suspects. Easterly again examined them, feeling her stomach churning.

Then she turned away from the artist-rendered features, bland and ordinary though they were. She did not want her own mind locked into a specific picture of the killers. She knew the recollection of an eyewitness could be totally inaccurate—especially a witness as frightened as Mrs. Loh.

She poured her coffee and glanced through the story and three sidebars. She cringed when she read an exclusive interview with Darryl's grieving parents, blaming "the police" for screwing up the ransom drop.

Stephen and Louise Childress also criticized "the police" for failing to inform them sooner of their son's murder; they had to learn of it from the TV news. They had retained a lawyer, Edward Bartholomew, a racially-motivated, militant African American who made a handsome living suing law enforcement agencies.

"Why did it take an hour for the department to notify my clients that the body was that of their son?" Bartholomew was quoted as asking. "Couldn't someone have called them as soon as they knew it was Darryl?"

Easterly felt sickened by that accusation. *Why didn't these pricks write a story about their TV cousins swooping down on the scene before the police? And why didn't they at least contact us for our side of the story? That's what an old-time reporter would have done.*

Now she was really angry. She remembered that not a single FBI agent had shown up at the murder scene. Demarest and his people had conveniently dropped "their" case as soon as it had gone bad. *Old Stan Jablonski sure called that one right.*

She checked the byline and vowed that she would have a private talk with the reporter, tell him whose fuck-up this thing really was. Then she caught herself: *No. Talk to David first. David has a good head about these things.*

Her annoyance with the sleeping David disappeared, and gave way to a renewed gratitude that he was in her life. *This is such a lonely world for so many people.*

As if prompted by this thought, Ralph Kane came to her mind. She was still puzzled by his behavior yesterday. When this thing was over, she'd have to figure out what to do about him.

But that was for later. Her thoughts returned to the murder. She said a bitter little prayer, to no God in particular: *Please help us catch these shits. Catch them or kill them.*

0632 hours

Isaiah Bell sat alone in the den, dark but for the glow of the television. The volume was down low, in order not to disturb his sleeping family.

Bell sipped coffee as he channel-surfed, seeking news of

the murder. He found "Morning in the City," a news/talk show on Channel 3. Chief Mosely and Mayor Webster sat together, expressing the collective horror and outrage of the community.

The "community." Whatever the hell that is.

Bell had long since given up the notion that there was anything cohesive holding this city together, or that there could be. The metropolis was a collection of political and ethnic enclaves that included differing and viciously competitive African American interests. The only thing they had in common was a fierce devotion to self-interest.

Maybe that's how it's supposed to be, everyone out for himself. Maybe that's the natural order of things.

Bell did not like to think that way. He *wanted* to believe in the goodness of man, *wanted* to believe the Sunday preachers. But he had been a warrior for too long.

His minded drifted back over his various wars. There was his childhood, of course, where just having black skin was dangerous. Then the Special Forces. Then the police department, always in dangerous inner-city assignments. And then the battle with his own demons. *That one continues every damned day.*

Bell turned his attention back to the television screen: Mayor Titus Webster was promising that "no stone would be left unturned" in the search for the killers. He would personally see to it, he pledged.

Bell watched the screen closely. The vacant expression on Webster's face troubled him. And the concern in his voice sounded rehearsed. *What has happened to this man?*

Webster had been the first non-white to break the old Irish and German stranglehold on city government. Prior to entering politics, he had enjoyed a great track record as a union organizer and civil rights advocate.

In his campaign, Webster had vowed to pressure Washington for the economic development of impoverished minority neighborhoods. Bell had been so convinced Webster would make good on his pledge that he had volunteered for his election campaign.

Then, two years into Webster's administration, rumors had begun to circulate within the police department about the mayor's use of cocaine. No investigation was ever launched, however, because no police administrator could afford to be wrong. That would have been political suicide. So the issue just died.

At first, Bell had ignored the rumors. Many of the old-line police brass were, in fact, rednecked bigots. He wouldn't put it past such people to destroy an ambitious black man by innuendo.

But Bell had been troubled by Webster's inept leadership, and by his lukewarm efforts with Washington. The inner city only decayed further. Webster seemed to have lost interest. His stock response to criticism was to blame "years of neglect under white administrations." However, he failed to mention his own neglect.

All of this, Bell realized, was consistent with the pattern of a cokehead. But it wasn't proof. And he still wanted Webster to succeed, if only to show that a black man could do it here, which historically had been one of the most racist cities in America.

Then, several weeks ago, an ambitious new U.S. Attorney had launched a corruption probe. The investigation was quickly leaked to the *Daily Times* and had been trumpeted in the media ever since.

The alleged scheme was a complicated one involving mayoral appointees—of both races—and kickbacks from municipal contractors. Bell's friends over in the Federal Building insisted that every word of it was true. But still, Bell didn't want to believe it.

Now, watching Webster on television, he began to suspect that he was looking at a once-decent man who had lost his soul. And narcotics were probably the reason.

That notion revolted Bell.

But, then he reflected on his own drinking history. Who was he to judge? Booze was the granddaddy of all drugs. He was blessed that Vera had stood by him, with the help of a loyal and steadfast support group. Without that woman, God only knew where he would be now.

On the television, Mosely continued talking about the Childress investigation. There were no leads on the suspects, he said, despite round-the-clock efforts of more than a hundred police officers and FBI agents. A businessmen's group had raised a $25,000 reward.

The announcer then said Darryl's grieving parents were too distraught to appear on camera. But "Morning in the City" had its own "exclusive":

With that, they played the video that Stephen Childress had taped for the searching police, while the boy was still alive. They played the whole thing, unedited, the parents' anguish on display for the whole world to see.

"We...We just wanted you to know a little about the kind of boy Darryl is, and why we miss him so much," the father was saying again.

Bell was sickened. *He made that tape for us, and now these maggots are using it for fucking ratings!* He muted the sound. *The vultures can't get to the parents, so this whore Mosely gives them the fucking tape!*

"Daddy?"

Startled, Bell turned around. There, in her pajamas, stood his daughter. "Cassie, what are you doing there?"

"I've been standing here. You didn't hear me."

Bell took a deep breath, gathering his thoughts. He beckoned for her to come to him. She crawled up in his lap.

"How much of this did you see?" he asked gently.

"Did something bad happen to that little boy?"

"You heard about it?"

"Daddy, what happened to him?" She was near tears.

Bell closed his eyes tight, wishing this weren't happening. He bit his lip. *I can't lie. If I could protect her by lying, I would. It's right there on TV.* "They killed him, sweetheart."

Cassie just stared at the television, not comprehending. "Why? Why did they do that? Why would someone kill him?"

"I don't know yet, Cassie, but we're going to find out." He stroked her hair. "There *are* bad people in this world, baby. It's why I'm a policeman."

"Are you going to catch the bad men?"

"Yes, baby. We're going to catch them. But we don't know how long it'll take."

Cassie put her arms around his massive neck and held on tight. "Please hurry. I don't want them to hurt Ikey."

Bell held his daughter, rocking her, hoping she couldn't see the fury on his face.

* * *

Ralph Kane did not read a newspaper or look at television this morning. Nor did he shave. He did not take a drink, smoke any weed, or plan to kill himself. He had only a minor hangover. That was remarkable, considering yesterday's excesses. He resolved not to drink at all today. He wanted a clear head for the business at hand.

Instead, he sat at the only table in his room, cleaning and oiling his Beretta. He prayed to a God he didn't believe in: *Let me get these bastards. Let me be the one.*

His cell phone rang. The readout said it was a private number. "Kane," he answered.

"Morning, Ralphie, it's Eric Klemmer."

"Don't call me Ralphie. What do you want?"

"Come see me. I have something. You know, that little memorial to your brother?"

Kane brightened. "Tell me now."

"No. I need to see you face-to-face. Sort of to cement our little agreement."

"How specific is this? It's a long drive."

Klemmer laughed, the maniacal laugh of a true psychopath. "What's the matter, you think I'm setting you up or something? We have a deal, remember? You coming or not?"

"We're going to be busy today. I don't want to waste my time if this is bullshit."

"I'll meet you halfway. There's a survival store in Danville, just off the Interstate."

"I know the place."

"Be there at 8:30. I'll meet you in the parking lot."

"Sure thing, Klemmer."

"Eric. Call me Eric."

"You know, if you don't mind, I'll call you Klemmer. You know, until we get to know each other better?"

Klemmer laughed. "Suit yourself, *Kane*. Too bad about the nigger kid."

"I figured you'd be heartbroken."

Kane hung up the phone and sucked in his gut. *Yeah, too bad.*

Just be there, pukeface. And if you are wasting my precious time, I'm going to drop you in the river...

He finished the job on the Beretta, wiping off the excess oil. He reloaded it, strapped on his shoulder rig, grabbed his mackinaw and headed out to the Pontiac.

0740 hours

Bell's Ford crept along in bumper-to-bumper expressway traffic. The sun had risen bright this morning. It looked as if the city might indeed enjoy a pleasant day for a change.

But Bell barely noticed the sun. He was brooding about Cassie's reaction to the murder. These monsters had done more than destroy a little boy and his family. They had damaged the innocence of his own daughter. And how many other children across this godforsaken city? He would gladly kill these savages up close and personal, the way he twice had done in Vietnam.

But the men I knifed in 'Nam weren't savages. They were soldiers serving their country, just like me.

He remembered the surprising ease with which he had dispatched those soldiers, both on dark trails in the jungle. His training had kicked in; he simply pulled out his K-bar knife and killed them with no reservation, and certainly no hatred. Now, whenever Bell thought of those men, he prayed for their souls.

But Darryl's killers—these assholes are different. Bell relished the possibility of being their executioner. He couldn't help himself. What would Scripture say about feelings like that?

As his car inched along, Bell momentarily regretted his return to Christianity. His religion robbed him of the opportunity for pure hatred. He could not legitimately entertain this desire for revenge. So he caught himself saying a perverse, involuntary prayer: *Lord, if vengeance is yours, let me be the instrument of it.*

Bell started to light a cigarette but again fought against it. How many times had Cassie and Ikey challenged his smoking? How much had it hurt Vera?

For the last couple of days, his wife had pretended not to notice the smoke on his breath. Bell knew she was pretending. She loved him too much to badger him while he was working on such a heinous case. But he knew how much it worried her.

In addition to the rage he felt toward Darryl's killers, he

now grew angry at himself for hurting his family. In a sudden burst of commitment, he rolled down the window and flung the cigarette pack out onto the expressway. The moment he rolled the window back up, a feeling of relief came over him. It was as if something had been lifted from his soul.

He recalled a similar sensation the day he'd finally surrendered his drinking. It was over. That was all there was to it. It was over and done with. The desire to drink was just *gone*. That had been some kind of divine intervention, he believed, a manifestation of grace. *So, is this how it happens with cigarettes, too? Will it be like that again, with this addiction?*

Bell vowed to get back to his meetings. His sobriety was too important to jeopardize. And, more than anyone he knew, Isaiah Bell needed to witness the redemption of others to sustain the hope that it could happen to *him*.

Flashing lights half a mile ahead suggested the reason for the traffic jam. Bell switched the department radio from Tac Four over to the Motor frequency, but all he heard was irrelevant chatter. However, an "eye in the sky" helicopter hovered overhead, from the local all-news station. Bell switched back to Tac Four and turned on the AM radio.

The chopper reported that an eighteen-wheeler had plowed into a compact car at the Harbor Breeze interchange. The car was pinned under the truck, the driver trapped inside. The fire department was performing an extrication. It was going to take awhile.

Bell was annoyed by the delay but corrected his thinking. *That poor bastard in the car...*

The AM station cut away from the helicopter back to the studio. The police department was reporting more good news this morning. The crime rate continued to decline. Overnight statistics now showed a full thirty-six percent drop over the same period last year. Christmas crime had not been this low since 1965.

To what did the police attribute the drop? "We believe it's

due to the added police presence throughout the city, in the wake of the horrible Childress case," the squint Dunsmore was parroting. "This proves our contention that additional police resources *do* make a difference in public safety. That's why Chief Mosely is asking the City Council for an increase in the department's budget next year."

Oh, bullshit…

The department radio beeped twice. "CP to Unit 2742. Come up on Tac Four for the command post."

Bell picked up the mike. "Twenty-seven forty-two, go."

"Call the CP on a land line, code two."

"Roger." He opened his cell phone. Roberta Easterly answered personally. "Inspector, this is Ike Bell. What's up?"

"Do you know a Tyrone Jones?"

"Yeah. By a different name."

"He wants a meet with you, right away."

Startled, Bell hesitated. "He does? Where?"

"The Pizza King at Fremont and 127th, in an hour."

Bell thought for a moment. *Is this a setup? And why is that asshole Malik using his slave name again?*

Easterly noted the slow reaction. "Is there a problem?" she asked. "Do you need backup?"

"No, I'll handle it."

"All right. Call me as soon as you're done."

Bell hung up, nervous about the call. What the hell *does* this asshole want? Maybe he *should* have asked for backup. But he didn't want to tie up another officer. At the same time, he was grateful for Bobbie Easterly's concern for his safety. *Now that woman, she's a cop.*

0802 hours

Easterly was indeed worried about Bell's safety. She returned to her office and asked Jablonski to run a discreet computer search of all suspects named Tyrone Jones. While she waited, she reviewed the Homicide file on Darryl Childress. Now the case belonged to *her*, no question about it. The FBI was out of this caper.

The file was thin, mostly duplicates of interviews conducted when the crime was still a kidnapping. The lab had found nothing of evidentiary value. The morgue reported only that the wound was a small caliber—a .22, mostly likely, or possibly a .38—and that it was "through-and-through." No slug had been found. Darryl had been killed somewhere else and dumped in that alley.

Still, reading the file gave Easterly an odd sense of relief. She had spent five years in Homicide as a young detective. There was something about the clinical nature of a murder file that distanced the investigator emotionally from the victim. A killing thus mutated from an atrocity to be deplored into a puzzle to be solved.

Easterly began sifting through McEwan's notes on the tips coming in. Already five dozen people had called the hot line. Several were the usual head cases—the Elvis sighters and conspiracy theorists—and a couple were clearly just trying to grab the reward. Many more tips had come from well-meaning citizens who thought they might have seen something. The latter would have to be checked out, of course, but none looked promising. This was shaping up to be a tough one.

The phone rang, the Seventh Precinct watch commander. A stolen gray Chevrolet Malibu had been set afire near the railroad yards. It fit the description of the kidnap vehicle. But arson investigators called it a total loss, with any evidence inside destroyed. The fire had been a hot one, fueled by an accelerant, most likely gasoline.

Damn it, Easterly thought, *why can't we catch a break?* She told the watch commander to impound the Chevrolet. She'd have the crime lab search it again, such as it was.

After fifteen minutes Stan Jablonski returned with a hard copy of the computer run. Past and present, there were sixteen known felons named Tyrone Jones in the metro area. One name leaped out. A hardcore drug-dealing Tyrone Jones had joined the Black Liberation Family in Statesville Prison. Now his alias was Malik Karanga.

"I wonder if this is the same guy Bell talked to," she said. "If so, why is he calling now?"

"You want me to get Sammy Grimes down here?" Jablonski asked. "He should know Ike's customers."

"Not necessarily. The BLF isn't a street gang. They would fall under OCI or Anti-Terrorism."

"And those cloak-and-dagger types don't even talk to each other," Jablonski said.

Troubled, Easterly leaned back and took a sip of black coffee. "Bell said he'd be all right. But he didn't sound convincing. Go ahead, talk to Grimes. Then take a surveillance van out to that Pizza King and keep an eye on things."

Jablonski left. Easterly closed her eyes and hoped she wasn't over-reacting. *Please, let's not get any more good people hurt.*

She got up and went back downstairs to the command post. She realized that she hadn't seen Ralph Kane all morning. Now she was worried about *him,* too.

0825 hours

A warm sun was climbing overhead. Some of the dirty snow was actually melting.

Kane pulled into the parking lot of the New Millennium Survival Store. He had arrived in Danville half an hour early, and had spent the last few minutes cruising around the decaying town, inspecting it. In his junior year at Northwestern High School, Kane had played shortstop against Danville High. So he still thought of the place as it had been back then. But a lot had changed since those days.

Danville was a blue-collar suburb northeast of the city, on the river. Once it had been a thriving industrial area. But the Rust Bowl economics of the Eighties had robbed the community of its industrial base. The population of the town was mostly aging and "ethnic"—Polish, Czech, Hungarian. Many were embittered by the economic depression which had befallen them, and by the failure of "the government" to do anything about it. Help would have been forthcoming, most believed, had they only been "minorities."

Consequently, several of the townsmen had formed a militia group. Anti-Terrorism had recently published a classified in-house intel brief which identified the New Millennium as headquarters for these angry men.

Kane parked the Pontiac and stood in front of the store, in plain view. The place wasn't yet open for the day. He wondered if the feds were watching. If not, they should have been.

The New Millennium sign was hand-painted. The front of the building, formerly a plate-glass window, was bricked up. Kane cupped his hands and peered through the iron-barred glass door. All he could see was an array of camouflage gear, K-bar and Swiss Army knives, bayonets and survival manuals. He checked his watch and waited.

Klemmer pulled up ten minutes later, driving a Hummer. He motioned for Kane to get in. "Are you alone?" Klemmer asked.

"Of course. Are you?"

"I have people watching from inside the store."

"I didn't think you hung with these militia fools."

"Times are changing. We have—how shall I say?—a certain commonality of purpose." He gestured in his rear-view mirror. "I also have backup down the street."

"A little paranoid, aren't you? You're the one who called

for the meet."

Klemmer grinned. "So I did."

Kane examined Klemmer's face and his soulless eyes. *This guy really is psycho.* "Why are we here, Eric?"

"I have a name for you."

"One of the killers?"

"It's not that simple. My man is a source. If he likes what *he* hears from you, *he'll* help you out."

"I'm listening."

"He's one of our people in Bryson Prison, doing life. He knows a certain black guy and a certain white guy who used to hang together in the joint. They paroled within a month of each other."

Kane forced himself to appear nonchalant. "Who?"

"My guy wouldn't say. He wants to see you, personally."

"Bryson's a hundred and twenty miles across the state line."

"You want these pricks or not?"

"Of course. I just don't want to waste valuable time on a wild goose chase. Lots of guys get paroled."

"Well, how about this? My man says the nigger used to see the dead kid on TV—they get our stations over there, you know, on cable. One time he mentioned that his mother lived near the boy. He bragged that she had his home phone number. Out of the clear blue, he bragged about a thing like that. Now does that get your attention?"

Kane sat forcing himself to be calm. "Yes," he said finally. "That gets my attention."

"I figured it might." He handed Kane a slip of paper with a name and prison number on it. "You'll find him in solitary. They're harassing him for his political activities."

Kane examined the paper. "Harold Heath. What's in it for him?"

"Harold's been spending a lot of time lately in solitary. That's a very cruel institution, Bryson. We'd like you to have a private word with the warden."

Kane thought about that, then nodded. "That can be arranged."

Klemmer smiled again. "I told him you were a friendly." There really *was* something demonic about his face. "Harold also knew your brother. Can't say they were friends. Harold's not the friendly sort. But there was mutal respect."

"I'll go see him."

Klemmer stuck out his hand for Kane to shake. "So now we're *officially* partners, right? *Now* you'll call me Eric?"

"Sure. Sure thing—Eric."

Kane opened the door of the Hummer. But Klemmer reached over and touched his arm. "One other thing, *Ralphie*. You ought to do something about your drinking. Yesterday, out at my place? Your breath stank like a distillery."

0838 hours

Easterly stood at the podium in the gymnasium, trying to contend with forty angry cops. She knew their anger wasn't directed at her. But neither Mosely nor Demarest had put in an appearance. So now, five minutes into the latest briefing, Easterly was taking the brunt of it.

She decided to let them ventilate. They were pros, and they would mount a full-on hunt for the killers. But first they needed to blow off steam to someone in command.

"Is it true the coroner made the mother come to the morgue to identify him?" one black detective asked.

"She came down, yes," Easterly said. "But..."

"Everyone in town knew that face!" the cop interrupted. "Why was that necessary?"

"The mother *asked* to see him," Easterly replied. "She's having a hard time letting go."

That calmed the hothead. But then a white cop chimed

in: "Who gave that video to the media?"

"I don't know," Easterly said. "You'll have to ask the Chief."

"Fucking whore, sucking up to the press," said a white cop in the back. There was a murmur of agreement.

"And why *did* the family learn about it on TV?" asked a bearded black cop. Easterly recognized him as an undercover narcotics agent, pressed into service for this task force.

"Because the cameras beat most of our own people to the scene," she said. She held her hands up for calm. "Listen, people, no one in this room is angrier than I am.

"We can sort out all of this later, tell our side of it. Right now our job is to catch the *bastards* who did this to Darryl Childress. Get out there and lean on every snitch you have. Paper this city with the sketches. Meantime we're emailing them to every law enforcement agency in the country."

Easterly studied the frustrated faces. "We do have one huge thing going for us. For once in this city's sorry history, the whole town is on *our* side. Something, somewhere will break. And then we'll get these savages.

"Now let's hit the streets."

The officers stood up, grabbed their gear and headed for the doors. Several carried assault rifles or shotguns. They were going hunting.

* * *

Bell circled the Pizza King restaurant three times, looking for suspicious men or vehicles. This neighborhood was dominated by the Camptown Crips. So normally there was no shortage of ominous characters on this turf.

Except at this time of day. Punks like the Camptowns were never awake before noon. So, Bell decided, the four thugs hanging around All State Liquors might be Karanga's BLF pals. On the other hand, the liquor store was at 129th

Street, two blocks up Fremont from the Pizza King. And these assholes were a hundred yards from the nearest vehicle. BLF torpedoes would be a lot more mobile.

Screw this paranoid mind-game, Bell finally decided. Karanga was waiting for him. He backed into a spot in the Pizza King lot and parked facing the street. If he had to leave fast, he didn't want to do it backwards. He picked a spot with large vehicles on both sides, in case he needed cover.

Bell removed the Beretta from his shoulder rig and shoved it in his belt, concealing it with his coat. Then he walked inside, avoiding the puddles formed by the melting snow. He stopped and his practiced eyes swept the room.

Karanga sat alone in a rear booth, next to the rest room. There were only four other customers, all of them at the counter eating the breakfast special. Pizza was not a big seller at this time of the morning. Two of the customers, Bell noted, were reading about the murder of Darryl Childress.

Karanga was just sitting there staring at him. Bell motioned him to a booth closer to the front. Then he sat down, facing the door. As he did, he covertly slipped the Beretta from his belt and clutched it in his right hand under the table. He gestured for Karanga to take the seat across from him.

"What's up, Tyrone?" Bell asked.

"Ain't *my* idea, this meeting," said Karanga.

"*Damn!* I was hoping we'd kiss and make up. Whose idea was it?"

"The Family—our chain of command. *They* told me to come see you."

Good. That means I have this motherfucker by the nuts. "Glad somebody has some civic pride. Are you strapped?"

"What do you think?"

"I think there's a 9-mm Beretta pointed at your balls right now. If this is a setup, you're going down first."

Karanga just glared at Bell. Finally he laughed. "You really are an uptight pig. You think I'd kill you in *public?* Would I call you at the po-lice station and leave my *name?"*

"Smarter people than you have done dumber things than that."

"Listen, my man, I'm a committed revolutionary. But I *ain't* a suicide freak. I know what cops do to cop-killers." He softened his tone. "Put the iron away, brother. I got something for you. About the little boy."

Bell re-holstered the Beretta just as the waitress approached from behind. She jumped back when she saw the pistol.

"Sorry," Bell said. He displayed his badge. "I'm a police officer. I was just showing my partner here my new weapon." He spoke pointedly to Karanga. "It leaves a large exit wound."

The girl smiled nervously. "What y'all want?"

"Two coffees," Bell said. "Police discount."

When she was gone, Bell leaned forward. "So why the change of heart? Why does the BLF want to help us all of a sudden?"

"We're all ex-cons. You know what convicts think of people who fuck with kids."

Bullshit. By helping us catch the killers, you figure you can legitimize the BLF to the world. Plus they're worried about heat as a result of your stunt yesterday. They hauled your ass in and had an in-house court-martial; this meeting is part of a disciplinary action.

All of that flashed through Bell's head in a burst. But his face revealed none of it. "So what do you have for me, Tyrone?"

Karanga looked around warily, even though there was no one within earshot. "Those drawings in the paper..."

"Yeah?"

"You know Bryson Prison?"

"What about it?"

"Coupla dudes got out recently, a chocolate and a vanilla.

They hung out together—probably fucking each other."

The waitress brought the coffee. They paused until she left. "Go on," Bell said, hiding his growing excitement.

"The black dude was a mouthy hype with a bad heroin jones. He'd brag to the assholes in the Narcotics Anonymous meeting about his mama knowing that little actor kid."

"You got names?"

"No. But our man inside will talk to *you*. No other cop, just to you, on my say-so. I told him how you saved my life. You've got to go over there, see him in person."

"That's good, *Malik*. What does he want in return?"

"He has two kids of his own. I think he wants you to blow the motherfuckers away." Karanga paused to let that sink in. "His name is Calvin Jones. Calvin's my cousin."

0915 hours

As soon as Jablonski called in to report that Bell was safely out of the Pizza King, Easterly went downstairs to Byron Slaughter's office. The Chief of Detectives had sent for her. As was her custom, she walked in without knocking. She found Slaughter at the window, looking down at the street three floors below. He turned slowly when she came in. His face was haggard.

"What's up, Byron?" Easterly asked.

"I have to say something to the press. You know, about the accusations from the Childress family."

"That's not fair! *Mosely* should take the heat on this one."

"Mosely's over at the City Council, giving them the department's 'input' on snow removal," Slaughter said. "He dumped this in my lap."

"The gutless wimp. What's a guy from Dallas know about

snow removal?"

Easterly's eyes surveyed the plaques on Slaughter's wall. She had seen them all, many times. Slaughter was a graduate of Airborne OCS. He had earned a Bronze Star in the Mekong Delta. He was valedictorian of his police academy class, had attended an FBI command school and a DEA drug interdiction school, and had been honored by the International Association of Chiefs of Police. The Chamber of Commerce once named him Citizen of the Year and his church had given him their Lifetime Contributors Award.

But now he looked defeated.

"What's the matter, boss?" Easterly asked. "Really?"

Slaughter sighed deeply. "I always told myself I'd give it up, pull the plug, when the weight of this work got too much. That time has arrived."

"What are you saying?" she asked, stunned.

"Bobbie, this one really got to me."

"It got to all of us."

"Do you know what I found myself doing last night? Weeping. Me! The last time that happened was when my mother died, sixteen years ago. I do *not* weep!"

"Skipper, you're not the first cop to shed tears over the death of a child." She forced a smile. "Not even a male cop."

He looked back out the window. "Do you know what depression is like?"

"This isn't a cheerful line of work."

"I don't mean that. I mean the total inability to see anything good in the world."

Easterly sighed. "I can see how that could happen."

"You're lucky. You have love in your life. It's the only thing that balances things out, for people like us."

Slaughter sat down on his couch, put his hands behind his head and looked at the ceiling. "When Marian died, part of me went with her. I've never gotten over it. She was the one who…"His voice trailed off.

"I know. Marian was a wonderful woman."

"I used to tell her the details of my job, did you know that? Most cops don't want their spouses to know the details, how ugly it can be. But she *wanted* me to talk about it. She thought it would lighten the load. And she was right." He shook his head. "I didn't tell her everything, of course…"

"Of course," she said gently, thinking of David.

"This depression's with me all the time now. It's like being in a black tunnel, not even a train in sight."

"Sir…?"

"I'm retiring, Bobbie. It's time to go fishing."

Easterly lowered her head and took a deep breath. This had turned into an utterly rotten week. "That might be a good idea," she said at last.

Slaughter beckoned for her to come closer. He spoke to her confidentially, even though no one else was in the room. "And I'm going to recommend that *you* succeed me."

Easterly could only stand there, dumbstruck. The surprises were coming too fast.

"I have influence with this Police Commission, a number of markers," he continued.

"Boss, what are you saying here?"

"What I'm saying, *Inspector Easterly,* is that I'm pulling the plug while I still have enough clout to make *you* Chief of Detectives."

"Me?"

"You, Bobbie."

Easterly started to argue. Slaughter held up his hand to silence her. "This isn't some favor to a friend," he said. "It's selfish."

"Selfish? What do you mean, selfish?"

"I'm a citizen of this community," Slaughter said.. "I want to know its police department is still in the hands of some real cops."

Driving back to headquarters, Kane seethed over Klemmer's comment about his drinking. *Who's that dirtbag to be judging me?*

Still, he was excited by the prospect of turning over a few rocks inside Bryson Prison. Bryson was one of the places where Billy had done time, prior to being sent to Statesville.

His cell phone rang. It was Vito Vitale. "Ralph?" the old mobster snapped.

"What's up, Vito?" He pulled to the curb.

"I wake up this a.m., I see the little colored kid on the front page. Terrible thing, just terrible. I just want you to know we're on the case, like you asked."

"Good. That's good."

"Were you at the crime scene?"

"Yeah." Kane closed his eyes, seeing it again. "Yeah, I was there." The craving for a drink welled up, full force.

Vitale must have sensed his pain, because he waited a few seconds before continuing. "Is it true the bullet went through his hand?"

"Aw, Christ, was *that* in the paper?"

"No. I have friends downtown. Tell me it's not true."

"It *is* true, Vito. It was like he was trying to stop the bullet —or not see what was happening."

"What a *fucked* thing to do to a child!"

"That it is. How about the street telegraph? You hearing anything yet?"

"No," Vitale said. "But my orders are on the wire. Anybody knows something, we find out they don't tell us, they get the same treatment the kid got. That's the word."

"We're hearing rumors about a couple of shitheads just out of Bryson."

"Give me more."

"Not yet," Kane said. "I'm going to the prison to nose around. I'll let you know what I find out."

"Give me everything you get, Ralph. Consider my people part of the police force."

"Thanks," Kane said. He hung up, then sat there reflecting on the conversation. *Consider my people part of the police force.' Well, well. Merry Christmas to one and all.*

The phone rang again. This time it was Tiny Lawless, of the West End Outlaws. "Hey, man, I just want you to know we're with you guys on this, all the way," Lawless announced. "Fucking bastards oughta be forced to eat their own nuts."

"You won't get an argument out of me. You hearing anything?"

"Not yet. But everybody in town's working with me—the Satans, Hell Riders, Road Killers... Man, we even got the Pagans out looking."

" The *Pagans?*"

"You believe that shit? How long them and us been fucking each other over?"

"Since about the time Christ was born."

"Don't mean we're gonna marry the scumbags. But those pricks got kids, too."

The Outlaws and the Pagans, riding together. Who says there are no miracles? "We may have a lead on the suspects," Kane said. "I'll let you know if it pans out."

"Hey, man, thanks for letting us in on this. It helps—you know, with the self-esteem."

Kane again signed off. *'Self-esteem?'; 'Thanks for letting us in on this'? What's that asshole been smoking, this early in the morning?*

Kane actually heard himself laugh, right out loud. He switched on the AM radio, but snapped it back off again as soon as he heard "The Little Drummer Boy." His smile disappeared.

B ell stopped in the gym to report to Inspector Easterly. But she was tied up on the phone. So he returned to the GIU office to check his messages.

Sure enough, Willis Henry had called. He actually left his number. This was the first time Bell knew how to reach him by telephone. Bell returned the call from his desk.

A sleepy woman answered. It took Bell nearly a minute to persuade her to get Willis.

As Bell waited, his cell phone rang. He recognized Garland McQueen's number. *All my flock.* He let the voicemail take the call.

Big Gun finally came on the line. "Yo, Bell-man. So who capped the little nigger?"

"Who you calling a nigger?"

Henry was taken aback; he was not used to being challenged. But Isaiah Bell was not one of his homies. "Man, it's just an *expression.*"

"Well, save the *expression* for someone else. A child is dead. A *black* child. Maybe you've seen too many drive-bys."

"Hey, brother, I didn't mean nothin' by it."

"I ain't your brother. Some white motherfucker with robes on his head calls us niggers, we want to kill him."

"Man, chill out! I said I didn't mean nothin' by it. I'm as pissed off as you are."

Bell caught himself. *He _didn't_ mean anything by it. It's just the way they talk.* He softened his tone. "Okay, Willis, why did you call me?"

"You ain't gonna believe this, Bell-man. But I got the Seven Nine Treys working with us."

"Bloods?"

"Ain't that a bitch? We had us a summit conference after you came to see me."

Bell shut his eyes. *He's right. I can't believe this.* "That's a good thing," he said.

"So what do you po-lice have? You got anything for us to be workin' on?"

"Nothing yet. But we may have something soon."

"Well, we up all night, every night. Leave messages here."

"Where's 'here'?"

"That was my mama answered the phone. I'm stayin' with her now."

"Sure thing, Willis. Next time, call my cell. You'll get me faster."

"I lost the number."

Bell gave him the number again and signed off. Then he laughed out loud. His *mama.* The city's number-one gangbanger, shotcaller for the Eastside Rolling Crips, a first-class street terrorist—and he stays with his mama! *He loses my number and he still lives with his mama!*

Then he remembered what Henry had revealed about his mother, that she, too, was trying to overcome a drinking problem. He found himself saying a little prayer for her to succeed, and that surprised him.

He returned Garland McQueen's call. "You're up kind of early, Queenie."

"Didn't sleep worth a damn last night," said the old racketeer. "I kept seeing the face of that sweet little boy." There was a catch in his voice. "Just tell me what you want, Isaiah. My people stand ready to help in any way possible."

"I may have something for you by tomorrow."

"Just ring me up, my man."

"Thanks, Queenie. Merry Christmas."

"Sure thing. Merry Christmas, Deacon."

Bell sat there for a long moment, reflecting on the two calls. *Now what do I make of that?* Then he walked downstairs, anxious to get on his way to Bryson.

He stopped short when he entered the gym. Easterly was standing in a corner with Ralph Kane. She spotted Bell and beckoned him over. He approached hesitantly. Stan Jablonski sat nearby, pretending not to hear.

"Detective Kane has developed some promising information out of Bryson Prison," Easterly said. "Something about two convicts who hung around together in there, a black and a white. The black guy's mother knew the Childress family."

Bell felt as if he had been slugged. "I'm hearing the same thing," he said quietly. "About the prison."

"Great!" Easterly said. "Then you need to go there." She looked back and forth between them. "You *both* need to go there."

"Yes, ma'm," Bell said, glancing over at Kane, who stared back hatefully.

Easterly just stood there, studying the aging enemies. "Okay," she said. "I'll phone the prison and tell them you're coming."

Now Kane and Bell were avoiding eye contact, afraid of what she was about to say. "We have a little logistical problem—a car shortage. Ike, I'm appropriating your vehicle for the task force. I believe it's a Ford."

"Inspector, you can't do that!" Bell exclaimed.

"I just did. I have two officers going to the same place at the same time. You can take the same car."

Kane looked at Bell in disgust. Easterly raised her hands. "I can't tie up a department vehicle unnecessarily. Work this thing of yours out, gentlemen. I don't care how you do it, just do it. Now go saddle up!"

She started to walk away, then stopped. "You're authorized code three to the state line." Then she continued on her way.

Kane and Bell stood there glaring at each other. Jablonski lowered his head, pretending not to be listening, trying to hide the amused expression on his face.

1035 hours

The sky had turned blue, surrounding a bright sun. Out here in the countryside, the snow was almost pretty. But neither Kane nor Bell even noticed.

The pavement had dried, so Kane raced along the Interstate, pushing eighty. He kept his eyes riveted on the road, not wanting to look at Bell. The rise and fall of the siren was the only sound inside the Pontiac. Kane was pleased that traffic was light, and he was grateful for the code-three authorization. The less time this fucking trip took the better.

He badly wanted a drink. But he had to keep a clear head and clean breath. He wasn't going to give this self-righteous prick Bell any ammunition to discredit him.

He also was grateful for the joint in his pocket. Taken alone, marijuana didn't screw up his thinking; that way he could catch a buzz without drinking.

Bell was sprawled in the right seat, pretending to doze. He had the seat pulled all the way back to accommodate his size. He hated being here, riding in the same car with this little asshole. But he was surprised that he didn't crave a cigarette.

They rolled like that all the way to the state line, fifty miles from town. Once they had crossed it, Kane shut down the siren and turned off the Kojak. But he did not slow down. Any state trooper could see the blue light on the roof. Even if they were pulled over, there wasn't a cop in the tri-state area who didn't know about the Childress case. If anything, they would get an escort.

But now there was no siren to drown out the thoughts of the two men. Bell, unable to keep up the pretense of sleep, reached into the back seat for his briefcase and pulled out his notes. Included was a glossy photo of Darryl Childress. He held it in both hands and examined it for the hundredth time.

"Do me a favor," Kane said. "Put that away."

Bell looked over at Kane for a long moment. "Sure thing. Whatever you say." He put the picture back in the briefcase.

"It makes me uncomfortable, " Kane said.

"Look, I put it away," Bell said. "I don't need any explanations." He looked out at the snow-covered farmland. "Not that you ever gave one."

"What the hell does that mean?"

"You know damned well what it means."

"Listen," Kane said, "I don't like being with you any more than you like being with me."

"Funny how life works, ain't it?"

Kane spotted a rest stop. "I gotta piss," he said. He pulled off at the exit ramp and parked at the men's room. He left the motor running for heat.

Bell sat and waited. At the curb, directly in front of the car, a newspaper vending box displayed *USA Today*. Darryl's picture was on the front page, along with the artist's sketches of the suspects. Bell leaned back to avoid looking at the paper.

Now it's a national story because he was a celebrity. How much attention would they pay if he were just another black kid killed in a drive-by?

Bell berated himself for his bitterness. Darryl had done nothing to deserve that. Maybe something good would eventually come of this. Maybe Darryl's death would make people care more about innocent black children.

Bell took a legal pad out of his briefcase and began making notes: "Mother knew family. How well? Mother in on it?"

His pen ran dry. Damn it, he thought, he was going to have to stop and buy a new one. Either that or borrow one from Kane.

Bell contemplated the reputation of Bryson Penitentiary, one of the most brutal and corrupt prisons in the nation, notorious for its racism. A few years ago there was a huge scandal when a newspaper revealed that several guards had been members of the KKK. How much could have changed since then?

Ralph Kane should be right at home there.

Speaking of Kane, what the hell was keeping him? This was turning into a mighty long piss. Maybe there was a pen in the glove box. Bell opened it.

There, in plain view, was a pint of cheap whiskey, three-quarters empty, lying alongside a plastic envelope containing the roaches of two joints.

Bell felt a surge of vengeful excitement. *I've got you, motherfucker.* He gingerly removed the items to avoid smudging any fingerprints, and dropped the bottle and the envelope into his briefcase.

As Bell turned to put the briefcase back on the rear seat, he looked up to see Kane staring at him through the driver's window. Kane yanked the door open, enraged. "What were you doing in my glove box?"

"It's not *your* glove box," Bell snapped. "This is a police car. I'm a police officer."

"What're you gonna do with that?"

"I don't know."

"Give it back," Kane demanded. Reflexively he put his hand on his shoulder holster.

Bell smiled sardonically. "What are you going to do, Kane, shoot me? That'll make a hell of a headline."

"You fucking prick. You're going to burn me, aren't you? How many years have you been wanting a piece of me?"

"A lot. A lot of years."

Kane slammed the door shut. He turned around and leaned with his back against the car, staring at the snow-covered hills. He regretted smoking that dope in the men's room. It didn't make him feel high, only angrier.

Bell got out of the car. He, too, slammed his door. "You gonna stand here all day? We have work to do."

"Will I still have a job when we're finished?" Kane asked bitterly. Then: *what difference does it make? I'm not going to be alive after we're finished.*

Bell leaned his elbows on the car roof and regarded Kane coldly. "Let me ask you something, Kane," he said finally.

"You gonna advise me of my rights? Because if you're going to arrest me, you'd better give me my rights."

"Like you and your partner gave James Caldwell his rights? That night in the alley?"

Kane just stood there for a long moment, knowing where this was going. "Why are you bringing this up now?"

"Can you think of a better time?"

"What do you want, Bell? You already have me by the balls."

"I just need to know, that's all. I been needing to know for damn near a quarter of a century. Why did it happen? Why did you let it go down that way?"

"What are you talking about?"

"You know damned well what I'm talking about. Why did you cover up for Frank Lucas?"

"A fourteen-year-old with a .38 can kill you just as dead as an adult."

"That gun was a throw-down and you know it! Everyone on the street—everyone on the job—knew Lucas kept a throw-down in the radio car. Everyone knew he was just itching to kill a nigger. He used to brag about it!"

Kane spun around, years of guilt and rage welling up in his chest. "What the hell was I supposed to do, burn my partner?"

"Your partner committed murder!"

"Bullshit! It was a righteous shooting! The review board said it was justifiable!"

"Because *you* lied to the review board! For Christ's sake, Kane, the kid was *fourteen years old!*"

"That kid…"

"James," Bell said. "*That kid* had a name! James Caldwell!"

"James Caldwell was a criminal! He was doing a B and E!"

"So a burglar deserves the death penalty? Tell the truth, Kane. Frank Lucas had the gun! And he planted it on James Caldwell, right after he shot him! You know that, I know that, everyone who was around back then knows that!"

Kane's eyes were fixed on the *USA Today* headline. "In Vietnam, you don't burn your buddies," he said softly.

"We're not talking about Vietnam! We're talking about an alley in the inner city!"

"What the hell's the difference?" Kane snapped. "Dead is dead. Turn your back on your own people, you can get yourself killed."

Bell glared at Kane. "You know, you're not the only one who was in Vietnam."

"I know that, Bell. That's why *you* should understand, for Christ's sake, you more than anybody!"

Kane's soul screamed for a drink. He wished to God Bell hadn't found that bottle. He walked away a few feet, his back to Bell. He stood there with his hands deep in his pockets. *Do it now. Do it right here. Put the Beretta in your mouth and pull the trigger. Make this prick watch.*

But the face of Darryl Childress smiled at Kane from the newspaper. *No. You have to see this thing through.* "'The Little Drummer Boy'," he muttered.

"What?" Bell asked.

Kane pointed at the newspaper. "'The Little Drummer Boy.' It was the kid's favorite song."

"What the hell are you talking about? By now the whole world knows that."

"I keep hearing that song, everywhere I go. It won't go away. It's like that fucking song is *following* me or something."

Bell pondered that in silence. All he could hear was the passing traffic. He reflected on his own hatred. Here, with Kane, the cumulative rage of all these years weighed him down like a rock.

But then he surprised himself. *What's the memory of James Caldwell doing to Kane? He seems tortured by it.* He was astonished by his own thinking. His wife's voice echoed in his head: *"Why don't you try loving him?"*

Kane broke the silence. "Bell, can we deal with this old shit later? It's been twenty-three years. It'll keep a few more days. We've got child killers to catch."

Still Bell said nothing. "For Christ's sake!" Kane pleaded. "This kid needs us! He needs both of us!"

"Okay," Bell said at last. "But I'm driving. Just in case you smoked some of that dope during your ten-minute piss."

Resigned, Kane nodded and tossed the keys to Bell, and the two detectives climbed back in the Pontiac.

* * *

Easterly sat in Jefferson Mosely's briefing room, listening to the horrifying report being delivered by Captain Angus MacKenzie. She was one of ten senior command officers present. MacKenzie, a ruddy-faced native of Scotland, was her Homicide C.O. He had come to America with his parents at the age of twelve but had never lost his Highland accent.

"There were a number of bruise marks on the body, consistent with the hands of one and possibly two adults," MacKenzie said. "It's our assessment that the lad was killed after putting up a terrific struggle with his captors. We believe they were holding him down when they shot him. The weapon —we're now convinced it was a .22—was fired at very close range."

Dead silence descended upon the room. MacKenzie looked around at the nine people listening. Only Mosely seemed aloof.

"We think the child must have fought very hard for one so young," MacKenzie added softly.

"Which means he was terrified," said Byron Slaughter. "That's why he tried to cover his face."

"Yes, sir, that's what we think it means," said MacKenzie. "His wrist was badly bruised. He must have pulled his hand loose from their grasp in the split second before he was shot."

"Bastards!" muttered Nick Georgiades. *"Fucking cowardly bastards!"*

Easterly glanced at Mosely. The son of a bitch was trimming his nails! She felt her face flush in pure, unalloyed hatred.

She recalled her phone conversation with David, an hour ago, just after her talk with Slaughter. David had congratulated her, but quickly added, "You don't have to take the job." He knew her feelings about answering directly to someone like Mosely. On the other hand, someone needed to keep this whore honest. Barring death or indictment, he would be here for a long time.

"Any chance of DNA samples left on the corpse – blood, skin or hair from the suspects?" Slaughter asked. "If the boy put up that much of a struggle…"

"The lab is working on it, sir," Gus MacKenzie said. "I'm afraid that's all we have so far."

Mosely turned to Easterly. "Inspector Easterly, I understand your intelligence officers have a promising lead. Anything we can tell the press?"

"It involves confidential informants," she said.

"Is the information credible? The public is hungry for us to solve this."

"Sir, at this point it's just rumor," Easterly said. "If

anything does pan out, you'll be the first to know."

Mosely stared at her as if appraising a specimen. He finally nodded, not wanting to alienate the others.

"All right," Mosely said. "Chief Slaughter, I trust you've delivered the department's apologies to the Childress family."

"They're too distraught," Slaughter replied. "As you no doubt can imagine." He barely hid his contempt.

"That's not what I asked you."

"Chief, when the time is appropriate, I'll speak to them personally."

"The sooner the better," Mosely said. "I'm just hoping they don't sue us. This lawyer Bartholomew has an impressive reputation. A publicized lawsuit won't be a good way for me to start my tenure here. See if you can head it off."

The command cops exchanged hateful glances. This asshole was thinking only of *himself!*

Mosely dismissed the group. Easterly started to leave with the others, but the chief beckoned her back into the room. "Close the door," he ordered.

Puzzled, she complied. Mosely smiled patronizingly. "The Chief of Detectives informed me that he's decided to retire."

"Sir?"

"You are his logical successor. Don't tell me he hasn't spoken to you about that."

"Yes, sir, he mentioned it." *Where is he going with this?*

"Well, as a woman, I think you'd make a sound political choice," Mosely said. "But there's a certain attitude on your part."

Easterly felt her face flush again. "Attitude? What do you mean?"

"You were quite belligerent yesterday, with Agent Demarest. I will endorse your promotion, but I expect you to be a team player."

"I've been a team player throughout my career."

Mosely just studied her, as if trying to make up his mind. To him, it was all a show, reaffirming the pecking order. "Good then," he finally said, extending his hand. "Congratulations—Chief."

Easterly paused before shaking it. The hesitation was not lost on Mosely. "I have to get back to work," she said. She saluted loosely and walked out into the hall. She took a deep breath, then headed for her office.

'Sound political choice'! What a prick! How about a damned competent cop?

At that moment, the young television reporter, Nanci York, was rounding the corner, headed for Mosely's office. On impulse, Easterly stopped her. "Nanci, I apologize for the way I talked to you yesterday."

The reporter nodded. "I understand. You were upset about the boy."

"How would you like to make your bones in this market?"

"What do you mean?" York asked.

"Can we talk off the record?"

"Of course."

"Come to my office. The public should know who *really* screwed this thing up."

1206 hours

Bryson State Penitentiary sat on a bluff overlooking a polluted river and dominating a barren, icy landscape. Even to the two hardened detectives, the place looked forbidding.

Bryson was not one of those modernistic, glass-and-steel "humane" institutions with the false promise of rehabilitation.

This place had been built in the late nineteenth century. Thirty-foot walls gave it the appearance of a medieval fortress. The walls were topped with razor wire and surveillance cameras, and guards with assault rifles manned the towers.

Before entering the front gate, Bell pulled the Pontiac to the side of the road. He opened the trunk and stashed the briefcase containing the whiskey bottle and marijuana. Then he and Kane presented their credentials at two separate checkpoints. They surrendered their sidearms to the chief guard, and passed through a final metal detector. Throughout the clearance process, the two men didn't speak to each other.

The deputy warden who met them was a career bureaucrat named Gardner. Gardner was not a happy man. He was annoyed that his routine had been interrupted on short notice by a pair of out-of-state detectives, whose names he barely caught. Gardner showed Kane and Bell to his office. He collected Siamese fighting fish. There were six of them in different tanks around his office.

Gardner sat down at his desk and leaned back, hands behind his head. He was trying very hard to look important. "So you want to interview Messrs. Jones and Heath," he said. "I'm sure you're aware of their histories."

"We know they're not candidates for Citizen of the Year," said Bell.

Gardner held up two thick files. "Both of these clowns are serious trouble. Mr. Jones, the *Afro*-American, is a career criminal with a fondness for armed robbery of convenience stores. Jones considers himself a political prisoner and loudly promotes that view within the black population. He's been attending AA and NA meetings. But that's a con job to get us to lighten up on him.

"Mr. Heath is a redneck, a leader of the white supremacist movement. He's doing life on his third strike. On the outside, Heath dealt drugs and stolen guns. He's also a self-styled political activist, on the white side of the street. To us, he's a major troublemaker. He requires constant supervision and discipline."

Kane checked his watch. "What's your point?" he asked.

"These two men are the kind who would love to kill each other, slowly," Gardner said.

"Yeah, we sort of figured that," Bell said.

"I find it peculiar that these two are your informants," said Gardner. "I mean, these are the last guys I'd expect to cooperate with the police. Tell me: How did you pull it off?"

"That's confidential," said Kane. *This prick is really beginning to get on my nerves.*

Gardner studied Kane, feeling the hostility. "All right," he said at last. "I'm having them brought up to the interview rooms. Follow me, gentlemen."

As they walked out behind Gardner, Bell and Kane passed three white trusties in his outer office. They were watching a television set tuned to CNN that was once again playing Darryl's Santa Claus commercial, filmed a year ago.

Out in the corridor, Gardner laughed. "Pizza King's sure getting a lot of free advertising. You don't think *they* killed the kid, do you?"

Kane and Bell glanced at each other. For a split second, their eyes locked in mutual contempt for this asshole. Gardner caught their expressions. "Hey, it was a joke. You need a sense of humor in a hellhole like this."

"Let us get on with our work, okay?" Bell said.

"Right," Gardner said. He started walking, irritated.

The corridor seemed endless. The trio passed a dozen convicts on a work detail, painting the corridor. All were black. Gardner noticed the quizzical look on Bell's face. "It's not what you think," he said.

"What *do* I think?" Bell asked.

"Yes, we do segregate inmates by race, quite often,"

Gardner said, still walking. "It's necessary to maintain order, with all the racial tensions in here. If you ever worked in a prison, you'd know what I mean."

"You don't say," Bell said.

Gardner now was even more defensive. "Look, contrary to what the NAACP says, we didn't cause those tensions. The separation policy has been upheld by several courts."

"Do I look like I'm from the NAACP? Why are you telling me all this?"

"Because I can tell you're wondering. And, no, we don't give all the dirty jobs to the blacks. The white work details get their share of grunt work, too."

"Mr. Gardner, I have other things on my mind," Bell said. But he glanced at the dark faces covertly watching them pass. He noted the hatred in their eyes. *What is it like to be a black man in a place like this?*

Gardner was anxious to change the subject. "So you think the killers are Bryson alumni?"

"That's what we're here to find out," answered Bell.

"It wouldn't surprise me a bit. Here we get the worst of the worst. Men sent to Bryson are less than human, that's the truth. Animals, most of them."

Kane, silent until now, abruptly stopped walking. Gardner also stopped, as did Bell. "Did I say something *else* wrong?" Gardner asked.

"My brother did time here," Kane said evenly, fixing Gardner in a murderous glare. "In this very institution."

"He did? What was his name?"

"Kane. Same as mine. It works that way with brothers."

"*Billy* Kane?" Suddenly Gardner was frightened.

"Yeah. Billy Kane."

"I—I *thought* you looked familiar."

"'Less than human,' is that what you said?"

"Come on now, don't twist my words! I said *most* of them. I didn't mean *every* one…"

"No, don't backpedal, Mr. Gardner. *Animals*, that's what you said. I think my partner here, Detective Bell, heard you say the same thing."

Gardner looked at Bell imploringly. "I said *most* of them. You heard me say that." But Bell just shrugged. Gardner reflexively stepped back one pace from Kane.

Kane held Gardner in a hateful stare. "So if Billy was an animal, and since we were brothers, I guess that makes me an animal, too. Right? Do you see anything wrong with my reasoning here?"

"Jesus Christ, I didn't mean it that way!" Gardner said. He looked again at Bell for a sign of support. Like most bullies, Gardner was a coward. Bell said nothing, just kept watching Gardner, now flushed and looking down at the ground.

"You're a gutless piece of shit," Kane said. He resumed walking. "Like my partner said, let's take care of business."

They walked the rest of the way in silence. Finally they reached the first interview room. Two guards stood at the door. "Jones is in here, Heath is down the hall," one guard said.

"We'll take them separately," Bell said. "I talk to Jones, he takes Heath."

Gardner gestured for the guards to open the door to Calvin Jones' room. Then he practically ran back to his office.

1230 hours

Easterly stood alone on the snow-covered roof of police headquarters, ten stories above the sprawling city. It was here that she came when she needed to think. A rare winter sun warmed her face, but she barely noticed. Sirens wailed in the distance. She scanned the horizon and spotted a black smokehead. Yet another of the city's decrepit buildings was going up in flames.

Easterly reviewed her anonymous-source conversation with the young reporter, York, during which she had laid out the details of how the attempted rescue of Darryl Childress had been botched. She hoped to God she had done the right thing. The public had a right to know these things. That's how democracy worked. At the same time, she wondered what, if anything, she should tell David about it.

There were no personal secrets between her and David. But he never pressed her for details of her job. He left it to her discretion how much she chose to tell him. He, too, was in a trade requiring confidentiality.

But this leak to York crossed between her two worlds, the professional and the personal. If York turned out to be unreliable, their conversation could cost Easterly dearly.

Easterly did not regret what she had told York. But now she wished she had thought out her decision more carefully. In her outburst at Demarest yesterday she had all but threatened to go to the press. Mosely would remember that.

I have to be more careful. I'm about to become Chief of Detectives in one of the nation's major cities.

On the other hand, she reasoned, she could simply deny being the source. York could have gotten her information elsewhere. Any number of disgusted cops could have talked to her. What could Mosely do, polygraph his new Chief of Detectives?

Easterly shoved her hands deeper into her pockets. *At least Nanci York is photogenic. If she does do a story about the FBI screwing up this case, it'll get noticed.*

She walked back to the stairwell and returned to work.

* * *

The bespectacled Calvin Jones was showing off his

intellect, testing Bell politically. Bell was prepared for it. Calvin's kind always pulled jive like this. *Motherfucker probably doesn't even need glasses.*

The first minutes of the interview were devoted to Jones' monologue justifying his membership in the BLF—the slave mentality of the black race, the inherently oppressive nature of the white ruling class, the racist history of capitalism, the Black Panthers, the old Black Liberation Army, the passion of Brother Malcolm... During the tirade, Calvin Jones quoted Ellison, Baldwin, Richard Wright and Angela Davis. Predictably, he condemned Martin Luther King, Jr. as an Uncle Tom.

It was the kind of rhetoric Bell had been hearing since his own youth. But he let the punk run his mouth. Intelligent thugs need to flaunt their self-perceived superiority, since they have nothing else going for them in their sorry lives. Somehow *sounding* intelligent made them feel morally superior.

They also need to rationalize their crimes, to absolve themselves of responsibility and thus fend off guilt. You can't be an effective criminal if you feel guilty. Class Struggle in America always provides a great rationalization. A common street crime becomes a political act, a statement against the establishment. So a common street criminal can now define himself as a political hero—at least *to himself.*

But Bell wasn't here to win a political argument with a dirtbag. He let his thoughts run as he waited for Jones's lecture to wind down, so he could try some flattery, which often works well with suspects who admire themselves too much. "Tell me something, Calvin," Bell said at last. "How come you kept your slave name?"

The question surprised Jones. "What are you talking about?"

"Well, Calvin Jones is a pretty common name for a man of your talents. You need something more *distinctive.* You know, for the history books. Like your cousin Malik."

Jones considered that. "Well, it happens that I *am* looking for a better name—something from African history. Or maybe something American but more distinctive—like, say, 'Eldridge.' Have you read *Soul on Ice?*"

"Everyone has." *It's working. This idiot thinks I respect his mind.*

"So what's your opinion of Brother Eldridge? From a *po-lice* perspective?"

Bell shrugged, indicating indifference. "By the time he died, Eldridge Cleaver was a born-again Christian Republican. I'd select a different name." Bell looked at his watch. "Look here, my passionate friend, time's getting short. Malik said you have some information about this dead child."

"First you tell *me* something, Brother Bell. Why did you become a cop?"

Bell smiled. "I could give you the usual speech about criminals oppressing our race, or about stopping black children from falling into a life of crime. But do you want the real reason?"

"I asked, didn't I?"

"I enjoy shooting people."

For a long moment, the young blowhard just stared at the huge detective. Then he laughed, missing the joke. "Oh, man, an honest pig."

Pig. Am I in some kind of time warp here? Bell leaned forward in his chair. "Listen to me, brother, all this bullshit aside: who killed the little boy?"

Jones hesitated. "I've never snitched before—not ever."

"This ain't *snitching*, Calvin. Someone killed an innocent little child. They shot him in the head, right through his hand—the hand he was holding up to ward off the bullet." Bell paused. "Malik tells me you have children."

"That's why you're sitting here."

"Then let's not waste any more of my time."

Jones lit a cigarette and held the burning match for a

lingering moment, working for a dramatic effect. Bell waved the smoke away from his own face. *God, don't let this asshole set off the craving.*

"There was this punk on my cellblock, name of Frederick Whitman," Jones said softly. "His color was about the shade of yours, but everyone called him 'White Man.' He hated that name, but the brothers wouldn't let up on him.

"Everyone laughed at him because he was AC-DC, hit from both sides of the plate, you know what I'm saying? He was a little short guy who did B and E's on the outside, probably for sex thrills.

"The little motherfucker had a boyfriend over in C Block named Thomas Blackstone. Blackstone was a white guy but everyone called him 'Blackie.' He was in for drug dealing, used to sell crack to kids at the university.

"So Blackie and White Man—we all knew they were punking each other. Everyone thought the names were funny because of the color reversal, you hear what I'm saying?"

"Yeah. I hear what you're saying."

Jones stood up and started pacing. "I'm listening," Bell said quietly.

Jones stopped and faced the wall. He took another deep drag on the cigarette. "One time—it was around Easter—there was this Pizza King commercial. That little dead kid, what's his name, Darryl, he was in it—with the Easter Bunny."

"My kids saw that one," Bell said. "Cost me twenty bucks for pizza that weekend."

"Yeah. So White Man is on a high that night, drinking or smoking some shit. We're at a recovery meeting, waiting for it to start. He's one of those phony dirtbags goes to meetings to impress the staff, trying for an early parole.

"Anyway, we're watching the tube and there's the kid. White Man starts bragging about how his mama knows the boy's family, has their private phone number, some white dude married to a sister. And then he starts bitching about how much money those people must have, how it ain't fair for a kid like that to get all the breaks, just because he's cute." Jones took another drag on the cigarette. "White Man resented people who were better looking than he was."

"And?"

"He said he thought the kid should pay for it. 'What goes around, comes around,' that's what he said."

"When did he get paroled?"

"Two weeks ago. His boyfriend got out three months before that." Jones turned to face Bell. "Man, I knew it was those two motherfuckers the minute I read the paper. We all did."

Nice of you to tell us, asshole. Bell hid his reaction: "How close are the sketches?"

"Close enough. Get their mug shots, judge for yourself."

"I intend to."

"One other thing you need to know. Remember that big shootout in L.A., between the bank robbers and the cops? These two assholes are crazy like that. White Man talked about that shootout all the time. He bragged about the heavy weapons he has, how he'd love to take down some po-lice."

"Did you believe him?"

"Yeah, I believed him. Why else would I tell you?"

"Much obliged."

"So you probably ought to watch your black ass, you hear what I'm sayin'?"

"Thanks, Calvin." Bell stood up. "Tell me one other thing: What time is the AA meeting?"

* * *

Kane was having yet another hateful reaction, this time to Harold Heath. Heath looked like a grown-up version of a neighborhood bully who had regularly beaten up the ten-year-old Ralph.

Heath towered over Kane, bigger even than Isaiah Bell. He rippled with muscles from years of lifting weights in prison yards. He was covered with amateurish tats; both forearms were adorned with swastikas. "My, oh, my, Billy Kane's brother," he drawled. Kane guessed East Texas. "Small fucking world."

"Small fucking world," Kane echoed.

"The word's out all over the institution that you're here."

"Is that so?" Kane was coming down from the dope he had smoked, and his belly ached for a drink.

"Yeah. And every jackoff in here knows I'm the one talking to you."

"What are you trying to tell me, Heath?"

Heath laughed. "Just the humor of it—whaddya call it? —the *irony*. This, me talking to you, this makes me a *snitch*. Officer, I'm sure you know there's only two kinds of people these guys hate more than a cop. One's a snitch."

"And the other is someone who fucks over a kid."

"Exactly." Heath smiled, the same demonic smile Kane had seen on the face of Eric Klemmer. "So that's what makes this little visit of ours kind of a historic event. See, in this case, every con in here thinks it's *okay* that I'm snitching to a cop. Makes me a hero, in fact. As far as anyone can tell, this is the first time this has ever happened in the history of Bryson Prison."

"We're all mighty obliged," Kane said sarcastically.

"Yeah, but here's what's *really* ironic: unlike most of the sentimental fools in this place, I personally don't give a flying fuck *what* those two guys did to some nigger kid. I'm talking to you out of enlightened self-interest, period. Eric says you're a friendly."

Kane's stomach turned at the word "friendly." But he had long ago learned to tell an informant what he needed to hear. "Yeah, we have an agreement, old Eric and I."

"Did he tell you how much you look like your brother?" Heath asked.

"How well did you know Billy?"

"As well as anyone knew Billy. He was a good man, right to the end."

Right to the end? What does this guy know?

Feigning indifference, Kane checked his watch. "So what do you have for me, Mr. Heath? I have time problems."

"Ralph, call me Harold."

"Okay, Harold. What do you have for me?"

"Blackstone. Thomas Blackstone."

"Come again?"

"The white guy you're looking for. That's his name, Thomas Blackstone. He's a nigger-lover—literally. His fuck buddy is named Frederick Whitman. 'White Man and Blackie,' that's how they were known in here. The black guy was called 'White Man,' the white guy was 'Blackie.' Kinda cute, huh?"

"'White Man' and 'Blackie.'"

"Yeah. Everyone thought it was funny. White Man is bisexual, but Blackie's only a jailhouse fag. Out in the world, he's into pussy, big-time. Spends half his life in tittie bars."

Heath then repeated comments that Blackstone made about Darryl Childress. "He bragged to the white inmates that he had a friend who knew where the kid lived and that the kid's parents were loaded."

"That's pretty thin information," Kane said.

"There's more," Heath continued. "Blackstone studied history. He admired the Colombian drug cartels—guys like Pablo Escobar, that bunch, talked about them all the time, wanted to be like them."

"You just lost me."

"Colombia leads the world in kidnapping. That's how those cartel guys make extra money. Blackie used to talk about how easy it would be to get rich like them, just grab someone who was loaded." He smiled demonically again. "Ralph, he did everything but *spell out* this caper."

"Did this Blackstone asshole return to the city when he got out?"

"Check with the parole board," Heath said. "I do know one thing: he has an arsenal stashed somewhere, maybe even a machine gun. He swore he'd go down in a blaze of glory, like his hero Escobar."

"So we'd better watch ourselves, is that what you're saying?"

"Both of these creeps are two-time felons. Next time around, they're coming back for life. So if they're cornered, what do they have to lose?"

"Except each other," Kane said dryly. "That's good information. Thank you."

"You're going to do something for me, aren't you?"

"I said I would. It may take a few days." Kane stared at the ceiling for a long moment. "Harold, tell me something else: who killed my brother?"

Heath looked at Kane in disbelief. "Jesus Christ, man, I thought you knew."

"Knew what?"

"Some detective you are."

"Until now, I've never given a shit. Now maybe I do."

"It was a race thing, man. You know how things are in Statesville, even worse than here. A nigger shanked Billy in the shower, some BLF guy."

Kane felt his stomach churning again. "What happened?" he asked softly.

"Near as we can figure, the coon came up behind him, grabbed him around the neck and slit his throat."

Kane shut his eyes, picturing his kid brother lying in a prison shower, his blood running down the drain. "How do you know the killer was black?"

"The BLF had a hit on Billy. Everyone knew that." He

shook his head in disgust. "They never shoulda let any of those niggers near us."

"What did the prison officials do about it?"

"They didn't give a fuck. So we took care of it ourselves."

"Whaddya mean, *we* took care of it?"

"The Brotherhood." He smiled. "No one knew which nigger it was, exactly. Coulda been any one of three. So we put down all three of them, just to be sure."

Kane just stared at the wall, trying to take this in. *"All three of them, just to be sure." Jesus, is this the code my brother lived by?*

"I figured you knew all of this," Heath said. "Didn't Eric tell you about it? We settled things for you."

"For me?"

"For your brother. I can't believe you didn't know."

Kane's hands suddenly felt clammy. He realized he was sweating. "I always figured he'd get it sometime," he said. "It was the path he chose."

"Don't tell me you buy *that* shit. Our paths choose us." Heath shook his head. "You're a piece of work. If he were my brother…I guess *we* were more kin to him than you were."

"Yeah, it kind of looks that way."

"So what are you gonna to do for me?" Heath asked. "You gonna talk to the warden? That was your agreement with Eric, wasn't it?"

"Yeah. I'll talk to him."

"You're sure about that?"

"I said I would, and I will." Kane stood up. "Thanks for the information," he said quietly. He did not extend his hand. Instead, he opened the door and walked out.

"Ralph, don't forget our deal," Heath called after him. "You owe me a big one."

Kane didn't answer. Once outside the cell, he stopped walking and leaned against the wall, fighting nausea as the guard watched curiously. *Billy, can you ever forgive me?*

1305 hours

Bell and Kane were together in a prison interview room. Kane stared out a window at convicts in the exercise yard, listening to Bell's end of a phone conversation with Easterly. On the table were prison photos of Frederick Whitman and Thomas Blackstone.

Easterly was excited by the call. "And you both came up with the same names?"

"Yes, ma'm," Bell said. "So far it's all circumstantial. But they do look good for this. The mug shots aren't far off the sketches. Parole records indicate they were returning to the city."

"That's wonderful!" Easterly exclaimed. "Fax me everything the prison has. I want pictures, aliases, physical descriptions, last known addresses, relatives, occupational histories, skills, known associates in and out of prison, everything you can get."

"The deputy warden's putting all that together," Bell said. "He's a jerk but he's cooperating."

"Good," Easterly said. "Bring the original pictures back with you. Meantime, we'll see what R. and I. can dig up. I'll have Jablonski track down the detectives who locked up those guys, talk to the prosecutors who convicted them. We'll start a full-court press to run them down."

"Warn our people to be careful," Bell said. "The bad guys are Ramboed-up—seems they were big fans of that Los Angeles bank shootout."

"What about weapons?"

"There's a rumor about a machine gun. My guess is an assault rifle converted to full automatic. Also, I don't think we oughta door-knock Whitman's mother too soon. We should plant on her place for awhile, at least 'til the word's out that we're looking for them."

"What's your reasoning?"

"Mama may be in on it. They had to keep Darryl somewhere. It could have been her house. They might even be going in and out of the place. If we hit the house when they're gone, we'll just scare them off."

"But if we wait too long, they could destroy any evidence."

"Yeah, it's all timing and luck, isn't it? The timing's your call, Inspector. That's why they pay you the big bucks."

"Well, I do have one thing going for me," Easterly said. "I have some of the best detectives in the country."

"That's only because we get so much practice."

"You did good work, Ike."

"Kane did good work, too," he said. Kane turned to listen.

"Tell him I said thanks," Easterly said. "How's it going with you two?"

"Oh, we're getting along just fine," Bell said, looking over at Kane. "In fact, as soon I get off the phone, Ralph and I are going to his first AA meeting."

Kane spun around and glared at him in disbelief. Bell smiled sadistically.

"Good," Easterly said. "Take your time getting back. I've got forty cops to chase down these leads."

"See you late this afternoon, Inspector." Bell signed off.

"What the hell is *this* bullshit?" Kane demanded.

Bell smiled again. "My man, I've been thinking. See, that bottle and that bag of dope, they've got your prints all over them. Internal Affairs would love to have that stuff."

"What the *fuck* are you driving at?"

"But me, I'd rather mess with your head. You're coming to meetings with me, twice a week for a month. You come along, I toss the shit. You don't, I give it to IA." Bell laughed. "AA or IA. It's your call."

"You can't do this!"

"Who you gonna complain to? The ACLU? Chief of Police? Easterly? Man, she's on *my* side." He laughed again. "Think of me as your probation officer."

"I can't believe this shit. What's in this for you?"

"Maybe it'll help me stay sober."

"I heard about you guys," Kane said bitterly. "Holy-roller do-gooders." He sneered. "Where do you plan to find a meeting around here?"

"A hundred feet down the hall. The inmates have one every day at two-thirty."

"*Inmates?!*" Kane pointed at the men in the yard. "For Christ's sake, they're *criminals!*"

"So was your brother. And so is a cop who keeps dope in a police car." He grinned. "Relax, Ralph, you'll be right at home."

1419 hours

Back in the gymnasium, Easterly and Slaughter stood before the re-assembled task force, briefing them on the new developments. The tech people had done a first-rate job enhancing the electronically-transmitted mug shots of White Man and Blackie. Jablonski circulated among the detectives, handing out copies. Now there was excitement in the gym, a sea change in mood.

"First off, Homicide will bring in our eyeball for a photo show-up," Easterly said. "She's a lousy witness. But unless she definitely rules them out, we'll assume these are our boys. It's possible they're already on the run. We've put out the mugs nationwide through NCIC. But it's equally possible they're still in town, since they don't know what we know.

"Your team leaders will coordinate assignments. We're going to stake on the mother's house, as well as the addresses of their associates. We'll have teams cover the airport, the bus terminal and railroad station. We'll contact the car rental companies—neither of these heroes has a car currently registered to him."

"They'll just steal another one," said one detective.

"Some things we can't control," said Easterly. "Canvas them anyway."

"The black suspect has a big heroin habit," interjected Slaughter. "So Narco will surveil shooting galleries. The white suspect hangs out in strip joints. Vice'll check those places."

"We gonna put their mugs on the street?" another cop asked.

"Not until word gets out that we're looking for them," Easterly said. "That won't take long. In the meantime we go low-profile, try to snag them before they know we're onto them. If that doesn't work, then we start handing out pictures."

"Including the media?" a third cop asked.

"Especially the media," Easterly said.

"Physical evidence is vital," Slaughter said. "We need to find where they kept the child, as well as the murder scene. They may be one and the same place—but they may not. Once we find those places, seal them tight so no one can mess up any possible evidence."

"Here's the last thing," Easterly said. "These guys were fans of that big Los Angeles bank shootout. They may even have automatic weapons. So watch yourselves." She let that sink in, then looked around. "Any questions?"

A florid-faced old detective named Buford raised his hand. "Chief Slaughter, is it true you're retiring?"

Slaughter was startled by the question. He looked accusingly over at Stan Jablonski, who shrugged innocently.

"Yes, that's the decision I've made," Slaughter said.

"You letting Mosely run you out of here?" Buford asked.

"No one is running me out of here. It's time to go. When it's your time to go, you'll know."

"Well, sir," the old detective persisted, "is it true that Inspector Easterly here is going to replace you?"

Despite his grim mood, Slaughter laughed. "The worst place in the world for secrets is a police station."

"Is that a yes?" Buford asked.

"Luke, no wonder you get so many confessions. Yes, I'm recommending that she replace me."

With that, the gymnasium erupted in raucous cheers and whistles. Easterly just stood there, overwhelmed.

She did not see Jefferson Mosely standing in the back doorway, listening. The chief was not smiling. In fact, he was seething.

* * *

Kane was also seething. He sat on a folding chair in the last row of Bryson Prison's Twelve Step room, his back to the wall and his arms crossed. He watched an assortment of thugs and thieves drift in for the meeting. They were white and black, about equal numbers of each, along with a scattering of Hispanics. All were clad in prison blues. Without exception, they checked out Kane and Bell, strangers in the room.

Kane glanced over at Bell sitting silently next to him. This was surreal. He thought he detected a smirk on Bell's dark face.

Calm down, Ralphie; he's got you by the balls. You don't want to be yanked off the last job of your life. When this is over, none of it will matter. You'll be just as dead as Darryl, Billy and Pete.

Kane stood up and moved around the room, inspecting

the place like a crime scene. On one wall was a poster listing the Twelve Steps, riddled with references to God. That confirmed Kane's view that this was some kind of cult.

In the front, next to a podium, stood a sorry-looking artificial Christmas tree next to a rack of pro-sobriety propaganda and a worn table with a battered coffee pot and styrofoam cups. Above the podium was a crude, hand-lettered sign, "WE CARE." It probably had been painted by some graffiti tagger.

Kane realized he was attracting attention. The last thing he wanted was these dirtbags watching him. So he sat back down.

The room was filling with smoke. Bell waved it away with his hand. "They don't smoke in the outside meetings," he said.

"Then what the hell are we doing here?" Kane demanded.

"I've been fighting a drink for two days. Being with you hasn't helped."

"So you're not just trying to save my soul."

"Screw your sorry-assed soul. I'm here to save myself."

"Then why are you forcing me into this?"

"That's *how* I save myself."

"Onward Christian soldiers," Kane said bitterly.

"Look, Kane, this has nothing to do with religion. That's a separate matter. In here we have every kind of human being there is. We have Catholic priests, Jews, atheists…"

Kane gestured contemptuously at the inmates. "And here we sit, hand in hand with God's chosen people." He leaned back against the wall, enraged by his own powerlessness.

Bell, annoyed, went for a cup of coffee. Ten minutes remained before the meeting was to begin. Kane decided just to watch, as if undercover, or working a surveillance. He started examining the faces of inmates as they entered, looking for criminals he recognized. *Maybe I'll get lucky and fuck up some asshole's day.*

Then a tiny old man with the face of a ferret sat down on Kane's other side. "Hi," said the old man, extending his hand. Kane ignored it. "You're from the outside," the ferret observed.

"No shit," Kane muttered.

"You're a lucky man, living a free life."

"Yeah, that's me, just a lucky son of a bitch."

The ferret wouldn't leave him alone. "I know you from some place," he said.

Is this moron trying to save me, too? "If you did, I'd remember you," Kane said. "And I don't."

The old man wouldn't take the hint. "Yes, sir. You look real familiar."

"My brother did time here," Kane muttered.

"That's it! Billy Kane! You're his brother." He again extended a hand. Kane again ignored it. "What's your name?" the ferret persisted.

"Kane," he said. "His name was Kane, my name is Kane. That's how it works with brothers."

"S-sorry," the ferret stammered. "I didn't mean to pry."

"I thought this was anonymous."

"It is," the little convict said. "My name is George Wyatt. In here they call me George W."

It was clear to Kane that the ferret wasn't going away. All of the seats now were taken, so he was stuck with the old man. Kane needed a distraction from his own dark thoughts, so he decided to play with the guy. "So what brought you here, George W?"

"Drinking," Wyatt said. "What brought you here?"

"I meant prison. Why are you in here?"

"Murder One. I decapitated my wife."

Startled, Kane looked hard at Wyatt. The old man was so matter-of-fact that Kane actually heard himself laugh. "You don't say."

"At least they tell me I did. I don't remember. I went into a blackout after I found her in bed with my best friend. They claim I used a machete." He smiled. "Someone did, that's for sure. She was missing her head, no doubt about that."

Jesus Christ, what have I gotten myself into? But Kane couldn't leave it alone. "So what happened to your best friend?"

"Oh, it wasn't quite so bad for him. He ran, but I chased him down and shot him in the balls. Or so they say." The ferret laughed. "He died too. But at least *he* had an open casket."

"George, are you putting me on?"

"I wish I were. Then we wouldn't be having this conversation."

This was the most bizarre discussion Kane had had since his days on patrol. In spite of himself, he felt his mood lighten. It had been a long time since Ralph Kane had laughed. "So how long have you been in this place?" he asked.

"Thirty-three years next week. And I'll be here all day—that means life without parole."

"I know what it means."

Wyatt shook his head. "Funny part is, before that, I never committed a crime in my life. Professional criminals, they get paroled. A drunk like me has one bad day and he's here forever."

One bad day? This is a fucking looney bin. "If you're going to be here all day, why bother with this? What's the point?"

"To help the others," Wyatt said. "This is my little island of sanity. It's where I come to watch men change. That's a rare thing in Bryson. This can be a savage place."

The old con gestured around the room, now filled with inmates and smoke. "Most of these kids, they're just trying to impress the parole board. They don't stay sober on the outside." He smiled. "But once in a while some guy does get it, someone you helped. He goes out into the world and makes a good life for himself. That makes it all worth it."

Kane suddenly realized that he had been enjoying the little bastard. But then the old man spoiled it: "Billy could have used this program, you ask me. I'm glad to see his brother got it."

Christ! Kane scanned the room for Bell. He spotted him in a corner, drinking rotgut coffee. Bell lifted his cup in a sarcastic toast. *Smug motherfucker.*

"Tell me something, Mr. Kane," Wyatt said. "What are meetings like in the outside world?"

"I don't know. I've never been to one."

Wyatt stared in surprise. "I don't understand. You came to your first meeting in a prison?"

"It's a complicated story. You don't need to hear it."

"Well, God works in strange ways."

God. I can't get away from that crap.

Wyatt gave Kane another curious look. "And what do you do, Mr. Kane? Out there in the outside?"

"I'm a cop."

"A *cop?*"

Kane put his finger across his lips. "Keep it quiet."

Wyatt pondered that. "There was a rumor Billy had a cop in the family."

"Well, the rumor was true." Kane covertly flashed his badge. "I'm just pretending to be an alcoholic. I'm here on an investigation."

Wyatt frowned. "You do know this is a closed meeting."

"What the hell does that mean?"

"It means you have to be an alcoholic to attend."

Kane pointed across the room at Bell. "My partner over there, *he's* an alcoholic."

"You're still not even supposed to be in the room unless you're an alcoholic."

"No, George W., you're wrong." Kane pointed to a wall poster. "See, it says right there, 'The only requirement for membership is a desire to stop drinking.' It doesn't say anything about being an alcoholic. And right this minute I have a desire to stop drinking."

"We should bring it up for a group vote. I mean, you being a cop and all…"

Kane leaned over and whispered in Wyatt's ear. "George, you bring this up for a group vote, if you reveal who I am, I'm going to break you in half. I'll break you like a dry twig. And then I'll arrest you for interfering with a police officer. Let's see how well you do in solitary."

George frowned. "Well, I guess it's okay."

"I knew God would help you see it that way."

At that point, a buffed-out skinhead banged a gavel on the podium. "Welcome to the Freedom Group of Alcoholics Anonymous," he announced. "Please take your seats."

Bell returned and sat down next to Kane, who looked at him bitterly. *You win, you self-righteous prick. Here we are, one big happy family.*

1528 hours

Easterly sat in her office, trying to concentrate on the information coming in about Blackstone and Whitman. But her mind kept returning to the latest ominous in-house development: Jablonski reported that Mosely was furious because no one had notified him about the break in the case. In the rush of events, both Easterly and Slaughter had assumed the other had done so.

It was an understandable oversight, in light of the investigation's urgency. But, considering the chief's sensibilities, this could be a very bad blunder indeed. And, since Slaughter was retiring, it all would come down on her. She had promised the chief he would be the first to know about any major developments.

To hell with it, she finally told herself. The investigation took precedence over Mosely's ego. She would try to mend fences later. For now, she needed to put her total attention on the capture of two child killers.

Faye Yang was with Lin Loh again, now interpreting a photo show-up. Easterly had little hope the frightened immigrant would provide a positive ID. This case would have to be proven without her help.

Spread out on Easterly's desk were rap sheets, parole reports, and the investigative files on various past felonies attributed to the two men. Mostly it was just garden-variety stuff—several burglaries by the twenty-four year-old Whitman, low-level drug dealing by the twenty-six year-old Blackstone.

Both men had been transferred to Bryson for disciplinary problems in other institutions. Probably, Easterly speculated, Whitman's bisexuality also had been a factor.

Both men also had southern accents; Whitman was from Alabama, Blackstone from Texas. If they were apprehended, the FBI voiceprint should reveal which one had made the ransom call—unless, of course, some third party had placed it.

She also noted that neither man had ever been charged with a violent crime. Was it possible that these dirtbags were not right for this one?

Easterly had long ago learned to play devil's advocate with herself. The worst sin of an investigator—other than prejudice or laziness—was sticking with a hypothesis so stubbornly as to rule out other possibilities.

She had seen that happen more than once, where a detective was so convinced of his theory of a case that he blinded himself to all other scenarios. That's the way innocent people sometimes get convicted—or, far more often, a guilty one simply gets away with his crime. And, since violent criminals are almost always repeat offenders, a botched investigation inevitably puts more innocent people at risk.

So Easterly had a gospel she preached to her troops. Of course you construct a theory of a case. But then you remain open, willing to abandon that hypothesis if you discover contradictions in the facts. And then you follow that new trail, wherever it leads.

So now Easterly began inspecting her own reasoning. Was there anything here that ruled out White Man and Blackie as suspects? No, she finally decided, these two still looked good for the crime. Certainly no other leads had appeared.

She just sat there for a couple of minutes, holding the mug shots. She tried an emotional exercise she frequently employed while working Homicide. She tried to put herself inside the mind and heart of a murderer. What kind of a person is capable of shooting a helpless child through the head? What does it feel like to *be* such a man?

But today the old exercise just gave Easterly the creeps. She went back to reading the files.

Whitman's mother, Felicia Harris Whitman, lived two miles from the Childress house. Criminal Conspiracy's best stakeout team already was planted on her place. This was not an open surveillance, like the one on the White Brotherhood. The CCB people were professional trackers, and they were good. They could follow the pope and not get noticed.

The Whitman place was ramshackle, sticking out in a neighborhood of old but well kept properties. The surveillance officers reported back that the house was quiet. The snow was piled up in drifts, shades were drawn on all sides, and two newspapers were on the porch. Either no one was home or no one was going out.

As Easterly pondered these facts, Jablonski walked in without knocking, carrying a stack of investigative files. "Bingo," he said. "These all belong to mama. She's a righteous crook herself."

Easterly examined the file jackets. "Welfare fraud, welfare fraud, larceny from a store, extortion."

"Family values," said Jablonski.

"Any current warrants?"

"Not under that name. She has a string of aliases, so R. and I. is still checking."

"Tell them to look hard. If her Freddie doesn't fall into our arms by tomorrow morning, a warrant for her will give us an excuse to search that house."

"We'll need a search warrant, not just an arrest warrant."

"Old Judge Delancey still owes us a favor. I don't think he'll split too many hairs in a case like this."

"Boss, I like the way you think."

Then there was a knock on the door. Jablonski opened it. Angus MacKenzie, the Homicide captain, stood there smiling. "I come bearing good news. The Chinese woman fingered our boys."

"No *shit!*" Easterly exclaimed.

"She picked them both out," MacKenzie said. "She says she's sure of it."

Easterly slapped her desk jubilantly. "Who says there's no God?"

"I thought the lady was seriously scared," said Jablonski.

MacKenzie nodded. "She is. But she told Faye she's also 'deeply offended'—that's Faye's translation—by what was done to the lad. And she's feeling very guilty. Now she wants to help in any way she can. Rather heroic, I'd say."

The three veteran detectives just looked at each other in silence. "This'll be enough for arrest warrants," Jablonski said quietly. "Since Felicia's house is Freddie's home of record, we shouldn't even need Judge Delancey."

Easterly shut her eyes in gratitude. "Keep the stakeout going through the night. If we don't score by morning, then we'll raid the place."

MacKenzie nodded. "This all started with Kane and Bell, from what I understand."

"Yes," Easterly said. "Kane and Bell."

"I thought they hated each other."

"They do."

The big Scot just shook his head. "Sometimes amazing things happen in this life."

1602 hours

Bell and Kane headed back to the city, with Bell again behind the wheel. The sun was dropping rapidly. Dark clouds again were forming in the north, and a cold wind had come up. For several miles, the two men barely spoke. Finally, Bell broke the silence, his eyes fixed on the road, "So what did you tell that asshole Gardner about your pal Harold Heath?"

Kane bristled. "Heath's no pal of mine. Is that asshole Calvin Jones a pal of yours?"

"It was just an expression." He looked over at Kane. "I heard a rumor you cut some kind of deal with Eric Klemmer."

"I bullshitted Klemmer and Heath for information, nothing more," Kane said. He rolled the window halfway down for some air. "It worked."

"So what *did* you tell the prison? You really gonna intercede with the warden on behalf of this genocide freak?"

"Fuck no! I told Gardner that as far I'm concerned Harold Heath can spend the rest of his sorry-assed life in solitary. Or maybe put him in a pen with the BLF, sell tickets. You think I'm going to honor any promise I make to psychos like these?"

"You don't need to get so defensive."

"Listen, just because my brother was tight with those scrotes doesn't mean I am. I may be a jerk about a lot of things, Brother Bell, but I'm no white supremacist!"

After another half mile, Bell softened his tone: "I never knew you had a brother in prison."

"It's not the kind of thing a cop brags about. Internal Affairs knows. That's why they're always looking to nail me. Guilt by association." He rolled the window back up. "Lotta that going around these days."

Bell did not respond. Kane brooded as he looked out the window. "You know," he finally said, "I didn't have a choice about it."

"About what?"

"That thing in the alley. With the Caldwell kid. I didn't have a choice."

"Bullshit."

"Goddamn it, Bell, what was I supposed to do, snitch off my partner? You think *I* wanted to die in some alley?"

Bell looked over at him. "That sure makes it sound like Frank Lucas *was* a murderer."

"Haven't *you* ever done anything you were ashamed of? Any dirty little secrets? Something you covered up, maybe?"

Surprised by these questions, Bell clenched the steering wheel tightly. Kane noticed. He leaned toward him. "Oh, yeah, looks like I might be hitting home! Tell the truth, Bell! Did *you* ever do anything you were ashamed of?"

Bell grimaced, remembering the execution of the young Viet Cong, and the silence he kept. "Once," he said.

"In 'Nam or on the streets?"

"In 'Nam, goddamn it!"

"What happened?"

"None of your fucking business!"

"Then maybe that's why you still hate *me* so much."

Bell boiled over, hating both Kane and himself. He steered the Pontiac across three lanes, then screeched to a stop on the shoulder. He activated the emergency flashers. He got out of the car, slammed the door violently, then just leaned his back against it, facing traffic.

Kane sat in the car watching him and craving a drink. *I really nailed the pious asshole with that one.*

But, after two full minutes, Kane began to grow concerned. He opened his own door and got out. "You're not going to do something stupid, are you?"

"Like what?"

"Who knows? Like that bottle in the trunk?"

"What the hell do you care?" Bell asked.

"Hey, I was asking, that's all," Kane said. "Family man like you, it'd be a fucking shame."

"You think I'd give *you* that kind of satisfaction?" Bell turned slowly and faced Kane, studying the man he had resented all these years. The two old cops stared at each other, both of them wondering what the hell was going on.

"Look, man, I haven't eaten since breakfast," Kane said at last. "I don't know about you, but I need something to eat."

Bell pondered that. "Yeah," he finally muttered. "Me too."

"Then let's hurry up and get across the state line."

"Why the state line?"

"In case the restaurant gets held up. That way we can shoot the son of a bitch. Think of the paperwork if we do it in the wrong state."

Bell just glared at him. "Hey, man, it was a fucking joke, okay?" Kane said.

He got back in the Pontiac and slammed the door, hard.

* * *

Easterly was combing through Thomas Blackstone's probation file when the intercom buzzed. It was Mosely's secretary. The chief wanted her immediately.

Christ, here it comes. This guy just can't wait.

Easterly took her time walking down to the third floor. She was accustomed to the egos of ambitious police executives.

But Mosely took ego to a whole new level. This asshole was Machiavellian. *People like this make you feel like a criminal.*

She was startled to find a television crew waiting in Mosely's outer office. The chief's secretary took her aside and cautioned her that Nanci York was inside with Mosely and the FBI's Francis Demarest. Easterly felt her heart start to pound. She pulled herself erect and walked in.

Mosely and Demarest rose smiling when they saw her. She knew it was a show for York's benefit. "You wanted me, Chief?" Easterly said. She avoided looking directly at York. With her peripheral vision, she could see that the young reporter was equally nervous.

"Inspector, I believe you know Miss York here," Mosely said.

Easterly extended her hand. "I've seen you on the tube. You're taking the town by storm."

York's palms were clammy but her smile was perfect. "It's good to see you again," the kid said. "Anything new on the investigation?"

"Not that we can talk about." She noticed that Demarest's smile had vanished now that York's back was turned.

"Sit down, Inspector," Mosely said. "Miss York is doing a piece about our response to the ransom demand. Some disgruntled officer—she won't reveal her source—has alleged that the situation was botched."

"Botched?" Easterly prayed that her own palms were dry.

"Yes," Demarest said pointedly, "something about how we usurped the lead in the case, and that the failure of the operation was thus somehow our fault." His eyes were riveted on Easterly's face, studying her reaction.

"But the Bureau always takes the lead in a kidnap," Easterly said with pointed irony. She turned to York, sending a cautionary message with her eyes. "We all *did* work together…"

"That's what we tried to explain to Miss York," Mosely said. "Since you command Major Crimes, we were sure you wouldn't mind going on camera to refute whatever this unnamed source told her."

Easterly was appalled by this Orwellian move. But she *had* to keep her composure. "What do you want me to say?"

"Just answer her questions, truthfully," Demarest said. "Tell the public how the arrest went bad despite our best *collective* efforts, that it was something that could not have been prevented, that it was an act of God—whatever comes to mind."

An act of God! What a cynical prick! "Sir, I don't know if I'm the appropriate person…"

"Inspector, you are the responsible command officer," Mosely said. "Mr. Demarest and I, we're simply administrators." He smiled again at York.

"Well, Inspector?" Demarest said. "Shall we bring the cameras in?"

"This is taking me by surprise," Easterly said weakly. "Can I have a few minutes to review the facts?"

"Miss York is on a deadline," Demarest said. He feigned sadness, another show for York. "The family is quite upset, as you can imagine. We'd like them to get it from the horse's mouth—how local and federal law enforcement combined resources in a professional manner to try and effect the safe recovery of their child. The tragic fact that it went bad was not for a lack of effort on our collective part."

"We've explained all of that to Miss York," Mosely said. "But it will sound self-serving and defensive if Mr. Demarest and I say it on camera."

"Like most reporters," Demarest said, "she's not familiar with police techniques. So we want her to get it from the command officer in the trenches. That's you."

Easterly felt perspiration on her face. She prayed it didn't show. *My God, I would never pass a polygraph!*

She turned to York and spoke slowly. "So what you want from me is a response to what your confidential source told you, is that correct?"

Confused, York looked back and forth between Mosely and Demarest. "If she does that—if she contradicts what the source told me—then I'll have to kill the story."

"Well, we wouldn't object to that at all," said Mosely. "We didn't think it *was* a story." He smiled at Easterly. "What about you, Inspector? Do you see a story here?"

Easterly thought for a long moment. Then she said, "I'm sorry to disappoint you, Miss York, but your source is mistaken. This thing went by the book."

York shrugged. "Then I guess the piece is dead."

Mosely and Demarest smiled covertly at each other, relieved. Disgusted with them, and herself, Easterly checked her watch. "Now, if you all will excuse me, I have work to do."

"Just one moment," Mosely said. He turned back to York. "For the moment, this is off the record. You *will* be getting a real story from us, in just a matter of days, concerning Inspector Easterly. She's about to become Chief of Detectives, the highest-ranking woman in the history of this department."

York didn't know how to react. "Is this a leak?"

"I guess you could call it that," Mosely said, turning on the charm. "I'll give you a one-day jump before we make the official announcement. Provided you lay it on 'informed sources', of course." He grinned, pleased with himself. "We'll call it a consolation prize for what happened here today."

"Congratulations," York said, trying to force enthusiasm. She extended her hand.

"Let's wait until it's official," Easterly said. She turned and walked out.

The sun was starting to set. The wind shifted, bringing dark clouds in from the north, fast, causing the temperature to plummet once again.

Kane and Bell pulled into a truck stop bedecked with Christmas lights on their own side of the state line. A blast of frigid wind greeted them as they emerged from the Pontiac.

"Christ, I hate this weather," said Kane.

"I hate these short days," Bell said.

"Everyone's days are short."

"What?"

"Never mind. It was a stupid comment."

They crossed the parking lot between two tractor-trailer rigs. Near the door of the diner was another newspaper box. The two detectives paused momentarily, gazing once more at their victim's innocent smile from the front page. Then they walked inside. Most of the other customers were interstate truckers. On a jukebox Bing Crosby sang "Jingle Bells."

"We don't have to sit together," Kane offered.

"Don't be ridiculous," Bell said.

The only available booth was beneath a festive Christmas wreath. The paper napkins were decorated with little figures of Santa Claus. The two cops sat down and studied the menu. A middle-aged waitress came over, wearing mistletoe on her blouse. Kane ordered a cheeseburger, Bell a salmon patty.

When she was gone, Kane reached into his coat pocket and took out the mug shots of Frederick Whitman and Thomas Blackstone. He studied them intently, memorizing the faces, picturing them with beards, eyeglasses and other disguises. "I'd sure like to be the one who takes down these two fucks," he said.

"Get in line behind me." Bell watched Kane continue to examine the pictures, avoiding eye contact. "I'm trying to remember when you were in Vietnam."

"Seventy-two and again in seventy-five," Kane said. "Right there at the end."

"I was there in sixty-seven and sixty-eight." Bell looked off into the distance, remembering. "Tet."

"It was a different war."

"Wars are all the same when they're shooting at you."

"Special Forces, wasn't it?"

"Yeah. Covert operations."

"With the spooks."

Bell pondered that ambiguous word. "Yeah," he said quietly. "With the spooks."

They sat in silence again, each lost in his own thoughts. The jukebox switched to "Rudolph the Red-Nosed Reindeer." The waitress brought the food. "Where you boys headed?"

"Nowhere," Kane muttered.

The waitress looked at him curiously, recognizing a profoundly unhappy man.

"He means we're not truckers," Bell explained.

The waitress smiled, the genuine smile of a kindly soul. "Well, Merry Christmas, gentlemen—two days early. God bless you."

"Thank you," Bell smiled. "The same to you."

Bell and Kane started to eat. "Tell me something, Bell," Kane said. "You really believe all this God stuff?"

"Most of the time."

"Most of the time?"

"Sometimes I have my doubts," Bell said. "I wouldn't be human if I didn't."

"Where was God for Darryl Childress?"

"I don't know. When I meet Him I'll ask Him."

"Was God in Vietnam?"

"Where are you going with this, Kane?"

Kane buttered his roll. "I stopped in a church yesterday. It was a church I went to as a kid, a Catholic church. St.

Michael's. We called it St. Mike's. I stopped in just to see what it was like now."

"Yeah?"

"While I was in there, I said a prayer for the kid. Then, six hours later, they find him with a bullet in his head, dumped in an alley like a piece of trash."

Bell sat in silence, equally tormented by that image. "I don't know how to answer that," he said at last.

Kane looked at him intently. "But you're a believer."

Bell sipped his coffee. "Doesn't mean I don't wrestle with the same questions."

"So how do you make sense of these things?"

"Sometimes I can't." Bell stopped eating and looked into Kane's eyes. He saw the pain there. He leaned forward and lowered his voice. "Here's what I do know. I'm a drunk. Two years ago I was at rock bottom, sitting on the edge of my bed with my pistol in my hand. I was trying to get up the courage to blow my brains out."

Kane took a long swallow from his water glass, trying to hide his surprise. Bell noticed. "I had everything," he continued softly. "I had my health, a good job, merit citations, a decent pension ahead of me. Most of all I had a wonderful family who loved me."

"Then why would you want to cap yourself?"

"It's where my disease took me. My alcoholism. I got to where I couldn't see any point in living any more."

"Disease? You think it's a fucking *disease?*"

"Ask a doctor. Ask the AMA."

"Those guys back there in the prison, they have a *disease?*"

"Just like me. It's a soul-sickness, Kane, a spiritual cancer. No one asks to catch it. It's something that happens to us."

Kane also lowered his voice. "So how come you didn't pull the trigger?"

"I don't know. At the time I thought I was a coward.

Now I believe it was divine intervention. For just a second, something opened my eyes. I could see what my death would do to the people who loved me."

"Did you really think you were a coward?"

"Everyone's a coward sometimes."

Kane looked up at the wreath, avoiding Bell's eyes. The jukebox switched to "Angels We Have Heard on High." "That's what happened to me, you know, that night in the alley," he said at last. "I was scared. *That's* why I didn't do the right thing—I was a *coward.*"

"That's what I figured."

Then Kane did look at Bell, imploringly. "Then you have to forgive me, right?"

Bell stared at Kane. *"What?"*

"Forgiveness. You're a Christian. Doesn't your faith require you to forgive me?" Bell had no ready response. "Well?" Kane asked.

"It's not my place to forgive," Bell said finally. "It's God's place."

"But *you're* the one who hates me."

Bell just sat there, confused. *He's right. The son of a bitch has got me there.* "Look, man," Kane persisted. "Frank Lucas is dead. James Caldwell is dead. I'm the only one left. Can we bury this thing? You and I are getting old."

"Are you sorry?" Bell asked.

"Sorry? Sorry it happened? Of course I'm sorry it happened. There hasn't been a single fucking day I haven't thought about it." He lowered his eyes. "Along with lots of other things."

Bell thought for a long moment. Then he took a deep breath. "Then, yes, I have to forgive you," he said softly He could barely believe the words coming from his own mouth.

Without warning, Kane's eyes flooded with tears. He stood up hurriedly. "I have to go to the john."

As Bell averted his own eyes, Kane turned and headed

for the washroom at the rear of the diner. He staggered like a drunk, barely able to see.

Once inside, Kane leaned against the washbasin. He fought for breath, trying to focus through the tears. *What in the name of God is happening to me?*

Then he became aware that "The Little Drummer Boy" was coming from the jukebox. Kane stood there listening, once again studying his face in the mirror. The tears surprised the hell out of him. A face overflowing with tears cannot be that of a corpse.

After what seemed to take a very long time, the song finally ended. Kane washed his face, and walked slowly back to Isaiah Bell. "Let's go," he said. "We have some killers to catch."

1719 hours

Easterly sat behind her desk, brooding about the afternoon's events. Mosely and Demarest had banished her excitement over the progress of the Childress investigation.

Her office was nearly dark. Night was again falling over the city. But she had only one small lamp burning, next to her sofa. The dim light matched her mood.

Easterly was pondering a phone conversation she'd just completed, with Nanci York. The kid had just lost her professional virginity.

"I didn't have any choice about going to Mosely," the distraught York explained. "I told my editor what I had. He asked who my source was. I told him it was confidential. But I did use the pronoun 'he.'

"He was pissed off by that. He demanded to know the race of my source. I asked what difference it made. He insisted, so I told him the source was white."

"Is your boss black?" Easterly asked.

"He's a white liberal. He said this was another attempt by the racist cops to undermine a black man."

"Jesus Christ!"

"He said the police department has a long history of racism, and that's why they're trying to sabotage Jefferson Mosely."

"Sabotage? The guy's a first-class asshole. He's in town ten minutes and everyone in the department has him pegged."

"So I've heard. But my boss *insisted* my source had to be racially motivated. He told me to get my butt over there and get their side of it—before he'd even consider running the story."

"Welcome to the world of political correctness," Easterly said, trying not to sound bitter. "Thanks for covering for me."

"I just wish there was some way to get this on the air."

"I wish a lot of things," Easterly said as she signed off.

I wish I lived in a world that was fair. I wish people could get along with each other. Most of all, I wish evil people didn't hurt little children.

Now, ten minutes after finishing with York, Easterly was startled by the sudden appearance of Stan Jablonski at her door. He noticed the dimness of the light. "You all right, Inspector?"

"No." She beckoned for him to come in and close the door.

"What's wrong?" he asked, genuinely concerned.

"Stan, I want your thinking about a couple of things."

"Sure thing." The old sergeant sat down. "What's up?"

"I know you talk to the troops, gossip a little…"

"Only harmless stuff. I never reveal anything sensitive."

"I know that, too. I trust your judgment. So help me understand something."

Easterly told Jablonski about the situation with Mosely, Demarest and York. He listened sympathetically. "I understand, skipper. If I were in your shoes, I would've done the same thing. What is it you don't understand?"

"Why Mosely and Demarest are sucking up to each other like this. They barely know one another."

"Mosely's a career chief of police, hopping from place to place," Jablonski said. "This won't be his last stop. He has his sights on something bigger, maybe New York or L.A.—some city that needs a black face at the helm—like we did.

"But he can't afford to look bad. So he can't admit any screw ups—especially one that helped kill a child."

"Jesus," Easterly groaned. "That figures. Why am I not surprised?"

"As for the FBI, they're in constant contact with police administrators all over the country. Mosely knows Demarest can help him with the right people."

"What about Demarest?" she asked. "What's in it for him? This went beyond just the usual FBI arrogance."

"My pals in the Bureau—I do have a couple; they're not all morons—they tell me Demarest is looking to become an Assistant FBI Director. That's why he grabbed this case—because it's high profile, the kid being a celebrity and all. And it's why he distanced himself when things went sideways."

"So they scratch each other's backs and cover each other's asses, all at the same time," Easterly said.

"Being a whore isn't always about sex. You know that. Guys like these, they're so mediocre they can't rise on their own merits. So they use whatever they have going for them. With Demarest it's a headline case. With Mosely it's his skin color."

Easterly stood up and turned on a light. She felt fatigue down to her bones. She needed a night with David. "So, tell me, Stanislaus, what does any of this have to do with crime, punishment and the public safety?"

"Nothing, boss. It never has and it never will."

"You're even more cynical than I am."

"That's because I'm older than you are." Jablonski smiled. "Inspector, these guys—the Moselys and Demarests of the world—*they're* the cynics. They don't even *think* about things like right and wrong. Guys like Kane and Bell, screwed-up as they are, they're the kind who worry about things like that."

"And people like us."

"Yeah, and people like us. The only time those Mosely and Demarest types feel pain is when things don't go their way. They're like those TV news creeps. They couldn't care less about the Darryl Childresses of the world."

"So what should *I* do?" Easterly asked. "I'm getting burnt out and jaded. I'm turning into a tired old cop."

"Hang in there for *us*," Jablonski commanded. "The real cops are counting on you. Chief of Detectives! My God, did you hear that cheer? Do you know how many admirers you have in this police department? You're the voice of reason."

Easterly sat back down and looked at her adjutant, feeling a swell of gratitude. "Thanks, Stan."

He smiled. "Now do you want some additional Father Jablonski advice?"

"Sure."

"Go home, spend some time with your husband, get a good night's sleep."

"As soon as Kane and Bell get back, I intend to do just that," she said.

"Kane and Bell. I like the way you handled that." Jablonski stood up. "Inspector, that's *why* the troops care about you. You have a great heart."

Easterly's throat tightened with emotion. "Get out of here, Sergeant."

Wet snow was falling by the time Kane and Bell arrived downtown. Rush-hour traffic was snarled. Bell crept along toward headquarters, peering through the windshield wipers. Kane, in the shotgun seat, was again scrutinizing the mug shots in the passing lights.

"Those faces haven't changed since the last time you looked," Bell said. "It's like you're *obsessed*, or something."

"You mean you aren't? Don't give me that shit."

Bell looked over at Kane. "I saw you in that alley last night."

"What do you mean, you *saw* me?"

"I saw you drinking," Bell said. "You had a flask, and you were drinking."

Kane felt a fresh surge of anger. "Man, you already have me by the balls. Why are you busting them all of a sudden?"

"And then I saw you crying. Crying about the little boy."

"Jesus!"

"That was the first time I ever thought of you as human."

Kane shook his head bitterly. "For God's sake, don't tell anyone."

"Then today I saw you *laugh*. You were talking to that old geezer before the meeting, the guy with a face like a mink. You were fighting it hard, but one time you actually *laughed.*" Bell shook his head. "Amazing what I've seen lately."

"Why the *fuck* are you so interested in my emotional well-being all of a sudden?"

"Well," Bell said, "you gotta admit we're sort of—what's the word? —*bonded* here."

"Like I had a lot of choice in the matter," Kane added." He turned to the snow-spattered window and looked out. Then, despite himself, picturing ferret-faced George W, Kane smiled. "You know what the old fart's in for? He cut off his old lady's head and shot his best friend in the balls. Just because he caught them diddling each other."

"The death penalty for adultery. It has a ring to it."

"He said he was in a blackout, didn't even remember doing it. Thirty-three years ago."

"Lotsa guys are there for things they don't remember. At least he's doing something about his problem."

"Fat lot of good it'll do him," Kane said. "He's serving natural life."

"Well, maybe he's a free man anyway." Bell rubbed his eyes. "Could be he's freer than you are."

"What does *that* mean?"

"When I was drinking, I was in a prison," Bell said, "the prison inside my own head."

"Listen, *Isaiah*, I'm cooperating, okay? Spare me the conversion speech."

"You're right. I'm sorry."

They arrived at headquarters, both of them exhausted. Platoon Two had gone for the night, so they found a parking spot in the basement garage. "Let's get upstairs before the Inspector leaves," Kane said.

"One minute," Bell said. He went around to the trunk and retrieved his briefcase containing Kane's bottle and his dope. Kane stood there glaring.

"What? You think I'd forget?" Bell asked.

"Well, I was sorta *hoping*," Kane said sarcastically. "You know, in light of our *bonding*."

"Kane, we have an agreement, you and I. You don't welsh on a deal with me."

"You know, Ike baby, I was right all along. You really *are* a prick."

In silence, they rode up the creaky elevator to the fifth floor. They walked down the hall to Easterly's office. Jablonski was doing paperwork. He smiled when Kane and Bell walked in. "Nice work, guys." He gestured toward her inner office. "She's waiting for you."

Easterly was behind her desk staring out at the falling snow. She swiveled around and greeted the two detectives. "Welcome back," she said.

"It's been a long day, skipper," Bell said.

"There's good news. We got a positive ID on your boys."

"The Chinese woman?" Kane asked eagerly.

"She's sure about both of them," Easterly said.

Kane and Bell looked at each other. "Good," Bell said. "That's real good."

"We're doing a citywide canvas tonight, based on the information you two provided. I've got most of Major Crimes out beating the bushes." Easterly looked back and forth between the two detectives. "It was a stroke of genius for me to bring you two in on this case."

"Yeah, brilliant," Kane muttered.

"Now go get some rest," Easterly ordered. "If we don't have these two in custody by morning, you'll have more work to do. Roll call is at eight."

Kane and Bell turned to leave. "Ike, you forgot something," Easterly said. She tossed Bell the keys to the Ford. "Thanks for your car."

"Sure thing," Bell said. He smiled at Kane. Kane just looked down at the floor, pissed off all over again.

2159 hours

Easterly lay in bed with David, reading. She was fatigued beyond her tolerance. At the same time, she was worried whether she'd be able to get to sleep.

She tried to concentrate on a magazine piece about the

state of the cinema. But her mind would not stop replaying every aspect of this hideous case—and the internal politics of local law enforcement. Images from the day's events kept flooding into her head.

Over on his side of the bed, David was reading a legal journal, brushing up on case law. Easterly covertly watched her husband. All these years, and she still could not comprehend how his mind could bend itself around material that boring. This was an aspect of the man which still fascinated her.

Finally he yawned and closed the journal. "Did you mean what you said?" she asked. "About how I don't have to take the job?"

"What's the matter? Something happen I don't know about?"

"No," she said. "I mean yes."

Then she blurted out the story about Nanci York, Mosely and Demarest. It came in a rush. Only when she heard herself telling it did Easterly realize how angry she really was.

"You weren't going to tell me this?" David asked. It was a gentle question, not an accusation.

"I didn't think I should bother you with it."

"Since when have your problems been a bother to me?"

"What should I do?" she asked.

"It seems to me the question is, how much can you handle? As Chief of Detectives you'll be right under Mosely's thumb. But even if you don't take it, even if you stay in *this* job, you'll still have to deal with him constantly. The only way to be rid of him is to quit."

"And that's not an option."

"Three more years you can retire. You can leave sooner if you don't take any sick time."

"I don't *want* to retire," she protested. "Besides, in three more years Mosely will have only two to go."

"Unless he's indicted or gets a better gig somewhere else." David smiled. "Or he dies. All the Homicide dicks you have working for you, you can't arrange that?"

Easterly laughed. "You're starting to sound like a cop."

"I've been married to you for too long."

"Seriously, David, what should I do? Give me a nice, reasoned, lawyer-like answer."

"Where can you do the most good for the city?"

"The Chief of Detectives is a lot more visible. And I'll have more juice with the Council and the Commission."

"Well, my dear Bobbie, there's your answer." He took her hand and examined it lovingly. "What's the worst thing that can happen?"

"I'll have a nervous breakdown and they'll cart me off in a straightjacket."

"Well, I'll love you anyway." He kissed her hand. "I'll even visit you in the nut house. If I'm not too busy with my teenaged mistress, that is."

She slapped him playfully on the cheek. They lay there for a long moment, looking into each other's eyes. *You really are a lucky woman, Bobbie. Don't ever forget it.* Then she kissed him, passionately.

* * *

What the fuck am I still doing here? I just wanted a couple of drinks, and here I am, shitfaced again.

Kane sat alone at the bar in Harvey's Place. Raunchy blues music again came from the little bandstand in the rear of the crowded saloon.

But he wasn't listening. He shifted his mind from his drunken self-recrimination and went back to reviewing the case. He reminded himself to call Vito Vitale first thing in the morning, get him the photos of the two suspects. He reminded himself to re-visit Tiny Lawless and the West End Outlaws. Now that they had solid leads…

I shoulda gone to see those fuckers tonight. I should be there now.

What kind of a sorry excuse for a cop am I?

He beckoned for another drink, then stared straight ahead at the mirror while Harvey reluctantly poured it.

"Hitting it kind of hard tonight, aren't you, Ralph?"

Kane focused his eyes. Harvey was looking at him with concern.

"What do you care?" Kane said.

"I have a license to protect. Are you driving?"

"I'm a cop, Harvey. You forget that or something?"

"How could I forget a little thing like that? But the laws, they've been changing. I don't want trouble with the LCC."

"You won't have any fucking trouble with the fucking LCC."

"Sorry, Ralph. This is your last one tonight."

"You're cutting me *off?*"

"Yeah, I'm cutting you off. I couldn't live with myself if you ran over a kid or something. Neither could you."

Harvey turned and walked down the bar to serve someone else. Kane beckoned weakly at him, then went back to staring at the mirror. Once again, his was the face of a dead man.

Kane checked the date on his watch and laughed. It would be *perfect* if they caught the two shitheads tomorrow. Then, the day after, that's when he would finish the job—*Christmas Day! God Himself couldn't have arranged better timing!*

Kane belted down his last drink. He tried to stand up but felt his knees grow wobbly. He beckoned to the barkeep. "You're right, pal. Get me some coffee."

* * *

Once again Isaiah Bell sat in the den with the television volume down low. But now Vera sat with him, her thin body curled into his massive arm. They had tucked the kids into bed an hour before.

"Do you really want to watch the news?" Vera asked. "It's

one horror story after the next. You need some rest."

"I want to see what they're releasing about the case."

An airline crash in the Atlantic knocked Darryl Childress out of the lead news spot. But the boy's story still got a huge play. Mercifully, they had stopped running his commercials.

Because they didn't yet know about Blackie and White Man, the television stations were scrambling for new angles. One reporter interviewed a popular psychologist, who warned of the story's damaging effect on children. Many kids already had voiced fears for their own safety.

"What hypocrites!" Bell said. "First they sensationalize the crime. Then they create a story about how the sensational coverage scares kids."

"Ikey told me tonight that he's frightened," Vera said.

Bell felt like he had been slapped. "What did he say?"

'I hope Daddy catches the bad men. I don't want them to hurt me.'

"Bastards!" Bell swore.

"I wish you wouldn't use that language."

"Sorry."

Vera took his hand. "Besides, which bastards are you talking about?" she asked gently, "the killers or the media?"

"All of them," Bell said. "Plus the politicians. Let's not forget the politicians."

"Baby, you know what resentments do to you."

"It's pretty hard not to have resentments in my line of work."

"Then maybe it is time to think about retirement. Find something less angry…"

"For God's sake, Vera, what am I going to do at my age?"

"What? You're going to be a cop forever? Ike, you're not a young man any more." She touched his face. "I sure hope you get back to your meetings."

Bell muted the television. "I went to one today, as a

matter of fact," he said. "In the prison."

"The prison?" Vera exclaimed.

He stroked her hair. "Ralph Kane went with me."

Vera sat up in disbelief. "You're *kidding!*"

"You heard me right. I took him to a meeting. With the convicts."

"My God, Ike! How?"

"It's a long story. I kinda tricked him into it. He wasn't happy. But I think maybe he heard something."

"Baby, that's—that's *wonderful!*" She shook her head in amazement. "I thought you hated him."

"I do. But he asked for forgiveness."

"Forgiveness?"

"For the Caldwell thing. He told me I *had* to forgive him. He said my religion required it. He pointed that out to me. The son of a bitch reminded me of my own beliefs."

Vera laughed. "That man sounds like a clever cop."

"He said it's been bothering him ever since it happened. The Caldwell thing."

"This is wonderful," Vera said. "This is *really* wonderful!"

"Vera, I can't stand the fool."

"Ike, do you realize what a big thing this is?"

Bell shrugged. "Maybe he'll get it, maybe he won't."

"Not for him. For you." She leaned against him and nuzzled his neck. "You really *are* my hero." She reached up and kissed him, passionately.

Then she closed the door of the den. She returned to her husband and changed the channel to MTV. They began to make love in the glow of the screen.

As Vera stroked his chest, Bell realized that he had gone an entire day without a cigarette. Maybe there was hope.

DAY 4 - CHRISTMAS EVE

0610 hours

Ralph Kane sat alone in the dark, staring out at the sky. The moon was just past full now, and seemed to be resting atop the quiet two-flat across the street.

This was Kane's least favorite hour, the silent time before first light. It had been that way ever since Vietnam, where first light had always been a time of fear, a time when anything could happen, a time for the realization of horror.

Now Kane was sick to the center of his very being. The physical hangover, bad though it felt, was the least of it. He felt desolate, cowardly, guilty and weak.

Why is life so smooth, so easy, for some men? They have no trouble with it, none at all. What the fuck happened to me?

A hideous loneliness came over him. He needed human contact. He hated himself for that weakness. He stood up shakily to turn on the radio atop the refrigerator. Christ, there it was again, "The Little Drummer Boy." He turned the radio off and sat back down.

Kane flashed back to yesterday, sitting with Bell in that diner. The memory embarrassed him, so he deliberately conjured up the girl in Saigon, then Darryl Childress, then his brother Billy, then his son Pete.

Pete. What would have happened to him if he'd had a decent father? God fucked him too.

Kane felt another wave of nausea come over him. He staggered into the bathroom. *No. God didn't do that to Pete. I did it.*

Leaning over the toilet, he earnestly wished he were dead. But he was determined to stay alive long enough to avenge Darryl Childress—and, in the process, all the others.

* * *

Roberta Easterly's clock radio woke her with a lively country tune about fresh new love. She had slept soundly, despite last night's anxiety. It was the lovemaking that had done it. Great sex was the world's most effective sleeping pill.

She turned off the radio and climbed out of bed. She looked over gratefully at the sleeping David, then went downstairs to call Homicide.

She already knew the task force had not yet made an arrest; they were under orders to notify her. But she wanted to know how close they were.

Angus MacKenzie came on the line. "You're in pretty early, Gus," Easterly said.

"I never went home."

"I hope you slept on something more comfortable than my office couch."

"I didn't sleep. I was out on the street with my people."

"Should I remind you that you're a command officer?"

"I'm a policeman who happens to be a captain."

Right answer. "How close are we to these guys?"

"We're not," the big Scot replied. "The Whitman house was dark all night. No one came or went. And no one on the street has seen a trace of these gents."

"Or they're not telling us."

"In a case like this, someone would tell us."

"I think it's time we raid the house, then go public with White Man and Blackie."

"That would be my suggestion," MacKenzie agreed.

"Okay, then. Leave the stakeout intact and send someone for warrants. I'll see you at eight."

After she hung up, Easterly felt her mood change. A wave of depression came over her. *Is this what Byron Slaughter lives with? No one should feel this way, not all the time.*

She went for the paper and noted that the snow had stopped again. Once more the sky had cleared, but the air was considerably colder than yesterday. *Damn this weather. Why can't it be consistent?*

Easterly fixed a quick breakfast and checked the front page. She vowed that the next time she leaked a story she'd first investigate the political views of the editors. The *Daily Times* had a strong anti-police orientation, so everyone knew that was not the place to take sensitive revelations. And now it was obvious that even photogenic television reporters operated under the same constraints.

This morning's paper led with the plane crash, naturally, along with sidebars about the history of the aircraft, horrified relatives, and the chilling last words from the cockpit. How much of the coverage was necessary, and how much pandered to the voyeurism of the public? Easterly had been to enough murder scenes to know the insatiable appetite of bystanders for gory details. To most people, violent death was just a big movie—until the victim was one of *their* loved ones.

Easterly hated to think like this. She had been doing it more and more lately. It was an occupational hazard, she reasoned, the cause of police depression. This work contaminated almost everyone in it. That was why she desperately needed David, a sense of humor and some heroes in her life.

Below the front-page fold was a piece about the fears of the city's children in the wake of Darryl's murder. Normally, the story pointed out, school psychologists would be out in droves counseling the kids. But this was Christmas vacation, so children were home where they could see and hear about the murder, over and over, in endless gruesome detail.

Of course, the newspaper itself had seen fit to send a reporter to the private school Darryl attended. So, there in print were the predictable quotes from his teachers, many of whom were openly weeping, as they described Darryl in the most glowing terms. In another sidebar, a reporter managed to track down some of Darryl's little classmates—no doubt with the help of the school. And, of course, all of the kids said they were terrified for their own safety.

Easterly felt like vomiting. But she felt professionally obliged to read through the entire article. An insert alerted readers to an op-ed piece about the Childress case. There Easterly found a *Daily Times* columnist lambasting the television stations for repeatedly playing Darryl's commercial. It was "shamelessly exploitative," the pundit thundered.

Easterly returned to the front page. She skimmed articles about violence in the Middle East and the midnight Mass in Bethlehem. But then she found a piece about the "anticipated indictment" of Mayor Titus Webster. The story quoted "federal law enforcement sources" predicting criminal charges would be filed by New Year.

There, that's it! That's why Demarest is sucking up to Mosely. His agents are the ones investigating the mayor. If there's any racial fallout, Mosely can shield him from it. Assistant FBI Directors can't be perceived as racist.

Now Easterly felt even more depressed.

Then a small piece on page three caught her eye: there had been a continuing, baffling crime drop over the past three days. Felonies were down nearly forty percent compared with the same time last year.

"Police officials"—the smarmy Lt. Dunsmore—still were attributing the drop to the increased police presence. But that was more self-serving hype by Jefferson Mosely. The extra cops were working the Childress case, not crime interdiction. They were detectives, traveling in civilian clothes and unmarked cars, and thus were barely noticed.

An old-time police reporter would have been all over the chief about such an obvious fiction. But no one in the lazy new-breed "media" had even noticed the fabrication, much less challenged Mosely about it. They all just accepted his word as gospel. That irritated Easterly even more.

Nevertheless, she also found the crime drop puzzling. Yesterday's pleasant weather should have brought an *increase* in certain felonies—purse snatches, street holdups, car clouts, convenience-store stickups, ATM rips. There was no logical reason why crime should be down, especially with so many Christmas shoppers out and about.

Some things are just a mystery, she finally concluded. If she lived to be a thousand she would never completely understand the peculiar species of which she was a member.

0732 hours

Isaiah Bell arrived at the gymnasium half an hour before roll call. The night watch guys were signing out. Only a couple of day watch detectives had arrived ahead of him.

Bell felt rested. He was grateful for that. The tonic effect of lovemaking is amazing. He also felt good about not smoking yesterday, and he resolved to keep it going. He was amazed at the ease with which he had stopped.

Bell tossed his coat across two folding chairs, one for himself and the other for Kane. Then he wandered over to the huge coffee urn and poured a cup. Stan Jablonski was sitting nearby, watching a portable television.

"Don't you ever leave this building?" Bell asked Jablonski.

"There are two of me. I'm identical twins."

"Good thing you're both bachelors."

Jablonski gestured at the television. The newscast was wrapping up yet another national story about the Childress case. Bell scowled: "If this was some street kid, how much attention would he get? We really do have a double standard in this country."

"You're just noticing?"

"Tell me something," Bell said. "When you were a kid— in Pittsburgh, wasn't it?"

"Yeah. Pittsburgh."

"When you were a kid in Pittsburgh, did you ever think this is what the country would turn into? The greed, the stupidity, the lack of respect, making role models out of thugs…?"

"Ike, you're bumming me out." Jablonski held up a paperback book entitled *You Are What You Think*. "I'm trying to re-program myself. I want to spend my old age as an optimist. I can't indulge that kind of negativity."

Bell laughed. "I should live so long."

"Go ahead, scoff," Jablonski said. "A man *should* aspire to greater things." He grinned. "While we're on the subject, how's it going with Kane?"

"We're working together, that's all. Thanks to your boss. When this is over, we get a divorce."

"He's still an asshole, that what you're saying?"

"Don't go putting words in my mouth. And this is not for your gossip network."

Jablonski pointed toward the door. "Speak of the devil." Bell turned and spotted Kane. He beckoned him over to join him.

The room was filling with cops. Kane stood there for a moment, then complied. Other officers noticed and exchanged curious glances. Kane, now with several days' beard, could have passed for a derelict. He tossed his own coat over the chair.

Bell looked Kane up and down, then laughed. "You musta done it up good last night," he said.

"Look," Kane snapped, "I agreed to go to those stupid meetings with you. I did *not* agree to stop drinking."

Bell laughed again. "You've got me there, pal."

"It thrills me that I amuse you," Kane said.

"The way you feel right now—Jesus, man, I don't ever want to go back there. Ralph, the mere sight of you fills my aging heart with gratitude."

"Where the fuck do you get off being so self-righteous?"

"You know, I thought about you a lot last night," Bell said. "I really *am* going to try to save your sorry ass."

"Who deputized you to be my guardian angel?"

"Yes, sir," Bell said. "You're going to be my own special project. I'm going to be all over you like a blanket."

"You're really enjoying this, aren't you?" His face was flushed, and he looked nauseous. "Let me tell you something, *Isaiah*. Once this case is over, I'm bulletproof. There won't be a goddamned thing anyone can do to me."

Something in Kane's voice alarmed Bell. "What's that supposed to mean?"

"You'll find out soon enough." Kane got up and crossed to the coffee urn. Bell watched him.

Just then Easterly entered the gym for the roll call briefing. Kane stood at the urn, staring into space. The look on his face gave Bell a chill, the chill of recognition.

0840 hours

Easterly waited in Mosely's office with Byron Slaughter and Captains MacKenzie and Georgiades. The four had convened to brief Mosely for the press conference.

Mosely was ten minutes late. This was a practice forecast by his former underlings in Dallas. Mosely loved to keep people waiting, then make a grand entrance. To his old staff, it was a symptom of his overweening ego. Men like Mosely want more than mere loyalty and obedience. Like all self-ordained gods, what they crave is adoration. And their drug of choice is *power*.

"Where's the FBI guy?" Georgiades asked. "You'd think he'd be here, now that there's something positive to report."

"He probably can't figure out a way for the Bureau to take credit," Easterly said. She heard a strange new bitterness in her own voice. She heard David's voice cautioning her: *"Careful, kid, it's not worth hurting yourself."*

She looked over at Slaughter, sitting slump-shouldered. The vitality seemed to have gone out of him. He had aged noticeably, just in the time since Mosely's arrival in town. *Is this what awaits me?*

Mosely finally entered, trailed by the sycophantic Lt. Dunsmore. The four command officers, raised in the military tradition, all reflexively rose to their feet. But everyone was stunned by the chief's dress. He was in full uniform, four stars on the collar. It was the first time anyone had seen him thus attired.

The four exchanged covert but very contemptuous glances. This asshole had never earned the right to wear that proud uniform, much less adorn it with *four fucking stars!* Slaughter's face reddened. For a moment, Easterly was afraid the Chief of Detectives was going to have a heart attack.

The collective reaction was not lost on Mosely. "Take your seats," he ordered, clearly annoyed.

The four complied. Mosely sat down behind his huge desk, and Dunsmore sat to his right. To avoid the chief's eyes, Easterly fixed her gaze on the young squint. A *Mosely in the making, Caucasian variety. God spare us.*

"All right, gentlemen and lady, what do you have for me?" Mosely asked.

Slaughter itemized developments in chronological order. He spoke in a fast, staccato monotone, fighting his rage. While Dunsmore took notes, Mosely sat listening imperiously, hands behind his head and eyes closed. He gave off the impression of an expert, patiently evaluating the correctness of the actions taken.

Easterly felt warmth on her face and knew it was red. She was, in fact, in a murderous boil. It was all she could do to keep from screaming. *This jerk doesn't know his ass from his elbow, and he's sitting there passing judgment on the actions of first-rate professionals.*

"So we now have warrants for these two men, is that correct?" Mosely asked when Slaughter finished.

"Murder warrants," Slaughter replied. "The DA says the Chinese woman's identification is sufficient."

"So when are you going to raid the mother's house?"

"As soon as possible," Slaughter said. "We wanted to brief you first."

"I think we should invite the TV people to come along," Mosely said. "In fact, *I* might even lead the raid."

Except for Dunsmore, everyone cringed. Mosely looked around. "Did I say something wrong?"

MacKenzie spoke up. "Sir, with all due respect, that house is a possible hideout for the murderers of a child. The element of surprise is necessary. We doubt if anyone is inside, but if they are they'll certainly notice television crews. That will give them ample time to destroy any physical evidence."

Mosely knew MacKenzie was right. But he was clearly upset about being called on his stupidity. He was feeling small, and he hated it.

MacKenzie lowered his voice and tried to sound conciliatory. "Chief, once we raid the place, then we can call in the FBI's forensics people to help our lads. They have all the hi-tech gadgets. Maybe they can find something our people can't. That will give Mr. Demarest an opportunity to share credit."

Mosely took several seconds to respond. "Whatever you say, Captain," he finally said in a low voice. "You know this city better than I."

"*Then* we can take the media to the scene," Georgiades offered. "*After* the raid."

Mosely smiled thinly. "Of course. That's what we'll do." He looked at his own notes. "Now what about these two detectives who led us to these alleged suspects? Kane and Bell, I believe their names are?"

"What about them?" Easterly asked.

"It would be good if they appeared with me at the press conference, said a few words about how they cracked this case."

"Again, sir, with all due respect," Easterly said, "those two officers should be out in the field trying to find the killers. They have unique skills…"

"An hour of their day won't hurt anything," Mosely said. "It'll be good for morale if I publicly acknowledge their accomplishment."

Slaughter finally snapped. "What will be good for morale is for us to put these two pricks behind bars. Once that's been accomplished, then you can hold your dog-and-pony show."

Mosely glared at the Chief of Detectives. But Slaughter no longer cared. "You think I'm being premature," Mosely said coldly.

"The time for self-congratulations is after the arrests— provided we make a good case!" Slaughter said. "That's what today's press conference should be about, providing the public with information that might help us catch the murderers of a seven-year-old child! It shouldn't be about *entertainment!*"

The silence in the room was palpable. Mosely looked around. "How many of you agree with Chief Slaughter?"

One by one, all of their hands went up. Easterly was impressed. *I guess we all hang together.*

0935 hours

Slowly shaking off his hangover, Kane drove out to Vito Vitale's mansion on the North End. The expressway had been plowed and the sun was out again. But the air was still cold.

On the seat next to Kane lay two packages, each containing mug shots of Blackstone and Whitman. But Kane was distracted by other matters:

Moralists; the world was full of them. They seemed to fall into two categories. There were those who seemingly had never yielded to ethical temptations, like that insufferable young lieutenant, Van Horn. And then there were those who had reformed, like Bell. Kane wasn't sure which kind was worse. Both were quick to point fingers at fuck-ups like him. Both were pains in the ass.

He resolved not to drink at all that day, not a drop. He didn't want his post-mortem blood alcohol level to reflect intoxication at the time of his death. He'd be damned if he'd give either Van Horn or Bell the satisfaction.

As he drove, Kane reflected with bitter pleasure on a conversation he'd had with Van Horn half an hour earlier. He'd run into the college boy in the lobby of headquarters, next to the Christmas tree. Van Horn demanded to know what Kane was up to and where he was headed, right now.

"You must be getting reports from the surveillance community," Kane said. "About my unsavory comrades."

"Don't get smart with me, Detective. This is not a joking matter. If you're palling around with known criminals…"

You want to know what I'm up to, all you have to do is ask the new Chief of Detectives, you idiot.

Instead, right there in the headquarters lobby, Kane decided to fuck with Van Horn's head. He revealed that he was on his way to seek assistance from his old, dear friend, Vito Vitale. He wanted to see the punk's reaction to that.

Van Horn had yet to get his hands dirty in a real Mob investigation. But the smug little bastard believed OCI officers had to be pristine. He assumed you made cases against mobsters with evidence that somehow fell from the sky. He didn't understand how a cop like Kane could be on a friendly basis with a criminal—for whatever reason.

Predictably, Van Horn reacted strongly. He ordered Kane take along a partner, so there could be no questions later on about his motives. Kane refused.

Then Van Horn demanded that Kane wear a wire, to fend off possible allegations that might come later. Again Kane refused.

With that, the enraged Van Horn all but accused Kane of corruption: "So what kind of *relationship* do you have with this man?" he demanded. "This is totally against department policy! Are you on his pad or something?"

"Lieutenant," Kane snarled, "you say something like that again, you'll be swallowing your teeth."

"Are you threatening me, Detective?"

"Yes, I'm threatening you! Take *that* to your pals in IA! It's your word against mine—unless you're wearing a wire right now."

"They'll put *you* on the polygraph," Van Horn said.

"Fuck the polygraph and fuck you!" Kane said. He turned and walked out of the building. Van Horn just stood there, fuming.

Now, heading north to Vitale's place, Kane reviewed the conversation with perverse satisfaction. Van Horn, of course, hadn't a clue that Ralph Kane planned to celebrate Christmas by blowing his brains out.

Then Kane reflected on the other major asshole currently in his life, Isaiah Bell. For a while yesterday, he had almost found himself liking the guy. Then Bell came on with all this holy-roller ex-drunk bullshit, mocking him for his hangover.

Kane recalled a crusty old gunnery sergeant in Vietnam who had despised religion. He had his own prayer, which he would quote over beers: "God, protect me from your followers."

That's for goddamned sure.

Bell sat alone in the back of the Red Bird Pool Hall, waiting for Willis Henry to arrive. Only two other people were in the joint at this hour, a solitary young hustler sharpening his game and the grey-haired proprietor, Dizzy Dean Jackson.

Jackson was born in St. Louis of racially-mixed parents during the 1934 World Series. He bought this place in the sixties, when he was still a young man and this was still a safe neighborhood. If you gave Dizzy Dean an ear, he would lament endlessly the passing of both his youth and his safety. Bell, who knew him well, did not intend to give him an ear.

Jackson walked back to Bell with a glass coffee pot and a cigarette dangling from his lips. He poured Bell some fresh coffee. "Who you waitin' for, Deacon?" he asked.

"Po-lice business," Bell replied. He made a show of waving the smoke away.

But Diz was undeterred. "Want some company?"

"Thanks, but I've got something I'm trying to figure out."

"I can dig it." Diz scowled. "Whatdya think of that little boy gettin' kidnapped and killed?"

"I'm glad it's not my case," Bell said.

"I hope they put the motherfuckers in the electric chair."

"This state doesn't have an electric chair."

"Well, they oughta buy one." Diz brightened. "That's it! I'll start a fund-raiser, buy the state an electric chair! Lethal injection is a pussy way to die. How much you figure a good electric chair costs?"

"I haven't the slightest idea."

"Probably could buy a good used one from Florida or Texas, one a them places."

Bell pulled a notebook from his pocket and pretended to read it. Jackson took the hint and went back to his cash register.

Bell waved away the remnants of Jackson's smoke and looked up at the clock. Willis Henry was late, the way dirtbags always are. *Laziness,* that was the primary characteristic of street thugs. *Laziness and cluelessness.* Bell felt his mood turn sour again.

His mind drifted to thoughts of Ralph Kane. He had discovered an utterly baffling feeling: he found himself worried about the little motherfucker. There was something about that look on his face a couple of hours ago...

Bell's detective instincts took over, as if Kane were a criminal he was hunting. He began reviewing the clues to the man's emotional state. He recalled Kane's reaction yesterday, when Bell revealed the secret about his own near-suicide. Then he reviewed Kane's words:

"Everyone's days are short..." , "Did you really think you were a coward...?", "Once this case is over, I'm bulletproof. There won't be a goddamned thing anyone can do to me..."

Bell was alarmed by the picture he was getting. He recalled those cops he had known who "ate their guns." Brannigan, in the Eighteenth Precinct. Smith, in the Twenty-Ninth. Roskoff, in Holdup. Bishop, in Auto Theft. Graham, in Special Investigations. And almost all of them had been drinking when they did it.

Suddenly Bell realized that his palms were sweating. *I came on too strong. I shouldn't have laughed at him. I remember how dark it was, near the end.*

He found himself profoundly surprised by this thought. Where did this come from? He resolved to make things right with Kane as soon as he could. It had nothing to do with goodness. He wouldn't be able to live with the guilt if Kane did something drastic.

Willis Henry finally strolled casually into the Red Bird,

wearing sunglasses and an expensive leather jacket. He stopped at the door like a cop, scanning the room, a study in cool. *Another asshole who's seen too many movies.* Bell beckoned to him. The shotcaller sauntered over, looking around to see who might be watching. Bell did not rise. "Mornin'," he said, sipping his coffee nonchalantly.

"Bell-man." Chewing a toothpick, Henry turned a chair around backwards and straddled it. "You got something for me?"

Bell reached under his jacket for a manila envelope. He removed a dozen of the mug shots. "Thomas Blackstone and Frederick Whitman," Bell said. "AKA 'Blackie and White Man.' White Man is black, Blackie is white."

"They the killers?"

"Looks like it." Bell replaced the pictures in the envelope and handed it to Big Gun. "There's some confidential stuff here – street monickers, tats, scars, names of friends, shit like that. You never got it from me."

"Sure thing, brother."

"So how's your mama, Willis? She staying sober?"

"She havin' problems, but she tryin'." Henry nodded. "Thanks for askin'."

"Anything I can do?"

"I'll let you know." The gangbanger pointed to the envelope. "These motherfuckers—We run across them, what you want us to do?"

"What do you think? I want you to call me."

"Before or after we kill them?"

"*Instead* of killing them."

Henry laughed. "Man, you takin' all the fun out of it."

"I have rules to play by."

"Too bad," Henry said. He brightened. "Crime still goin' down?"

"Why you asking?"

"Well, it's like I told you, we got this little alliance with the Bloods. Just for this thang about the little boy, you follow me?"

"I follow you."

"*That's* the reason crimes be down. Not the bullshit your phony-assed Uncle Tom chief is puttin' out." Henry laughed. "Crimes be down 'cuz *we-all ain't doin' them!* Sort of a Christmas present to the city."

Bell also laughed. "I don't suppose there's any way to keep it going..."

"*Hell,* no." Henry said. "Once this shit be over, it's business as usual."

"A man can always hope."

"True enough, Bell-man. What's life without hope?"

Bell stood up and clasped hands with the gangbanger. "Obliged, Willis."

"Sure thang, officer." Willis Henry turned on his heel and sauntered out of the pool hall, king of his universe.

* * *

Kane cruised Vitale's tree-lined neighborhood for a few minutes, killing time until the appointed hour. Then, promptly at ten, he pulled into the driveway of the mansion. He rang the buzzer and was admitted by a Vitale bodyguard. He removed his galoshes before entering. Once again, the servant girl led him down the long hallway to Vitale's study.

This time the old *capo* was wearing a jogging suit. "I'm getting ready for the treadmill," Vitale said. He poured Kane a cup of coffee. "The doctor tells me to get in shape. My heart is going to explode unless I take care of it." He smiled. "It proves I have one, Ralph. That'll surprise your buddies down at the cop shop."

"I don't have any buddies down at the cop shop."

"So I hear."

Kane was startled by the comment. "I guess you do have

wires everywhere."

"That's why you came to me, is it not? My network of friends? Too bad you don't have friends of your own. It must be lonely."

"I get by."

The mafioso shrugged. "It's your life. You got the pictures?"

Kane handed over the envelope. "There's a note with names, descriptions, associates, that sort of thing. We'll appreciate anything you can do."

Vitale examined the mugshots. "Sure. I'm putting these pricks on the internet. Their maggoty faces will go out all over the world. They won't find a safe place on this planet."

Kane actually smiled. "You people have your own web site?"

"'Certain of our associates, yes, they're 'on line.' Everyone is, these days." The old hoodlum pointed to a desk globe. "We're everywhere now, Ralph. You should know that, a man in your line of work. We're with the cartels in Cali, the Russians in Moscow, the yakuza in Tokyo, the Chinks in Hong Kong—the world's shrinking. We're now a huge, transnational business."

"An idea whose time has come."

"A man needs to keep up with the times he lives in. A man who won't change with the times is in trouble."

Kane shrugged indifferently. "Not me."

Vitale shook his head. "You're a very strange fellow, my friend. You really should get some love in your life—while you can."

"I'll take it under advisement." *What the hell is this, Fix Ralph Kane Week?*

"Christmas," Vitale mused. "A time for an old man to reflect on his life, where he's been, what he's done, what he hasn't done. Sometimes he doesn't like what he sees."

"I suppose not," Kane said, itching to get out the door.

"I was an orphan. When I was ten, my parents' car was hit by a train."

"I've read your file."

"I'll tell you what's not in that file: I used to *pray* my old man would die. Especially when he was beating my mother. I prayed that one of his *goombahs* would put a .22 round in the back of his neck."

Kane smiled bitterly. "Sounds like we had the same father."

Vitale snapped his fingers. "That's it! I figured there was something about you, and that's what it is! You understand!" He pointed his thumb at his heart. "In here."

"I have a rough idea."

"When the accident happened, you know, with the train? I figured it was God answering my prayers. But he took my mother, too. So I felt I was responsible for killing *her*, by praying like that."

"Heavy shit for a ten-year-old," Kane said. "Why are you telling me this?"

"I don't know. I guess because it *is* Christmas, and I don't have much time left."

"What do you mean?" Kane asked.

"Like I said, I ain't in the best of health."

"I'm sorry," Kane said. To his surprise, he realized the statement was true.

"Just getting a few things off my chest," said the old racketeer. "Ain't no big deal. We're all gonna leave at some point. It's just the where and the when that's the mystery."

"Sounds like something for your priest, Vito."

"Maybe you *are* my priest." He laughed. "Believe it or not, Ralph, I like you. I like you because you're a square shooter. You may be fucked up, but you're honorable. I figure I can talk to you, as a man who understands."

Vitale poured Kane another cup of coffee. "Not much of that left any more—honor. The do-gooders, they get up in their pulpits, yell about sin and vice, go before Congress and give lectures about us, how bad we are, how we fuck over people. We're the scumbags."

Vitale began pacing around his office, talking expansively with his hands. "But look who's running the country, my friend. Corporations. Banks. Advertising agencies. Liars, all liars! And no fucking heart! You ever heard of a corporation with a heart?

"You want to talk organized crime? We give money to a politician, it's bribery. A corporation gives money, it's a campaign contribution. Who fucks over the little guy more than the corporations? Hell, at least we come from the people."

"I guess that's one point of view," Kane said quietly.

Vitale stopped pacing and calmed himself. He examined his old adversary thoughtfully. "So what was it like for *you?* Growing up, I mean?"

"It sucked."

"Yeah," Vitale said. "It's all over your face. You never lose that pain, do you?"

"I guess not."

"You know, when I was a kid? You won't find this in your intelligence files, either, but I loved poetry, art, opera – those great Italian singers. But my old man, he said those things were for faggots—no place in the family for that kind of bullshit. So, he beat it out of me."

Kane checked his watch. "Listen, can we talk about this some other time?"

Vitale again studied Kane's distressed face, then shrugged. "Sure thing, officer. You have work to do. Important work." He smiled. "You might even say it's God's work."

"Yeah, you could say that." Kane stood up to leave. "Thanks for the help."

But then he stopped at the door and turned back to the old mobster. "Vito, there's something I've been wondering about for years. You don't have to answer if you don't want to."

"You mean that shit about the drill through the shylock's head?"

"How did you know?" Kane asked.

Vitale laughed. "That's the one question everyone is afraid to ask. You do have balls, Ralph."

"Well?"

"That story's the biggest joke of my life. It never happened."

"What do you mean it never happened? I've seen the pictures."

"Oh, the murder happened all right. But it's Jimmy Delvecchio does that one, not me. He's Santo's chief button. I'm a kid learning the ropes, so I'm along for the ride. But Jimmy makes me wait in the car. I don't even see it happen— which is okay with me. Who wants to witness something like that?"

"No shit?"

"No shit. Now Jimmy's a stone psycho. He gets clipped by the Purples a week later. So I kinda take the credit, you see what I mean? It adds to my legend, helps me build my empire."

"Well," Kane said, "live and learn. I'm glad I asked."

"Don't tell nobody," Vitale said. "I'd like to keep the legend, in case someone writes a history book."

"It's been half a century, Vito. I don't think anyone gives a shit any more."

"Probably not." Vitale rang for the servant girl. "Good hunting, Ralph. God be with you."

Kane followed the girl back to the front door, considering the old don's commentary. Very few things surprised him any more. But this visit was pretty amazing.

He thought of Vitale's personal advice: "Get some love in your life…God's work…God be with you."

Jesus Christ, how many more weirdos are going to give me free advice?

1023 hours

Byron Slaughter rang Easterly on her private line to tell her the raid was set for fourteen hundred hours. They agreed it should be a joint Crime Suppression-Homicide operation. A Crime Suppression SWAT crew would hit the dwelling in a lightning raid. After they secured the house, the detectives would seal and search it.

Slaughter instructed Easterly to assign the best crime-scene people in the department. After they had gone over the house meticulously, then—and only then—would Demarest's FBI agents be allowed inside.

Then Slaughter startled her. He dropped his voice and requested a private meeting, somewhere away from either of their offices. "It's important," he said.

His tone worried her. So Easterly suggested the roof of headquarters. Ten minutes later, she casually walked out of her office without a coat, in order not to arouse Stan Jablonski's curiosity.

Slaughter was already on the roof, waiting in the shadows between a huge generator and a cluster of radio antennas. Easterly walked over to join him, looking around to make sure they were alone.

The sun was even warmer now. Melting snow had created huge ponds on the streets below. "From up here, the city looks almost beautiful," Slaughter said. His face was a study in melancholy.

"Skipper, why are we sneaking around like this?"

"I found out Mosely had his own internal spying system within the Dallas P.D. Some Dallas cops believe he even planted bugs in the offices of his command staff."

"Oh, for God's sake," Easterly said. "This is turning into a bad movie."

"I don't think he's that bright. But you never know."

"So what's on your mind, Byron?"

"When you take over my job, you'll have enormous power."

"I'm familiar with the organization chart."

"Bobbie, you'll have far more power than even you realize." Slaughter sighed. "As you know, the clandestine units also answer to the Chief of Detectives. Internal Affairs, Special Investigations, all of the intelligence bureaus..."

"What are you driving at?"

"As you may also know, those cloak-and-dagger types have unofficial alliances with their counterparts all over the country—in some cases, all over the world."

"So I've been told. I've always found the idea disturbing."

"But it's effective." Slaughter pulled a folder out from under his suit coat and handed it to her "One of my best OSI officers has a friend in Dallas. The friend provided him with these."

Easterly opened the folder. Inside were dozens of black-and-white surveillance pictures. The first two photos were of a black man and a white woman entering and leaving a motel. The man was Jefferson Mosely.

"As you know, our new chief is a married man, with a wife and three teenaged kids," Slaughter said quietly. "He promotes the family image. But the word in Dallas is that he was a major player. He's especially fond of white women."

Easterly was stunned. "What difference does it make?" she blurted out. "The race, I mean."

"Only in the motivation of the rednecked officer who gave these to our OSI. Dallas, as you know, is not a model of social progressiveness. They hated Mosely from the start, and this behavior clinched it."

"Boss, this *really* bothers me. Not the screwing around so much as the spying. You're offended by Mosely running a spy operation. What do you call *this*? And what right do I have to this material?"

"Other pictures in that envelope are far more explicit. There's also an audio tape of Mosely, from a room bug."

"You're dodging my question."

"Bobbie, there were a *lot* of women. Several were themselves married."

"Why are you giving me these things?" Easterly cried.

"For your protection."

"My *protection?*"

"In case this creep tries to sabotage you."

"I don't like this. I don't like this one bit." She glanced at more of the photographs, then looked out at the city. "Skipper, I can't play this game. It's like something Nixon might have dreamt up. Or Stalin."

"You don't have to play *any* game unless he forces you to." Slaughter gently touched her shoulder. "This is for your own sake, Bobbie. Keep these in your safe—in case you ever need them."

Easterly did not answer. Slaughter walked over to the edge of the roof and looked down. "The problem with being a career police officer is that you learn things you'd rather not know."

"I already have too many of those," Easterly said. "I don't need any more." She walked over and forced him to look at her. "You know, this is the same kind of thing J. Edgar Hoover did to Martin Luther King,"

"Jefferson Mosely is *not* Martin Luther King."

"The principle's the same. We're cops, all right, but we're cops in a democracy. Since when are we the morality police?"

Slaughter looked out at the city and smiled sadly. "The

irony of this conversation is that your high-mindedness is the main reason I respect you so much." He turned to her. "The problem with that is, few in the police world are as high-minded."

"Does that mean we descend to their level? Is that the price of ambition? What does that do to *our* souls?"

"Now you know the primary reason I'm depressed." He checked his watch. "I need to get back. Make your own decision. If you don't want the pictures, burn them. But think it over carefully first. You never know."

Easterly leaned her back against the rail for a long moment, clutching the manila envelope. Then she followed Slaughter back to the stairwell.

1113 hours

Bell located Garland McQueen in the back room of the deserted Lucky Deuce Lounge. Today McQueen's Motown suit was a festive red and green. He was eating take-out Chinese. The old hustler was an expert with chopsticks.

"Where'd you learn that shit?" Bell asked.

"Taiwan," McQueen said. "With the Air Force."

"I never could get my fingers to cooperate."

"Well, it's not exactly a black thang." McQueen licked his fingers. "You have a line on the assholes?"

Bell handed over a package of mug shots. "We have warrants. We're going public today." He gave the old bookie a quick rundown on the two suspects.

McQueen examined the photographs. "Pretty average looking dudes. Don't look like killers to me."

"And you don't look like the owner of a tittie bar."

"You say the Caucasian frequents establishments like this?"

"Yeah, but white joints, most likely. I doubt he wants to be conspicuous. But you never know. His prison wife was a brother."

"You imagine being that horny, Deacon? Man'd have to be real horny to be punkin' another male."

Bell shrugged. "Who am I to throw the first stone?"

"Yeah," McQueen said. "I heard you found religion, real and righteous, not just that play-acting Deacon shit."

"Pretty hard for a man to keep a secret nowadays."

"Hey, I wasn't judgin' that, neither. Ain't nothin' wrong with knowing the Lord. My mama was a believer, God rest her."

"It's hard to imagine you with a mama, Garland."

"Kindest woman ever lived. Worked her whole life as a cleaning lady in white folks' homes, over to Chicago. That's where I was raised."

"I know. I memorized your jacket."

Bell was astonished to notice McQueen's eyes misting up. "Sweetest, lovingest woman ever did live, my mama," McQueen said. "This is the time of the year when I miss her the most."

McQueen opened his desk drawer and poured a shot of bourbon. This time he did not offer Bell a taste.

"No daddy, just a mama," McQueen continued. "Her name was Lucille, died right before Christmas one year. She worked her fingers to the bone to give me and my two sisters an education. Died when she was only forty, some kinda cancer she got from toxic chemicals. She worked herself to death, on her knees all day, scrubbing floors and toilets for the white folks."

"There were lotsa black women like your mama," Bell said.

"Thousands," McQueen said. His eyes were even wetter now. "Invisible heroes."

"Yeah," Bell said softly, "heroes, sure enough."

"Me, I was a hopeless fuck-up when I was young. Mama finally gave up on me, said it was because I was a boy."

"Where are your sisters?"

"Damnedest thing, Isaiah. One went to medical school at the University of Michigan, the other became a hooker. Died of a heroin overdose when she wasn't but thirty."

"Sorry, man."

"Hey, one success out of three ain't bad, for black folks. My baby sister, she did good, a pediatrician in Detroit. Works with AIDS and crack kids. So who knows how things turn out?" He sipped his bourbon. "How about you, Deacon? How many years I been knowin' you? And I don't know a *thang* about you."

"Some other time, Garland. I have work to do."

"Of course." McQueen smiled. "I didn't mean to get emotional. There's something about this time of the year."

"It's okay, man."

"You know the trick to life?"

"No."

"The trick to life, my friend, is to live in a way that'll give you happy memories when you're old."

Bell smiled, then looked at his watch. "I have to go."

"I figured that out way too late." McQueen pointed at the pictures of Blackstone and Whitman. "I'll put the word out among my colleagues. Maybe we can come up with these motherfuckers."

"Much obliged," Bell said. He started out the door.

"Hey, Deacon," McQueen called after him. "You know, I really like you a lot better now that you're on the wagon."

"Merry Christmas, Queenie."

"Find those baby killers, mister po-lice."

Out in the street, Bell considered the irony of that expression, "baby killers." That's what some anti-war protesters at the Los Angeles airport had called him and other Special Forces guys the day they returned home. They'd put it on hand-lettered signs and waved them at the troops. TV cameras caught it all; it had made for great theater. *Those fuckers were lucky we didn't kill <u>them</u>.*

Then he thought of all the dead children he had seen in Vietnam. *I didn't kill any of them, as far as I know. At least it was never my intention.*

Not like these bastards who killed Darryl Childress.

* * *

In the Pontiac, Kane followed the El tracks out to the West End and arrived at the Outlaws' body shop. As always, summer or winter, the garage doors were shut. Kane doubted if they even could be opened. The only available parking space was next to a hydrant. Kane put the Kojak on the dashboard and got out, not bothering to hide his identity from any curious locals.

Weasel Warren and Mumps Rafferty stood around outside, stoned on weed, basking in the unusual sunshine. They acted nonchalant as the detective approached them. "I see you're working on your tans," Kane said.

"Keep parking illegally, you're gonna give us a bad name with the neighbors," said the Weasel.

"Where's Tiny?" Kane asked.

"In the office," said Rafferty. "I don't think he's expecting you just yet."

Kane walked inside and negotiated the obstacle course toward Lawless' rear office. Several strands of Christmas lights had been strung around the garage. Marijuana smoke hung in the air. "Hey, Lawless!" Kane called out. "It's the police!"

The huge biker appeared shirtless, rolls of fat hanging over his belt, sporting two fresh tattoos. From force of habit, Kane found himself memorizing them. One was a naked woman, the other said "Semper Fidelis."

Another fucking phony. The closest this asshole ever got to a Marine was the time I arrested him.

"You're here early," said Lawless.

"I like to sneak up on people,"

"Well, come on back, meet my new squeeze. Wait'll you see the tits on this one."

Kane followed the big slob. The walls of his office were decorated with *Penthouse* and *Hustler* girls, spread-legged. Sitting on Lawless' desk was the real thing, a nearly-naked teenaged girl with silicone breasts. Each tit was adorned with a tattoo—the right a butterfly, the left a coiled snake.

"This here is Rachel Fenner," Lawless said. "We were just doing a little fucking."

"Good morning," Kane said. He pulled out his badge. "Miss Fenner, my name is Detective Ralph Kane, assigned to the police department's Organized Crime Intelligence Bureau."

"Aw, man!" Lawless bleated. "What you doin' that for?"

"I'm sorry, Mr. Lawless. I would simply like some assurance that Miss Fenner here—I take it that's spelled F-e-n-n-e-r—is of legal age."

"I'm twenty," the girl muttered. "You want to see my ID?"

"He's jerking you off, Raitch," Lawless said. "He wants you to go somewhere, put on some clothes."

Pouting, the girl slunk off. "Best pussy I've had in months," said Lawless when she was gone. "Jewish kid, too, believe it or not. Her old man's a big-shit downtown lawyer."

"So what does she see in a guy like you?"

"The golden tongue, my man."

"Plus all the dope you give her."

"Just weed, Kane, and *you're* in no position to judge that. Man, we don't even do coke or crank around here any more."

"Why not? You find religion?"

"Man, the stuff that's out there these days, that shit's poison. I lost too many friends already."

"Sounds like you're getting old, Tiny."

Lawless laughed. "Your ass, Fosdick. Twenty-year-old Jewish chicks with lawyer fathers still give me head. Just like Clinton. Bet *you* can't say that."

"I don't want to say that." Kane reached under his coat and took out the envelope with the mug shots. "Here are our boys. There's a lot of information in there about them."

Lawless examined the pictures. "The drawings were close," he said. "Cocksuckers better hope us or the Pagans ain't the ones who find them."

"The black guy's AC-DC, leans mostly to homo," Kane said. "The white guy hangs around tittie bars."

"Which ones? There must be a hundred in this city."

"We don't know. But between you and the Pagans and the Road Killers, you probably have people inside most of them, day or night. That's how I figure it."

"That's about right." He put the pictures back in the envelope. "I'll have these all over town by late afternoon."

"We're obliged."

Lawless opened a desk drawer and took out a huge joint. "Want a hit?"

Kane shook his head no. "I need a clear head. There's a rumor these guys have a machine gun."

Lawless fired up the joint, laughing. "I always smoke a joint before I go up against a machine gun."

"You really are full of shit."

"Seriously, Kane, I hope you do watch your ass."

"Why is that, Tiny?"

Feeling the buzz, Lawless studied Kane's face. "Because I'd miss you."

"Please don't go telling me how much you love me. I've had enough sentimental horseshit already today."

"Naw, nothing like that. The guy who replaces you could

be a real prick."

Kane gestured at the nudie pictures. "The guy who replaces me will be a *woman. A feminist.*"

"Then I'll have to shoot her," Lawless said. He held out the joint again, in offering. Again Kane shook his head no.

"How come you're so different?" Lawless asked. "From other cops, I mean?"

"The curse of Kane."

"Come again?"

"Some other time."

Kane was getting a contact high from the smoke, which was making him lightheaded, chasing off the last of his hangover. "So you tell me something else, Tiny."

"If it's serious, you'd better read me my Miranda warning."

"What kind of a childhood did you have?"

"What mutants spawned a freak like me, that what you're driving at?"

"Just curious." Kane smiled. "I've been curious for years."

"Don't you guys keep a file on me?"

"Hate to disappoint you, but bikers don't qualify for that kind of attention."

"Well, that's fucking discrimination. We're as bad as the fucking Mafia any day." He giggled, stoned now. "I was born rich, believe it or not. Winnetka, Illinois."

"No shit?"

"No shit. Black sheep of a perfect family. Four kids, private schools, father a millionaire business man."

"Tiny, are you putting me on?"

"It's all true. But I was fucked up from the gate. I couldn't read worth a shit, and I had a weight problem. So they called me stupid and lazy and ugly, along with a bunch of other loving things."

Lawless again inhaled deeply on the joint. "They have

names for it now," he said. "'Dyslexia.' 'Attention deficit disorder,' shit like that. They didn't have those names then. You were just the school dummy and the neighborhood fat face."

"That must've been rough," Kane said. For the first time, he was seeing Leonard Lawless as a child in pain.

"Hey, it's ancient history," Lawless said. He gestured toward the clubhouse. "At least *these* creeps don't judge me. This is my real family. Other losers." Lawless picked up the envelope containing the mug shots. "Some day, officer, I'll buy you a beer. I'll tell you my whole shitty story and you'll tell me yours. Meantime, you and I both have things to do."

"We're obliged," Kane said. He started to leave.

"Send Rachel back here, will you? We have some unfinished business."

Kane just shook his head in mock disgust. Lawless grinned. "You know something, Kane? Something I notice about you? You don't laugh very much. Anyone ever tell you that? You really oughta laugh more. Life's just a big fucking joke anyway."

"I'll take it under advisement." *Another expert heard from.*

Kane walked back into the garage and gestured to Rachel with his thumb. "Casanova's waiting." He continued walking out to the street.

1225 hours

Bell drove through the downtown streets on his way back to headquarters. As he passed the Acropolis Lounge, he spotted Kane's Pontiac at a hydrant. He pulled to the curb for a moment. Then he made a U-turn and parked in the red zone. He put his own blue light on the dash and walked through the slush.

Kane sat alone at the bar, eating a hamburger and drinking a coke. Bell sat down next to him. Kane spoke to him in the mirror: "Well, look who's here. The sobriety police."

"I saw your car," Bell said. "I came in to apologize."

"Apologize?"

"For ragging on you this morning. I was wrong."

Kane went back to eating his burger. "Okay, you apologized. You can leave now."

"Man, can we talk about this shit?"

Kane turned and raised his glass for inspection. "See? Coca Cola. The last I heard, even twelve-steppers approve of that."

The bartender walked toward Bell, but the big detective waved him off. "Kane," he said quietly, "I'm worried about you."

"*Worried* about me? Two days ago you hated my guts. Why is everybody so goddamned worried about me all of a sudden?"

"I told you: I've been where you are."

Kane turned and glared directly at Bell. "What the fuck does that mean? Just where exactly do you think I am?"

"I told you how I almost blew my brains out."

Kane threw the hamburger down on the plate. "Jesus Christ, is that what you think?"

"I noticed your reaction when I was telling you about it. You've been there, too." He shut his eyes in pain. "Here's what I didn't tell you: my own father did shoot himself. I loved him, and he killed himself. I never got over it."

"Well, you don't have to worry about me, goddamn it," Kane snapped. "I won't give the do-gooders around here the fucking satisfaction."

Bell nodded. "Okay, I'll leave you alone." He stood up. "The raid's scheduled for two."

"Good. Maybe we can have these scrotes in custody in time to celebrate the alleged virgin birth of your Jesus."

"I came in here to make peace with you," Bell said. "Please don't mock my beliefs." He started for the door.

Kane watched him in the mirror. He swiveled around on his stool. "Hey, Bell," he called.

Bell stopped. "What?"

Kane just sat there, as if wanting to say something. "Never mind," he finally said.

Bell walked back to him. "Listen, there's a police AA meeting at seven tonight. It's in a guy's house. You and I should go."

"What? Run into bigger assholes than the ones in Bryson?"

"It's not like that. They're good guys, most of them. A lot of them got into jams with the department. You oughta hear their stories before you close your mind."

"This is Christmas Eve," Kane said. "I've got plans."

Bell shook his head. "Have it your way. I'm still holding that shit for Internal Affairs. We're going to get seriously into this when Christmas is over."

Kane raised his glass in a sarcastic toast. "Thanks for sharing."

Bell walked out of the bar, silently praying for guidance. He found himself simultaneously hating Kane and fearing for him.

1355 hours

A block from the Whitman house, Easterly and Angus MacKenzie sat in the rear compartment of a surveillance van that had been disguised as a gas company repair truck. Nick Georgiades, dressed as a meter reader, slouched behind the wheel. Easterly and MacKenzie peered out through blackened windows, awaiting the raid.

The van belonged to Georgiades' Criminal Conspiracy Bureau. It was rigged with telephoto and night-vision cameras, sophisticated communications equipment and state-of-the-art body armor. It reminded Easterly of how old-school she was. She was barely able to handle a computer.

Easterly had decided to come along as an observer. She was dressed in jeans and a sweat shirt instead of her business suit. She also wore a bulletproof vest and a raid jacket, but only because MacKenzie had insisted on it.

MacKenzie, similarly protected, checked his watch. "Five minutes," he said.

Easterly wiggled around, trying to get comfortable in the warm gear. It had been a long time since she had suited up like this. She was beginning to perspire.

More adrenaline. How many gallons have I pumped over the years? No wonder older cops have so many heart attacks.

"We should get a flood of tips after the press conference," MacKenzie said.

"I hope one pans out fast," Easterly said. "The precincts are squawking about the borrowed manpower."

"I thought the crime rate was down."

"What do you make of that, Gus?" Easterly asked. "I mean, for real?"

"Well, if crimes aren't being committed, it means the criminals aren't committing them," mused the big Scot. "So what have they been doing instead?"

"Collecting Christmas donations," chimed in Georgiades from the front. "Toys for Tots, Little Sisters of the Poor…"

"You're too cynical," Easterly said.

"Inspector, it's not *possible* to be too cynical…"

He was interrupted by radio traffic—terse, coded messages from the raiding party. Easterly peered out, watching for the SWAT crew. If they were out there, they were invisible. The radio went silent again. The banter in the van stopped.

Easterly found herself drifting over a list of truly great

cops she had known over the years—two of whom were sitting with her at that very moment. Certainly police officers were no angels. She had known her share of corrupt and brutal ones. But there was something special about the great ones, the ones with brains, courage and great hearts. It was like a priesthood—a priesthood of the deeply flawed.

Cynicism in law enforcement was inevitable and pervasive. It wasn't so much the perversity of the low-lifes you dealt with. That much you expected; you were trained to deal with it from the first day in the academy.

No, the greater cause of cynicism was the duplicity and venality of the people in power. Easterly had had a partner once, a crusty old detective who insisted that, per capita, there were far more criminals among the rich than among the poor. Over the years, she had come to believe he was right.

But, on the other side of the coin, Easterly also saw heroism, plenty of it, practically every day. And it wasn't just physical bravery, although she had seen a great deal of that. The true, day-in, day-out heroism of big-city cops lay in their struggle to keep their hearts intact in the face of relentless evil.

Her thoughts turned to Byron Slaughter, and the compromising photographs now locked in her office safe. She realized that Slaughter was right. She ought to hang onto them, for insurance. God only knew what Mosely was capable of.

She wondered what to tell David about the pictures. David fancied himself a realist, but underneath he remained an idealist. She was not sure David would understand why Slaughter had given her those pictures. But she did know what he would say if he knew she had decided to keep them.

So now, for the first time in their marriage, Easterly considered the option of concealing something truly important from her husband. She could tell herself that this was a sensitive operational matter, and thus exempt from their conversations. But that was a cop-out and she knew it. *I don't even have this new job yet, and already it's affecting my integrity and my marriage.*

She next thought of Kane and Bell. They certainly had come through. When this was over, she would put both of them up for commendations. But she also would have to separate them again, and return them to their units. That idea bothered her.

More than once in the past couple of days a strange notion had occurred to Easterly. It seemed that some powerful and mysterious force was suddenly at work in the lives of Kane and Bell, something healing, and that she somehow played a part in it. Maybe something good could come out of this horrible case. That by *itself* would be a miracle.

But Easterly had always considered herself an agnostic. This line of thinking was utterly irrational. Regardless, she mused, as Chief of Detectives she could assign Kane and Bell wherever she wanted them. She could even order them to continue working as partners, just to see what might happen.

Then, embarrassed by her own thinking, she forced all such thoughts out of her head. *Who am I to play God?*

The hand-held radio at her side crackled. "Cobra leader to all units. Go!"

"Hit it!" exclaimed MacKenzie. Easterly grabbed her field glasses to watch the street. With commando precision, a convoy of unmarked cars screeched up to the Whitman house. They slammed on their brakes and a dozen SWAT cops bailed out.

MacKenzie and Georgiades leaped from the van. MacKenzie carried a shotgun, Georgiades an M-16. They sprinted to join the Crime Suppression officers storming the house. With a single scream of "POLICE!" over a loudhailer, the entry team smashed down the front door.

Simultaneously, other officers crashed through the back

and side doors. Easterly noted that two of them were very young women. Still other officers covered the side windows with assault rifles.

Entry took less than twenty seconds. The team leader came up on the Tac channel: "We're in and commencing the search!"

Easterly emerged from the van and stood behind it, watching and listening to the hand radio. She uttered a silent plea that she would not hear gunfire. *I should be in there with them. Why am I standing out here?*

Then she answered herself: *Because I am the boss, the general. This is where I am supposed to be. I have been there and done that. I have paid my dues.*

Easterly stood there for three anxious minutes, until she heard the welcome words, "All units, code four! Building secure!"

With that, four homicide cars and the lab truck rolled up from a side street. Easterly walked to the house. Some of the raiding officers emerged, holding handkerchiefs over their noses.

"What is it?" Easterly asked Georgiades.

"Corpse in the living room," he said. "A female."

Easterly took out a handkerchief and started inside. "You don't need to go in there," Georgiades said. "It's not pretty."

"I did work Homicide," Easterly said. She motioned for the crime-scene investigators to wait outside.

She walked into the house. The first thing she noted was the wilting heat. Someone had left the furnace up full blast.

The body of a middle-aged black woman lay sprawled across the couch. She had already decomposed badly. A small-caliber revolver lay on the floor next to her hand. Also on the floor were a hand-scrawled note, an empty whiskey bottle and an overflowing ash tray.

Easterly felt herself go into the old detached emotional state. Her brain began automatically cataloging things. In the corner, she noted, was a forlorn Christmas tree, completely dried out. A fire hazard, she noted absurdly. "Open the windows, but be careful about prints," she ordered. "Don't touch the thermostat until we dust it."

She walked to the corpse and crouched down to read the note. "MY SON IS THE DEVILL!" was scrawled with a black felt marker, in childish capital letters. "I CANT LIVE WITH WHAT HE DID!"

Easterly went back outside to the waiting Major Crimes detectives. "It's all yours," she said. "We have either a second homicide or a suicide. Most likely a suicide. Either way, look hard for anything that'll put Darryl here. Remember those fibers from his jacket."

Then, fighting a wave of nausea, she went for a cell phone to call Byron Slaughter.

1502 hours

Once again the task force cops were assembled in the gymnasium, awaiting the brass. This briefing was to plan strategy.

Kane stood by himself in the corner of the gym, watching the others, isolated as usual. He watched Bell from across the room, his massive body draped over a folding chair he had turned around backwards. He was staring off into space, as if pondering some deep pain.

Kane found himself having some very strange feelings about his old antagonist. He actually felt something shift, deep inside himself. *What if I had had a father I loved, and then the man killed himself? How would I have turned out?*

The idea of having a loving father was almost impossible for him to comprehend. It was like trying to understand life on another planet. But, simply by making the effort, Kane felt a sudden, startling compassion for Bell.

Then that line of thinking mutated into a string of questions: *what's it like to be black?; what's it like to be aware that you're different, every minute you're alive?*

Kane, of course, had been an outsider all his life. But at least his difference was not readily visible to the world. To have coal-black skin in the body of a giant was to draw attention everywhere you went.

Kane shivered. He was not accustomed to feeling such empathy. True enough, his work often required him to go inside other people's minds. But this was the first time he had *tried* to feel the pain of another man—and a black man, at that.

Where's this coming from? What's happening to me? Kane made a decision. He walked slowly over to Bell, who did not see him approach. Kane touched him on the shoulder. Startled, Bell spun around.

"What?"

"I'm sorry," Kane said. "I apologize for mocking your beliefs. That was an asshole thing to do."

Bell studied Kane, trying to comprehend. Kane looked down at the floor. "I'm also sorry about your father—that thing with the gun," he said softly. "I respect what you've done with your life."

There was a long silence as the two men scrutinized each other. "Thank you," Bell said finally. "I appreciate that." He gestured at the chair next to him. "Sit down."

Hesitantly, Kane complied. Then he sat there with his elbows on his knees, looking down at his boots.

Bobbie Easterly, Angus MacKenzie and Nick Georgiades walked into the gymnasium. The task force officers all rose. Easterly was back in her business suit. MacKenzie and Georgiades were clearly exhausted.

Easterly walked to the rostrum. "Take your seats," she said. She looked around at the assembled cops. She paused, considering her words.

"We've come a long way on this case. Everyone has worked magnificently. The citizens of this community owe you a debt of thanks. Special credit is due to Detectives Bell and Kane, who first got us on the trail of Blackstone and Whitman."

Every cop in the room looked over at Kane and Bell.

"It appears certain that those two are, in fact, our killers," Easterly continued. "Whitman's mother shot herself, probably two days ago. We figure it was right around the time our victim was killed. She left a note implicating her son.

"Forensics discovered promising physical evidence in an upstairs bedroom, fibers we believe will match those at the abduction scene. We also found items of a little boy's clothing, which have been taken to the Childress home for identification. That includes what looks to be the other red glove."

Easterly let the significance of that, and the visual imagery, sink in before continuing. "We're confident the victim was held in that house—but probably killed elsewhere."

Easterly lowered her voice. "We're also speculating that Mrs. Whitman was so horrified that she had no choice but to commit suicide." She looked down at the floor. "She was a criminal herself. But she was also a mother."

MacKenzie took over. "We're having a press conference in one hour, releasing the names of the suspects. Then we'll rely on the community to help us find these monsters." The big Scot rubbed his face in a gesture of fatigue. "If we're lucky, we'll be able to disband in time for most of you to have Christmas with your families. Are there any questions?"

"Yeah," chimed in a detective from Holdup. "Where's Chief Slaughter?"

"He went home early," Easterly said. "His adjutant said he wasn't feeling well."

Another detective raised his hand. "How much credit are

we going to let Mosely and those federal assholes take?"

Easterly smiled wearily. "That's what I hate about you, Norm, the way you mince words. Why don't you tell us what you really think?"

Then, at that moment, Kane's cell phone rang. He examined the number and turned to Bell. "Vitale," he said under his breath. He moved away from the group and answered. Bell came over and listened to Kane's side of the conversation. "Blackstone? Yeah, the white guy." Kane scribbled a note. "The Blind Pig? Thanks, Vito."

With a sudden surge of adrenaline he signed off and showed Bell the note. "One of Vitale's torpedoes says a guy who looks like Blackie just walked into this joint."

Then Bell's phone rang. It was Garland McQueen. "This is the Deacon," Bell answered. He, too, listened. He looked over at Kane and nodded. "The Blind Pig," he said for Kane's benefit. "Thanks, Queenie."

Within four minutes, the two detectives had received identical information from Willis Henry and Tiny Lawless. "Thanks, man, we're on our way," Kane said to Lawless. When Bell hung up from Henry, he turned to Kane. "You know this dive?"

"It's a couple of miles from here," Kane said, "a low-life tittie bar. Used to be the Diamond Cutter."

"I remember the place," Bell said. "A real shithouse."

"Still is. It's a hangout for ex-cons—black *and* white."

Bell went for their coats. Kane approached Easterly, discreetly interrupted the briefing, and handed her the note naming the Blind Pig. "The white scrote is in there right now, watching a skin show," he said quietly.

"Where's his partner?" Easterly asked.

"I don't know." He looked at her pleadingly. "Inspector, this one's mine."

"Not without backup."

"Look, give Bell and me a ten-minute head start," Kane

said. "This is a biracial joint. We'll slide in as customers and get a fix on the asshole. Maybe we can take him quietly."

"Okay. But I'm putting people all over the place, in case something goes sideways. Take a hand-held, stay on Tac Four."

"Thanks, skipper."

"Try to take him alive. We need to know about his partner."

"You don't have to tell me that."

He turned to leave. "Ralph," Easterly said.

He turned back. "Yes, ma'm?"

"Be careful, okay? You're a valuable man."

Kane stood there for a moment, trying to absorb the compliment. Then he ran to catch up with Bell.

1533 hours

Kane and Bell raced to the Blind Pig in the Pontiac. It took less than three minutes, code three. Kane shut down the siren four blocks before they arrived. Bell hid the Kojak on the floor.

Kane backed into a space in the bar's parking lot, near the side door, and secreted a hand-held radio under his coat. He and Bell got out of the Pontiac, stepped around some freezing puddles and walked into the club.

They stopped at the door to let their eyes adjust to the dark. At this hour on Christmas Eve afternoon, the dive was packed with dirtbags of every color. On the stage, a bored biker chick with a dragon tattoo on her pubis was gyrating listlessly.

"So this is where scrotes do Christmas," Kane muttered. Looking like a derelict, he fit right in.

"Yeah," Bell said. "But we know at least four of these

assholes are on our side."

"Yeah, but which ones? How many guns are in here?"

"You want to go back and get a vest?" Bell asked.

"No. I like to live dangerously."

"Yeah, I noticed."

They sat down at a rear table. A very young waitress sauntered over, wearing only pasties and a G-string. She was a dancer forced to do double duty. Her arms were covered with needle tracks and she chewed gum.

Both detectives ordered cokes. The waitress looked them over suspiciously. "High rollers, you two," she said.

Kane and Bell exchanged a glance, worried that she would rat them off. "We're in AA," Kane said. "We just came in to worship you."

"My old man was in AA," the girl said. "Went into a bar for a coke one night and I never saw him again."

"Well, I'm not your old man," Kane said. He stuffed a ten into her G-string. "Merry Christmas."

"Thanks, sport." The girl went for the cokes.

Pretending to watch the dancer, Kane and Bell covertly inspected the clientele. The smoke was heavy, despite the no-smoking ordinance. "You still off cigarettes?" Kane asked.

"Not if I stay in here much longer."

"Then let's find this asshole."

Bell touched Kane's arm. "Over there. By the men's room."

Kane picked out Thomas Blackstone, seated by himself at a table for four, mesmerized by the dancer. "There he is, bigger than life. The dumb shit." He lowered his voice. "Okay. I'll make like I'm going for a piss. When I'm behind him, you make like you're going to the pay phone."

"Do it."

Kane stood up and casually walked to the men's room, his eyes on the dancer but his peripheral vision on Blackie. He went into the john, then immediately came back out and stood in the shadows.

Bell rose and walked around the crowd in the other direction. As he moved, he pulled some change from his pocket and pretended to count it. He passed the waitress, carrying a tray of drinks. "Hey," she called, "you owe me for the cokes."

"We paid you, remember?" Bell pointed to the ten in her G-string.

"That wasn't for the cokes. That was a *tip*."

Bell wanted to get away from her, in a hurry. They were attracting attention. "Just leave 'em on the table. We'll pay you when we get back."

"No way," she said. "Cash on delivery." Then she laughed, giddily. "You guys are Vice, aren't you? I can smell Vice a mile off."

Bell motioned for her to come closer. He leaned down and whispered in her ear, savagely: "You shut the fuck up!"

But she pulled back and looked Bell up and down, stupidly. "*The cops are here!*" she yelled, loud enough for the entire room to hear. She raised her voice still more: "*Ya'll watch out, now, we've got the po-lice in here!*"

Blackstone looked up, alarmed. He got to his feet and started for the door.

Kane came at him from behind, a Marine all over again. He grabbed Blackstone's collar with his left hand and pulled him savagely to the ground. With his right hand, he jerked his Beretta from the shoulder rig. Then he knelt down on Blackstone's neck, pressing the pistol hard against the back of his head. "Give me an excuse!" he said through his teeth.

Several customers stood up menacingly. Bell elbowed two of them aside like rag dolls. He pulled his own Beretta. "*POLICE OFFICERS!*" he screamed. He waved the Beretta at the crowd. "Get the fuck out of the way!"

Kane keyed the hand radio. "Officer needs assistance, inside the Blind Pig!"

Everyone pulled back slightly but stood there watching, hostile. Then four of the low-lifes, acting individually, elbowed their way forward. Two were white and two were black. Together they formed a protective cordon. Bell realized that these were the informants.

Kane reached under his coat for his handcuffs. He knelt down on Blackstone's back and wrestled the cursing killer's hands into them. Then he looked up at the menacing crowd and made an announcement: "This is one of the *heroes* who murdered that little boy!"

A hush fell over the assembly, broken only by the sound of rapidly approaching sirens. "Give him to us," one voice finally said. The voice belonged to a white man whose neck was covered with prison tats. Blackstone looked up, almost weeping in panic.

"Forget about a motherfucking trial," echoed a black biker with gold teeth. He was even bigger than Bell, and thirty years younger.

Still lying face down, Blackstone twisted around to look at Bell. "You can't do this!" he said. "I know my rights!"

"Fuck your rights!" growled the white ex-con.

With that, the first backup officers came bursting in, guns drawn. Bell held up his hand to them. Kane keyed the radio again. "All units, code four. Everything is under control."

Then Kane leaned down to Blackstone's ear and spoke through his teeth, murderously. "You have thirty seconds to tell us where your partner is, or we give you to these people."

"Please!" Blackstone whimpered.

"Where is Whitman, fuck-face?" Kane said.

The ex-con whimpered. "Voyager Motel, 129 and Jefferson."

"What room?"

"Three-ten."

Kane again pointed to the hostile crowd. "Okay. Now

listen closely, you sack of shit. If you're lying, we're gonna bring you back here and turn you over to these guys. You can tell *them* why you executed that helpless little boy."

"Man, I ain't lying. That's where he's staying, the Voyager Motel." Blackstone started sobbing. "He's the one who shot the kid. I begged him not to."

"Horseshit," said Bell. He jerked the trembling punk to his feet. While the other cops watched, he dragged him through the hate-filled crowd.

"Hey, guys, cokes are on me," laughed the junkie waitress.

Kane reached over and yanked his ten out of her G-string. "The little bitch ripped me off," he announced to the crowd. "Whatever happened to honesty?"

The Blind Pig broke out in applause.

1602 hours

Easterly stood uneasily before Mosely's desk, flanked by MacKenzie and Georgiades. All three were under extreme stress. The squint, Dunsmore, stood next to Mosely. The chief was livid. "What do you mean, cancel the press conference? You're the ones who asked for it."

"Chief, circumstances have changed," Easterly said. "It happens sometimes."

"Half the city's media is waiting in my conference room," Mosely said. "We promised to name the suspects on the five o'clock news. And now we've even got one of them in custody."

"*One* of them," Easterly said. "Now we have a chance to grab the other one—*if* he doesn't know we're on to him."

"Look outside," Mosely said. "Look at all the TV trucks out there, waiting for live feeds. We can't call this off now."

"We don't work for the news media," Easterly said quietly.

Careful. You could be cutting your own throat here. But principle has to count for something, or none of this matters.

"Sir," she continued, forcing calm into her voice, "we think we know where Whitman is staying. If we reveal any of this now, he'll flee."

"Then he'll just turn up somewhere else," Mosely said. "They always do, his kind. With all the national publicity, it won't be long before someone catches him for something." He looked at his watch. "Let's hurry this thing up. It's Christmas Eve. I have plans."

MacKenzie and Georgiades looked at each other, speechless. Easterly lost it. "Plans?! For Christ's sake, this is a police department, not the Rotary Club!"

Mosely glared. "You're out of line, Inspector." He turned to Lt. Dunsmore. "What do *you* have to say for yourself?"

This was Dunsmore's big moment. "Sir, I have a plan to orchestrate the effect of the story to our advantage. I think it will maximize our favorable exposure."

Mosely nodded. "Let's hear it."

"We'll reveal the details incrementally. For now we go out with a story saying simply that we've cracked the case, and we identify the suspects. Then, later in the evening, in time for the 11 o'clock news and the *Daily Times* final edition, we reveal that one of them has been arrested—or, if we get lucky by then, both of them. That way we keep the story dynamic all night."

The three command officers looked at each other in disbelief. Easterly felt her stomach churn. *Keep the story dynamic.*

Dunsmore, oblivious, smiled and continued. "This being Christmas Eve, people will be home tonight, many of them up late with the TV on. This story will play well for Christmas."

"Chief…" Easterly started to interrupt. But Mosely

raised his hand to let Dunsmore continue.

"Sir," the squint went on, "I'd further suggest that you alert Mr. Demarest, in case the FBI would like to hold their own press conference later this evening. That way you won't have to interrupt your plans.

"The TV people can link it with footage from this earlier press conference. Then both you and Mr. Demarest will be visible and can share in the credit. Meantime, I'll stay around to deal with any late-breaking events. If need be, I can go on camera as your spokeman."

"I've heard enough of this shit!" Nick Georgiades burst out.

"So have I!" echoed Angus MacKenzie.

Mosely glared at them. "This is insubordination! I won't stand for it!"

"And we won't stand for you and that FBI squint fucking up this case any more than you already have!" Georgiades shouted back. "What if this asshole kills some other kid after you've scared him off?"

MacKenzie stepped forward. "We have a chance to arrest a cold-blooded child killer," he said. "If he escapes because of you, we'll conduct our own press conference."

"Whitman claims he's going to shoot it out with automatic weapons," Easterly added. "Once he finds out we're on to him, we lose the advantage of surprise. He just might kill some cops. How will you explain *that* to the troops or will you foist it off on someone else?"

There was dead silence in the room. Enraged but cornered, Mosely looked around at the three command officers.

Then Easterly thought of the photographs in her safe. She felt a surge of hatred. She stared directly into Mosely's eyes. "Chief," she said quietly but viciously, "why don't you just go on home—*or wherever it is you go when you leave this building?*"

Mosely instantly understood her reference to his sexual wanderings. She held his eyes. He looked away in fear.

Easterly felt a surge of power. *Got you, you pompous prick!* She immediately hated herself for sinking to this level. But she didn't pull back. She owed it to Darryl Childress, and to her cops, to neutralize this dangerous bastard. She stood still, awaiting the chief's response.

Mosely was perspiring, groping for words. "I am *still* the chief of police," he said weakly.

"And nobody will be the wiser, if you let us handle this," Easterly said. "None of it will leave this room."

She knew that no one else in the room knew what they were talking about. She pointed at the baffled Dunsmore. "I think the lieutenant here should just go on home, spend a nice Christmas Eve with his family. If we arrest Whitman, *I'm* perfectly capable of dealing with the press."

After another long silence, Mosely said, "All right. But I'll be back here the day after tomorrow, and I *will* be in charge of this police department."

Dunsmore did not understand what had just happened. "Sir, what do I say to the reporters?"

Easterly did not let Mosely answer. "That you made a mistake, that we had the wrong guys. I don't care what you tell them. Just don't say *anything* that'll make Frederick Whitman decide it's time to get in the wind."

Dunsmore looked over at Mosely. The chief nodded reluctant agreement. Mosely was crushed. The perplexed Dunsmore headed for the door.

MacKenzie and Georgiades were as bewildered as Dunsmore. But they also were profoundly relieved. Afterward, they did not ask Easterly about it. A smart cop knows when *not* to be an investigator.

Darkness was falling fast, along with the temperature. Kane and Bell sat watching the Voyager Motel from a panel truck that had been disguised as a UPS delivery vehicle. Kane was behind the wheel. He let the motor idle to run the heater.

The Voyager was a South End hot-sheet parlor. The ratty building was decorated with a single string of Christmas lights above the office door. Three of the bulbs were burned out.

Easterly had sent the exhausted MacKenzie and Georgiades home, then had assumed personal command of this operation. Homicide detectives had shown Whitman's mug shot to the motel manager, and the guy had made a positive ID.

Whitman, the manager told the police, was registered as a "Gregory Smith." The license number on the registration form came back to a stolen Honda. The car was in the lot, but Whitman was away from his room.

Easterly replaced the manager with an undercover CCB officer. Now she herself waited with Stan Jablonski and a Homicide team inside room 310, monitoring Tac Four.

Bell and Kane had plenty of company out on the street. Crime Suppression had deployed several plainclothes units in a tight but invisible perimeter. An aero unit was orbiting a much wider area to avoid attracting attention—but available to swoop in at a moment's notice.

Kane and Bell both wore bulletproof vests under their winter coats. Neither man had a long gun; they would leave the heavy artillery to the Crime Suppression specialists. But they did have a cheap bottle of wine in a paper sack.

The wine was a prop, part of the game plan: if anyone spotted Whitman approaching on foot, Kane and Bell would get out of the van and pretend to be winos. Then they would stagger up innocently and try to take him on the street. That would lessen the chance of gunfire penetrating the motel.

Now, in the van, Kane leaned back against the head rest. "That wine smells like shit," he said. "You ever drink anything that putrid?"

"I don't remember."

"I know I have."

"Lucky you survived."

They sat in silence for several minutes. Then Bell said, "I hear a rumor Vito Vitale's circling the drain."

"That old bastard'll live forever," Kane said. "He's indestructible." He looked over at Bell. "What's this I hear about a truce between the Crips and the Bloods?"

"Yeah, like a cease-fire in the Middle East."

"I don't understand those fuckers. I mean, they're all black kids, they all come from the same place..."

"They direct their rage at themselves. They've been programmed to do that. It's a form of self-genocide."

"Well, I don't get it."

"I'll explain it some time," Bell said.

Kane lifted his binoculars and watched a pair of black hookers leaving the hotel, waving goodbye to a white man in an upper room. "Looks like Santa came early."

"Another ten minutes, he'll be driving home to his loving family, out in suburbia," Bell said. "Out where I live. Out where everything is safe and life is sweet."

"What the hell are you talking about?"

"Never mind."

The two men sat in silence for several more minutes. Then Kane asked casually, "So what's your opinion of Titus Webster?"

"Is that a legitimate question or are you baiting me?"

"He *is* a crook, you know."

"You think I'm going to defend some corrupt politician

just because he's black? Is that what you're driving at?"

"Man, don't get defensive," Kane said. "We're just passing time here. I mean, we could talk about baseball, but I don't know shit about sports."

"We've been doing just fine the last little while. Let's not screw it up now."

Kane shrugged and picked up the binoculars again, scanning the street. Without lowering them, he asked, "So why *did* your father kill himself?"

Bell looked over at him, surprised. "Why do you ask?"

Kane shrugged. "Nothing personal. I've always wondered what makes a person do that."

"Pain. Unbearable, endless, hopeless pain." He stared into the distance. "It's not you you're trying to kill. You're trying to kill the pain." He looked back at Kane. "But I have a hunch you already know that."

Kane said nothing, just kept scanning the street. Finally he lowered the binoculars. "What was it like," he asked, "growing up black in the Deep South?"

"You mean you care?"

"No, Bell, I just say shit like that to hear myself talk."

"It sucked. It sucked big-time. That's what it was like. My grandfather was lynched by the Ku Klux Klan. My father was seven years old when it happened. He witnessed it. Then, when *I* was seven years old, my father blew his brains out." He closed his eyes, seeing it again. "I was the same age as Darryl Childress. He was my daddy, and I loved him."

"Jesus Christ!"

"As far as I'm concerned, the Klan murdered both of them. And they damned near murdered me, too, a coupla years ago when I came close to shooting my *own* sorry-assed self." He grimaced. "*That's* what it was like, growing up black in the Deep South, just a little taste of it. Ask any of us. Like I said, it sucked."

Kane shut his eyes momentarily. "I'm sorry."

"Suicide's a shitty thing, my friend," Bell added softly. "That's why I didn't do it. I couldn't do that to my own children."

Both men silently contemplated that. Then a real wino, a black man, came along and began rummaging through a dumpster. "Some life," Kane muttered.

"There but for the grace of God…"

"You really believe that stuff, don't you?"

"Most of the time."

"You go to church?"

"Some of the time. Listen, Kane, I'm not sure I want to talk about this."

"Well, *I* want to talk about it. It's important to *me*."

"I don't go to church because I'm impressed with the titles and vestments and rituals. I go to hear the *message*."

"'Blessed are the merciful, blessed are the peacemakers'— that kinda stuff."

"Yeah, that kinda stuff. I need to hear how love can redeem the world. I need *desperately* to hear that."

"The world?"

"Oh, for Christ's sake, Kane, I don't know about the *world*. But I believe it can redeem *me*."

"You don't have to be a churchgoer to believe that."

"No, but it *was* the Man's main message. Love your neighbor, forgive your enemy, feed the hungry, comfort the afflicted—you know, that kind of shit. Can we drop this now?"

"Sure thing, Ike. Let's drop it. I was just curious, that's all. I didn't want a big fucking debate."

Bell calmed down and studied his old nemesis. Four days ago, he would not have believed this. "Since you got so personal with me, let me ask you something."

"Fire away."

"What was it like being an abused child?"

The question caught Kane off guard. "What are you

talking about?"

"Ralph, I worked Child Abuse for two years. I know it when I see it."

Kane thought for a moment before he answered. "It sucked," he finally said. "It sucked big-time."

"I couldn't handle that duty, Child Abuse. Every night I'd come home and think about those poor kids. That's when my drinking really started getting bad, working Child Abuse." He looked at Kane. "So I guessed right, didn't I? You *were* one of those kids."

Kane just stared at the Christmas lights on the forlorn motel. "Yeah," he said, almost inaudibly. "I was."

Bell raised the binoculars again. "You know why I drank?"

"You just said it—to kill the pain," Kane said.

"Yeah. And to fill the hole in my soul that was the size of Rhode Island. No matter what, I couldn't fill that hole. It didn't matter what I did, or how many people loved me. The only thing that filled the hole was booze."

Kane laughed bitterly. "You want to hear a real pisser? I used to *pray* my old man would kill himself. Your father did what I prayed mine would do."

Bell thought about that for a long moment. Then he asked softly, "How *did* he hurt you, Ralph? What did he do?"

Kane turned on the dome light. He pulled back the hair on his wrist and showed Bell the old knife scar. "There's a bunch more on my back. Plus a few burn marks on the soles of my feet. Fun guy, old Howard Kane. He smoked Camels."

"That scar on your cheek?" Bell asked. "Was that him, too?"

Kane turned off the light. "No, that's from a little hand-to-hand tussle with a Viet Cong. I won."

"Had a couple of those myself."

"I figured as much."

"So your entire life's been a war."

Kane nodded. "I could say the same thing about you."

"Yeah, I guess you could. Where's your old man now?"

"He died of lung cancer. From what I hear, it was painful. He went down hard."

"Must've been all those Camels." Bell opened the door. "I gotta piss."

Bell walked over to a bush in the shadows. Kane picked up the binoculars and continued scanning the street.

* * *

Easterly sat on the bed in Frederick Whitman's room, a hand-held radio lying next to her. Stan Jablonski sat across from her, drinking a coke and reading *USA Today*. Jablonski wore a battered shoulder holster with a hogleg .357 Smith. Normally he carried only a snub-nosed .38 Detective Special, about the age of the two Homicide detectives sitting here with them. But tonight he was taking no chances. Jablonski was one of the last of the city's police to carry a wheel-gun.

The two young Homicide guys, Parker and Dalessandro, sat nervously on the floor, smoking and watching "It's A Wonderful Life" on the nearly-muted television. Half an hour ago, when they tossed the room, the detectives had found two assault rifles and two hundred rounds of ammunition. Now Easterly looked over at the rifles, bagged for prints and tagged as evidence.

This evil prick means business. God only knows what kind of a walking-around piece he's carrying.

Easterly now found herself saying a silent to-whom-it-may-concern prayer—for the safety of her own people and the safety of innocent bystanders. She glanced over at Whitman's suitcase, also evidence-tagged. In addition to a bag of weed and a bottle of methamphetamine, the suitcase contained neatly-clipped stories about the Childress case.

The clips were from the *Daily Times* and four other papers, including *USA Today*. The articles were circumstantial evidence, but Easterly knew how they would look to a jury. The last thing she wanted was to *need* Thomas Blackstone to make a case on Whitman. Sentencing-bargaining with an asshole like that, enticing him to betray his partner to save himself, was more than she could bear to imagine. She needed iron-clad, dead-bang evidence, on both men. *I want <u>both</u> of them on Death Row.*

She wondered what her deceased parents would have thought of such a wish. They had both been free-thinking intellectuals, university professors, active in the ACLU. They had been appalled when she dropped her law-school plans and joined the police department. Then, not long afterward, they were utterly terrified when they heard details of the shootout in which she had earned the Medal of Valor.

It took a long time, but her parents finally came to accept Easterly's chosen life. Eventually they saw how fulfilled she was by her work, and how the community benefited. Then, as she made rank, they even began to tell their friends how proud they were of her.

As she watched a roach scurry across the motel floor, Easterly second-guessed herself, wondering if her parents had been right in the first place. *What's a nice girl like me doing in a dump like this? If I had gone to law school, what would I be doing tonight, Christmas Eve?*

The thought of law school made her think of David. As soon as this caper was over—whichever way it went—they'd have to go somewhere for a nice, romantic dinner.

Love, she reminded herself, needs to be nurtured. Especially if so much of your life is a Horror Show.

* * *

Bell was out of the van for two minutes while Kane

watched the street. Suddenly a lone black male rounded a corner half a block away, headed for the motel. An overcoat hung below his knees, and his hands were deep in his pockets.

Heart pounding, Kane focused in with the field glasses. It was White Man! Kane tooted the horn discreetly for Bell, then picked up the hand-held. "Cobra Seven to all units, subject approaching from the east! We're out!"

Kane grabbed the wine bottle and slipped out of the van. Bell was waiting. "Here comes Satan," Kane said under his breath.

Both officers unholstered their Berettas and held them behind their legs. Faking intoxication, they laughed and staggered toward Whitman. Kane waved the wine bottle. "Yo, buddy, you know where a dude can cop some weed?" Whitman stopped walking and warily watched them approach, appraising them.

Then suddenly Bell slipped on the ice. As he reached out to break his fall, his pistol came into view. "Shit!" he yelled as he went down.

Whitman spotted the gun, then saw Kane coming toward him. He turned and ran, darting through the motel parking lot, slipping on the ice, splashing through puddles. Kane sprinted after him, screaming into his radio, "Officer in foot pursuit, rear of the motel!"

As Whitman ran, he pulled a MAC-10 from under his coat. He found himself blocked by a chain-link fence at the rear of the parking lot. Trapped, he spun around and blindly opened fire, the little machine gun on full automatic.

Kane dived for cover, skidding in the slush. Bullets were hitting cars all around him. The frenzied Whitman was looking everywhere, searching for Kane. With his peripheral vision, Kane saw Bell running toward him. "BELL! GET DOWN!" he screamed. Bell dived for cover, just as Whitman fired another burst.

Lying on his belly in a pool of water, Kane took fast aim and fired a single round. It struck Whitman squarely in the stomach. He fell back against the fence and slid down into a sitting position. The MAC-10 dropped from his hands, landing in a puddle inches from his fingers.

Now everything was in slow motion, dreamlike. Kane moved toward Whitman in a low crouch, holding the Beretta in both hands. He could hear Bell again rushing toward him, and sirens in the distance. Easterly, Jablonski and the Homicide detectives were racing down the motel stairway.

Kane reached Whitman. He knelt down and leveled the Beretta directly at the face of Darryl Childress' murderer. The now-unarmed Whitman was writhing in agony, gut-shot. "Shoot me, motherfucker!" Whitman screamed. "Shoot me!"

Kane began to squeeze the trigger.

"Don't do it!" he heard Bell say, from somewhere behind him.

"Why the *fuck* not?" Kane said without turning. His eyes were locked on those of Frederick Whitman, murderer of children, destroyer of innocence.

"Because then *you'll be just like him!*" Bell shouted.

Kane continued staring at Whitman's closing eyes, considering those words. Finally, he relaxed the gun.

As other officers ran up, Bell rolled Whitman over to handcuff him. Blood was gushing from the exit wound in his lower back. "He's circling the drain anyway," Bell said quietly. "Fucker won't last ten minutes."

Kane looked up and saw Roberta Easterly looking down at him. "I told you you were a valuable man," she said.

Bell sat on the living room couch with Vera curled into his arm, watching the Christmas tree lights flash on and off. "You going to help me put the gifts around the tree?" she asked.

Bell smiled. "Let's make real sure they're asleep first."

Vera looked up at him. "Was it bad?"

"It's never fun to watch someone die," he said.

"I know."

Bell looked at her lovingly. She *did* know, and that was a fact.

Vera got up. "How about some hot chocolate and cookies? Will that fix things up?"

"Hot chocolate and cookies would be real nice."

When she was gone, Bell just stared at the flashing lights. *Where is Kane tonight? What's he going through?*

Bell rose and followed his wife into the kitchen. He came up behind her and put his huge arms around her small waist. "I have something to thank you for," he said.

"What's that, big man?"

"*'Why don't you try loving him?'* You remember saying that to me? About Kane?"

"Of course."

"Where did that come from? Just then, at that moment?"

"I don't know, Ike. Inspiration, I guess."

"I can't get this guy out of my mind," Bell said. "All these years—it wasn't as simple as I thought."

"Baby, it never is. People are complicated. What they are is what their world made them."

He looked at her with love burning in his eyes. "Well, someone sure did a good job making you. I have so much to be grateful for. Why do I keep forgetting that?"

"Because you're human," she said. She smiled. "There's something I want to thank *you* for."

"And what might that be?"

"Like those signs say: thank you for not smoking."

"I didn't realize you noticed."

"I notice everything about you."

Bell took his wife in his arms and held her tight. Together, they rocked gently back and forth.

And then Cassie walked into the kitchen. "I can't sleep," she announced.

"Speaking of things to be grateful for," Bell said to Vera. He swept his child into his arms. "Then I guess we'd better go look at the Christmas tree."

"I'll make that *three* hot chocolates," Vera said.

Bell carried Cassie back into the living room. They sat down on the couch. She nestled into his powerful chest. "Ikey still believes in Santa," she said.

"That's okay," Bell said. "The spirit of Santa Claus, that's what counts." Cassie snuggled tighter against him.

Then another voice made itself heard. "Daddy?" Ikey called timidly from the stairway.

"Better make that *four* hot chocolates," Bell called to Vera.

Rubbing his eyes, the little boy walked over to his father and sister. He, too, crawled up onto the couch and snuggled into Bell's other arm.

"You know, little man, if you don't go to sleep, Santa won't come," Bell said, winking at Cassie.

"I'm scared," Ikey said.

"Scared?"

"I'm afraid of the bad men."

Bell hugged his son tight. "The bad men can't hurt you," he said gently. "Those bad men can't hurt any children any more." Bell's eyes suddenly misted up. The Christmas tree became a multi-colored blur.

Vera appeared quietly behind them. She just stood there in the doorway, looking down at her family. "Your daddy *caught* the bad men," Vera said proudly. "Your daddy and another policeman. Your daddy's a hero."

"Like on TV?" Ikey asked.

"Yes, like on TV. Only better." She smiled, her heart aching with love. "Because he's real."

2228 hours

Roberta Easterly and David Goldman lingered over a second glass of wine following a late dinner at Farber's, the neighborhood deli. Business was brisk, because so many other restaurants were closed for Christmas.

Normally there would have been a huge party tonight, in some cop bar, celebrating the victory. But tonight all of Easterly's people just wanted to get home to their families. So there'd be no celebration. *That's as it should be. This crime was too horrid for festivity.*

Easterly let the fatigue wash over her. She wasn't in a mood for much talking. She also didn't enjoy watching someone die—even when she herself had wished for it. David knew enough to let her be.

She reviewed the events of the last four days. It had been the most intense period of her life.

Then she remembered the discreet phone call she had placed from the motel as soon as the paramedics pronounced Whitman dead, giving Nanci York a jump on the story. Nanci had been overjoyed. Easterly hoped she'd been able to get at least something on the air during the six o'clock newscast. York would be a valuable ally. Easterly even gave York her home phone number.

Then Easterly reviewed the impromptu press conference

she had later held in the motel parking lot. She was pleased with herself for asking Stan Jablonski to arrange things. He had done an extraordinary job. The man was a wizard at detail, and he had shown a surprising flair in dealing with the reporters. They loved his crusty attitude and his old six-shooter.

Easterly resolved to bring Jablonski along with her; that way he could remain her confidant, her voice of reason. She would badger him to take the lieutenant's exam he had always scorned; that was the only way he could get the pay raise he deserved.

Then Easterly critiqued her own on-camera performance. She was glad she had remembered to credit Kane and Bell by name. But she was still worried about Kane. The guy was shaky already, and now he had just killed a man.

She also was pleased that she had mentioned her personal anguish over Darryl's death. She wanted Stephen and Louise Childress to know that she cared about them. She hoped the comments wouldn't come off as self-serving, in light of the lawsuit threatened by Edward Bartholomew. She also hoped the commentary wouldn't be edited out.

She was less pleased by the undiplomatic way she had handled a naive question about the FBI's role in cracking the case. "Absolutely none," she had responded tersely. She knew her anger had shown. That one might come back to haunt her.

To hell with all of it. These things are out of my hands. I can't control what other people do. My conscience is clean.

David, checking his watch, interrupted her thoughts. "We'll have to get home soon, if we're going to watch the news."

"I don't need to see the news," she said. "I was there, remember?"

"Don't you want to see how you come off in an interview?"

"I don't care," she lied. "I just tell the truth." *Most of the time.*

Then she thought of the pictures Slaughter had given her. She wanted in the worst way to tell David about them, to unburden herself of the sleazy secret.

But I'm not finished with Jefferson Mosely yet. And David doesn't really _need_ to know.

The thought of Slaughter jolted her. In all of the fast-paced events, had anyone informed the Chief of Detectives that this case was over? Or would he see it on the 11:00 news?

"Excuse me a minute," she told David. She stepped away from him and dialed Slaughter's number on her cell phone. He sounded groggy when he answered. He had been sleeping, he claimed. He sounded more as if he had been drugged.

Easterly filled him in on the details, and he congratulated her. But something about his voice bothered her. "Byron, is something wrong?"

"You're too good a detective," he said.

"What is it?" she asked, alarmed.

"I'm not coming back to work."

"What?"

"I'm finished, for good," he said.

"What are you talking about?" Easterly asked.

"I have four months of accumulated leave and sick time. I'm using it up and then retiring. As of today you are the acting Chief of Detectives. I'd planned to tell you tomorrow." There was a long pause. "Bobbie, I'm checking myself into a clinic for psychiatric care."

"Jesus, Byron…"

"It's not fashionable for a cop to admit he has a problem. But this depression—I need help. I've been taking heavy medication. But I need something deeper. It's all backed up on me—the war, the years on the streets, Marian's death…"

Easterly felt tears coming to her eyes.

"Bobbie, are you there?" Slaughter said.

"Yes, I'm here."

"What do you think? I value your opinion."

"I think this is the most heroic thing you've ever done. For you to admit that you're a human being…This might help some of these macho guys get over their foolish ideas about manhood…"

"I'm not trying to be a role model. I'm just trying to save my *own* life."

She considered that, then sighed. "You're right," she said. "I'm sorry."

"For the time being, I'm keeping this problem of mine low-profile. Tell David, but no one else." He laughed. "Especially not Stan Jablonski."

"Of course." Then she choked up. "Yours will be big shoes to fill."

"No offense, but your feet are big enough. Good luck, my friend."

After she hung up, Easterly found David paying the bill. "Maybe you don't want to see the news, but I do," he said. "Not every middle-aged Jewish lawyer in town is married to a gorgeous shiksa celebrity super-cop."

Barely hearing him, Easterly just shook her head. "David, you're not going to believe the conversation I just had."

2305 hours

Kane was the only patron left in Harvey's Place. Harvey was closing up early. He washed glasses listlessly while he and Kane watched the news. Kane was drunk again.

There, up on the television screen for the world to see, was the conclusion of Kane's last case. In the glare of the television lights, flush against the chain-link motel fence, lay Whitman's corpse, covered by a coroner's blanket. And there, with a battery of microphones stuck in her face, stood Bobbie Easterly talking about the valor of Detectives Ralph Kane and Isaiah Bell.

Kane sat on the bar stool, re-living the shooting. Then the segment ended, and the news shifted to a follow-up of the plane crash. "Nice job, Ralph," Harvey said softly.

"Then give me another drink," Kane said, fumbling in his pocket for money.

"You've had enough, my friend. Go on home. I have a date in the morning with my grandkids."

Grandkids. You lucky son of a bitch. "Sure thing, Harvey. See you around."

"Go straight home, Ralph."

"Right you are."

"Merry Christmas. Thanks for what you did for the city."

Kane waved listlessly, then walked out to the Pontiac. It was snowing again, hard. *Home? Tonight?* He got in the Pontiac and started it up. *Where the hell is home?*

He started driving aimlessly around the streets again. He turned up the volume on the police radio. There was something perversely comforting about knowing the shitheads were out and about, even on Christmas Eve. Somehow it made Kane feel a little less alone. But tonight the radio was quiet, just a series of fender-bender accidents, a DUI, and the predictable domestic violence.

Kane stopped at a liquor store. The owner also was closing up. "You're just in time," he said. Kane bought a pint of cheap whiskey and got back in the Pontiac. He drove some more, drinking, not even caring if some Motor officer stopped him.

Because tonight was the night. The job was done, and now it was time. The girl in Saigon. Billy. Pete. That kid in the alley, James Caldwell. Darryl Childress... Tonight was the night Kane would join them all. Where they were now—*that* was home.

Kane found himself again passing St. Michael's Church. Despite the snow, several cars were pulling into the parking lot.

Of course! Christmas Eve, Midnight Mass! Perfect!

Kane drove into the lot. He parked at the far end, in the only space available, directly alongside the life-sized, snow-covered statue of St. Michael the Archangel. *God Himself couldn't have picked a better place!* He left the motor running for heat.

The snow fell harder. Kane sat in the car and watched the people entering the church. He heard a choir singing, and then he caught a glimpse of that priest who had been kind to him, dressed in vestments.

Was that only two days ago? He laughed bitterly, right out loud. *Fat lot of good your prayers did, Padre.*

Kane looked up at the snow-covered angel and thought of the Virgin Mary statue in Vito Vitale's mansion, which in turn caused him to think of Vitale's last words to him. *"Get some love in your life—while you can."* That's what the old killer had said. *Well, it's too late for that shit now.*

Kane thought of his little flock of customers. Absurdly he found himself wondering where Tiny Lawless was tonight.

I'm insane. I've gone absolutely fucking insane.

Kane waited until after midnight, when the worshippers all were safely inside the church. Then he turned on the FM radio and began channel-scanning, looking for "The Little Drummer Boy." This was Christmas. Sooner or later, on some radio station or other, he would find some rendition of Darryl Childress' favorite Christmas song. For some reason, he wanted to hear it one more time.

And that will be my signal. That's when I'll go join them.

It took only ten minutes to find the song. And suddenly there it was, the original Harry Simeone version, loud and clear on one of the region's main stations.

Kane took another long pull on his booze. He drained the bottle and let it fall to the floor. Then he started singing along with the radio: *"the ox and lamb kept time, pa-rumpa pum pum…"*

As he sang, he pulled out his Beretta and snapped off the safety. He thought of Isaiah Bell. The love of family was what had stopped Bell. *But I don't have any family. No one will grieve for me. Thank God.* He sang louder: *"I played my best for Him, pa- rumpa pum pum…"*

Kane looked over at the face of the archangel. *Okay, pal, take me home.* He shut his eyes. He raised the barrel of the Beretta to his mouth, smelling the gun oil…

Then, through the boozy haze in his mind, Kane remembered his plan to radio for assistance, so it would be another cop who found him. *Can't do this to an innocent civilian.* He laid the gun on the passenger seat, turned up the volume on the police radio and fumbled to remove the microphone from its cradle…

And then he passed out cold. He slumped to his right and sprawled across the seat, knocking the gun onto the floor of the Pontiac, where it landed next to the empty bottle.

DAY 5 - CHRISTMAS DAY

A golden sunrise graced the city. Roberta Easterly lay in bed with David, reading the *Daily Times*. The headline trumpeted "CHILD SLAYING SOLVED, POLICE SAY: Suspect Slain in Shootout, Second Arrested."

Once again, the reporters had minor facts wrong. The article said Whitman and Blackstone were on parole from Statesville, not Bryson, and that they had been arrested by a joint police-FBI task force. The reference to the FBI rankled Easterly, especially in light of her own comments to the television people. "If they don't know something, why can't they just ask?" she groused.

David pointed to the op-ed page. "Here's a sociologist analyzing the crime drop. He's making pronouncements about age, demographics, socio-economic conditions and race relations. A criminology professor at the University of Pennsylvania." He laughed. "He admits he's never even been here."

In spite of herself, Easterly laughed, too. "The age of the talking head."

"Modern life's just a big football game, to be watched and commented about. And everyone's an expert."

"What do you say we go out again for breakfast?"

"You're on. But first…" He reached under the bed and pulled out a small gift-wrapped box. "Merry Christmas."

"David, since when are we observing the holidays?"

"It's just a little something I picked up. You don't have to be religious to love your spouse."

She kissed him on the cheek. "Thank you, my dear man." Then she reached under her side of the bed and retrieved a gift-wrapped box of her own. "Turnabout is fair play. Here's a little something I picked up. Happy Hanukkah."

David smiled. "Thank you, my dear lady."

Together they peeled off the wrapping. Each box contained a gold watch. "Same gift," David joked. "My, aren't we the cute little All-American couple?"

"Sickening, just sickening."

"Big-time lawyer and the Chief of Detectives. Good thing nobody can see what cornballs we are underneath it all."

"I love it," she said, laughing. "And I love you." She stroked his forehead, then he kissed her. Things grew passionate in no time.

0732 hours

The same golden sun shone on the fresh snow outside St. Michael's Church, giving it an orange hue. The morning was still and cold. The only car in the parking lot was Ralph Kane's unmarked Pontiac, sitting next to the statue of St. Michael the Archangel. The new snow was so thick that now the statue was almost unrecognizable.

A radio car on routine patrol, a blue and white Adam unit, cruised slowly into the church lot to check out the Pontiac. Normally a patrol officer wouldn't even notice such a vehicle. But these two bored young bluesuits were in the final hour of morning watch, looking for something to do. Dawn on Christmas Day is not a busy time in the Twelfth Precinct. And the Pontiac did stand out, still sitting there by itself seven hours after midnight Mass. The tracks of the worshippers' cars had been pretty much covered over.

The kid in the recorder's seat got out and made his way over to the Pontiac. He casually brushed away some of the snow covering the passenger's window. He peered inside. "Jesus Christ!" he shouted to his partner. "Come look at *this* shit!"

Roberta Easterly and her husband were dozing after lovemaking. The phone rang. "Let the machine get it," David said.

But she had already rolled over and picked it up, switching to a professional voice. "Inspector Easterly," she said, then listened. "What news?" Then she sat bolt upright. "*What?!*"

David, alarmed, also sat up.

"Oh, my God!" Easterly said.

"What is it?" David mouthed silently.

"Just a minute, Nanci," Easterly said. She put her hand over the mouthpiece. "Jefferson Mosely was in a traffic accident. He's in critical condition."

"You're joking!"

She shook her head. "This is Nanci York. He lost control of his car on the ice. He ran into a tree, out on Viaduct Road."

Easterly listened some more. Then she shook her head. "Oh, God! Thanks, Nanci. Call me later, on my cell phone, after you get more details."

She hung up and turned to David, still processing this. "It happened about three a.m. He was drunk. There was another woman in the car with him. She was killed."

"Oh, man! On *Christmas!*"

"It's even worse. The dead woman was a policeman's wife."

David shook his head in disbelief.

"The poor wife," was all Roberta Easterly could think to say, "the poor wife." Then she caught herself. "Both of them."

David took her hand. "Look, this is a terrible thing to say, but it sounds like Mosely's career just ended. You're out from under. He can't screw things up anymore."

"Oh, David, I can't let myself think like that."

"And that's one of the reasons I love you so much." He held her close, stroking her hair. "Bobbie, you're the finest human being I've ever known."

0935 hours

Isaiah Bell was just leaving for church with Vera and the children. All were dressed in their best clothes. Behind them, the living room was a festive place, with new toys under the tree and Ikey's bicycle propped up in the corner.

The phone rang. Bell thought about letting the answering machine take the call. But he picked it up. "Bell," he said.

Vera watched her husband. She saw that familiar look on his face. His job was calling again. "Ike, it's *Christmas,*" she pleaded under her breath.

"He asked for *me?*" Bell said to the caller. Then he listened. "Okay. I'll be right down." He hung up.

"What is it now?" Vera asked wearily.

"Ralph Kane's in trouble."

"Kane? What kind of trouble?"

"Drinking. They've got him locked up over at Number Twelve." He looked at her with amazement. "He asked for *me*. He told them I'm his *partner*. Can you believe that?"

Vera thought about that for a moment, then smiled. "When a policeman's partner's in trouble, he'd better go."

"My mother's plane gets in at two o'clock."

"The kids and I can find the airport. You just go. Go and do God's work."

Bell opened the door. Vera touched his arm. "Bring him home for dinner. The kids would like to thank him."

"You mean that?"

"Of course I mean that."

Bell kissed her cheek. "You know, you're my kind of woman." He headed outside to the Ford.

1025 hours

Easterly sat with Byron Slaughter at a booth in the coffee shop near police headquarters. But for the waitress and the cook, the gaily-decorated diner was empty. On the table sat the folder Slaughter had given her, the one containing the surveillance pictures of Jefferson Mosely and his lovers in Dallas.

"I used that information," Easterly said. "I didn't want to, but I did. I didn't actually show Mosely the pictures, but I let him know that I knew." She took a hefty swallow of coffee. "It was the last conversation I had with the bastard."

"I'm sorry it came to that. I figured you'd need all the ammo you could get." He smiled sadly. "I just didn't think it would be that soon."

"You know the worst part? The feeling of power I had over him. It was intoxicating." She shoved the folder over to Slaughter. "Take them back, will you, Byron? Burn them or something. It makes me feel sleazy."

"*He's* the one who did this, you know. *He's* the one who'll have to live with it the rest of his life—if he survives." He smiled sadly. "Those pictures are the *reason* he left Dallas."

Easterly shook her head in disgust. "So what are you going to tell the press?"

"The truth. What else?"

"You don't have to tell the whole truth."

"About the cop's wife? That's kind of hard to hide, Bobbie. The woman's dead."

"I mean all the background stuff."

"Of course not. We'll stick to the facts of *this* case." He rubbed his eyes wearily. "Hell of a time for the other two deputy chiefs to be on vacation."

"Boss, I hate to sound ghoulish. But the city's going to need a chief of police, and soon. You have another chance here."

"Didn't you hear what I said to you last night? I'm finished with police work."

"But you were one of the finalists. The Commission... Byron, this changes everything."

"I couldn't do justice to the position. The city deserves better."

"Aren't you selling yourself short? It wasn't that long ago you *wanted* the job."

"Things have changed. I've already talked to all three Commissioners, within the last hour. They did offer me the job and I turned it down. But I did make an alternative recommendation. It was so brilliant that they approved it on the spot."

"Yes?"

"You, Roberta."

"Me?"

"Congratulations," Slaughter said. "You're not going to be Chief of Detectives after all. As of now you are this city's acting Chief of *Police.*"

"My God!"

"And as soon as the City Council officially fires Mosely, you won't be acting anymore."

Easterly shut her eyes wearily and shook her head, again in disbelief... Then she smiled. "Merry Christmas."

I saiah Bell walked through the Twelfth Precinct lockup toward an interview room in the back of the station. His guide was the watch commander, a ruddy-faced lieutenant named O'Hara.

"Damned lucky he didn't freeze to death," O'Hara said as they walked. "The ignition was on and the gas tank was empty. So we figure he had the heater on much of the night. Fire Rescue took him over to Central Receiving, but the docs said he's okay. You believe in miracles?"

"Yeah, I do," said Bell.

"Personally, I'd just like to make this go away. I'm supposed to notify the duty officer, he's supposed to notify IA. I say to hell with all that bullshit. The paperwork would take all day. Besides, it's Christmas and the guy didn't hurt anybody."

"Plus, he's a hero," said Bell.

"Listen, Detective, let me give you a little word of advice," the lieutenant said, lowering his voice. "Your partner needs help. I've seen this before. Drink just about wiped out *my* people."

"I have a slight acquaintance with the problem," Bell said.

"I don't know *why* his weapon was out of its holster. But I can only guess. Next time this guy tries to cap himself, he just might pull it off."

They arrived at the interview room. "He's in here," the lieutenant said. "Tell him my hat's off to him. About getting those bastards, I mean."

"Sure."

Bell started to open the door. The lieutenant turned back. "Listen, you never heard my name, okay?" Bell gave him a thumbs-up and went inside.

Kane sat with his head in his hands. His beard was now five days' old and his clothes were rumpled. He looked up when Bell entered. "You came," he said quietly.

"I came."

"Sorry to fuck up your Christmas."

"Why did you call me, Ralph?"

"I don't want to die," he said. "Not any more. I tried, but I even fucked that up. Now I don't think I'm supposed to." He spoke through his hands, hesitantly. "I guess I need a little help."

Bell stood there, thinking.

"I wouldn't blame you if you said no," Kane said.

"Do you *want* help? If you don't, I'm not going to waste my time."

"Yes. I want help."

"Okay, then, come on, let's go home," Bell said.

"Home?"

"My house. My wife invited you for dinner..."

"I can't—I can't do that," Kane said.

"Why? Because we're black?"

"Black doesn't have a damned thing to do with it!"

"Then why can't you come? My mother will be here from Alabama…"

Kane put his head back in his hands. "A guy like me shouldn't be around decent people, not on Christmas. Not people with kids."

"That's crap, Kane! Pure self-pitying bullcrap!" He picked up Kane's coat and tossed it to him. "Look, man, my own children were scared of Blackie and White Man. Now they're not scared any more. They want to thank you for that."

Kane stared at Bell. "No shit?"

"No shit. Then, after dinner, I know a good meeting, some guys who can help you stay sober."

"On Christmas?"

"Can you think of a better day to start?"

Kane nodded. "Then let's go," he said. He stood up.

"There's just one thing," Bell said. "My wife doesn't like profanity." He shrugged. "You know how women are."

Kane smiled. "I think I can manage."

Bell opened the door and together they started back down the hall of the precinct station. As they walked, Bell put his huge hand on Kane's shoulder.

Kane let it stay there.

EPILOGUE

So that was it, our police version of a Christmas miracle. The next day, the Childress task force was officially disbanded. All officers, except Ralph Kane, returned to regular duty. By New Year's Day the crime rate was back up to normal.

Now if you're anything like me, you're a realist who recoils from words like "miracle." So I use the word in the broader, metaphorical sense, as in "the miracle of life." What I have done here is report the *facts* of the story—facts that Bell, Kane and Easterly individually related to me. I took the three accounts and wove them together into this narrative. Make of it what you will.

Here's the update, as we go to press:

Louise and Stephen Childress moved to California. She resumed her nursing career, and he is a teacher. When last heard from, they were expecting another child.

Jefferson Mosely survived his injuries but committed suicide before his manslaughter trial was to begin. He shot himself in the front seat of his locked car, which happened to be a Pontiac. But first he called 911 to make sure it was a cop who found him.

Lin Loh, the eyewitness, moved away from the city before Thomas Blackstone went to trial. Her whereabouts are unknown. Nevertheless, Blackstone was convicted of first-degree murder and sentenced to die by lethal injection. He is on Death Row in Statesville Prison while his case is under appeal.

Mayor Titus Webster was convicted on federal corruption charges. He was sentenced to probation and resigned. He has since disappeared.

Eric Klemmer moved to Argentina, where he joined a neo-Nazi organization. He, too, has disappeared from sight.

Tyrone Jones, a.k.a. Malik Karanga, moved to Los Angeles and converted to Islam. After 9-11, the FBI investigated him for suspected links to Islamic extremists in the Middle East, but nothing ever came of it.

Vito Vitale died of a heart attack four weeks after Christmas. His son, Vito, Jr., succeeded him as capo of the city's ruling organized crime family.

While eating Chinese take-out, Garland McQueen was assassinated by a rival with a high-powered rifle

Tiny Lawless died of a methamphetamine-induced heart attack during sex with a sixteen-year-old girl.

Willis Henry was convicted of assaulting a police officer. He was sentenced to Statesville, where he became a leader of the Black Liberation Family.

Lt. Van Horn left the police department to become a Special Agent of the FBI.

Lt. Dunsmore was transferred to Administrative Services, where he oversees logistics, procurement and vehicle maintenance.

Francis Demarest retired from the FBI after being passed over for Assistant Director.

Byron Slaughter was successfully treated for post-traumatic stress disorder. He retired to Florida, where he now runs a charter fishing service.

Stan Jablonski became Easterly's press officer. He met a thirty-two year-old former debutante with a millionaire father. At sixty, he married her and retired to a life of bliss.

Angus MacKenzie is Chief of Detectives.

Nick Georgiades is Deputy Chief of Police for Operations.

Nanci York quickly became a star in local television, then was lured away by ABC News, for whom she toils in Miami.

Roberta Easterly remains Chief of Police. She is one of the most respected law enforcement executives in the United States, and has introduced numerous creative innovations into the criminal justice system. She and David Goldman remain happily married.

Isaiah Bell retired and founded a private security firm. It is rapidly becoming one of the most successful African American businesses in the region. He remains tobacco-free and happily married to Vera. His brother, however, died of alcoholism.

The day after Christmas, Ralph Kane entered a chemical-dependency program at the VA. To this day, he remains sober and free of drugs. Kane is still an organized crime investigator, but six months ago Roberta Easterly promoted him to lieutenant and named him commanding officer of the Organized Crime Intelligence Bureau.

He fell in love with a woman he met at a recovery meeting, and they are now living together. Once a week he volunteers an off-duty evening as security officer at a battered woman's shelter. He also found a website run by other Marines who had been at the American Embassy that last day of the war, and has joined their group.

He no longer dreams of the little girl in Saigon.

ACKNOWLEDGMENTS

I would like to thank the following people, each of whom had something to do with the creation of this book:

Douglas T. Graham; Isabel Graham; Laura Graham; Helen Graham Moore; R. Del Brunner; Michael Butler; Gerald Chamales; Joan Churchill; Dennis Elleflot, USN; Eileen Foley; Leslie Fuller; Niel Hancock; Jack Hoffman; Anthony and Stella Hopkins; Robert Kahn, USMC; Mark Kroeker, Deputy Chief, Los Angeles Police Department; Michael Lally; Karen Lorre; Janiva Magness; Janice Mall; Midge Mamatas; Patty Markey; Jay McCormick; Sean McGrath; Jim McNally; Tim Meier, S.J.; Barney Melekian, Chief, Pasadena Police Department; Beryl Mick, USMC; Judy Muller; Jim Neubacher; Bonnie Olson, M.D.; Shirley Palmer; Chuck Patterson, USMC; Rev. Larry Peacock; David Peckinpah; Jim Reinitz; Kae Resh; Doug Ryan, USMC; Dan Schaefer; Hubert Selby, Jr.; Karen Struck; Tom and Lois Wark; Bob West; the West Los Angeles Vet Center; Ken Wilson; Bob Wolf; Verdi Woodward; and Barbara Young.

Also Lt. Robert Hislop, commander of the Detroit Police Homicide Division, and his tireless detectives—Thomas Peterson, Donald Carter and Robert Kanka.

Also the U.S. Marines who related their experiences at the embassy on that last day of the Vietnam War: Ken Crouse, John Stewart, Doug Potratz and J. Ghilain. Semper Fi.